D0730495

Kansas City, MO Public Library
0000186891461

BOOK THREE:
THE SHINING BLADE

MADELEINE ROUX

SCHOLASTIC INC.

If you purchased this book without a cover, you should be aware that this book is stolen property. It was reported as "unsold and destroyed" to the publisher, and neither the author nor the publisher has received any payment for this "stripped book."

© 2020 Blizzard Entertainment, Inc. All rights reserved. Traveler is a trademark, and World of Warcraft and Blizzard Entertainment are trademarks and/or registered trademarks of Blizzard Entertainment, Inc., in the U.S. and/or other countries.

All rights reserved. Published by Scholastic Inc., *Publishers since 1920.* SCHOLASTIC and associated logos are trademarks and/or registered trademarks of Scholastic Inc.

The publisher does not have any control over and does not assume any responsibility for author or third-party websites or their content.

No part of this publication may be reproduced, stored in a retrieval system, or transmitted in any form or by any means, electronic, mechanical, photocopying, recording, or otherwise, without written permission of the publisher. For information regarding permission, write to Scholastic Inc., Attention: Permissions Department, 557 Broadway, New York, NY 10012.

This book is a work of fiction. Names, characters, places, and incidents are either the product of the author's imagination or are used fictitiously, and any resemblance to actual persons, living or dead, business establishments, events, or locales is entirely coincidental.

Library of Congress Cataloging-in-Publication Data available

ISBN 978-1-338-53894-6

10 9 8 7 6 5 4 3 2 1   20 21 22 23 24

Printed in the U.S.A.   40
First printing 2020

Cover illustration by Vivienne To
Interior illustrations by Brandon Dorman

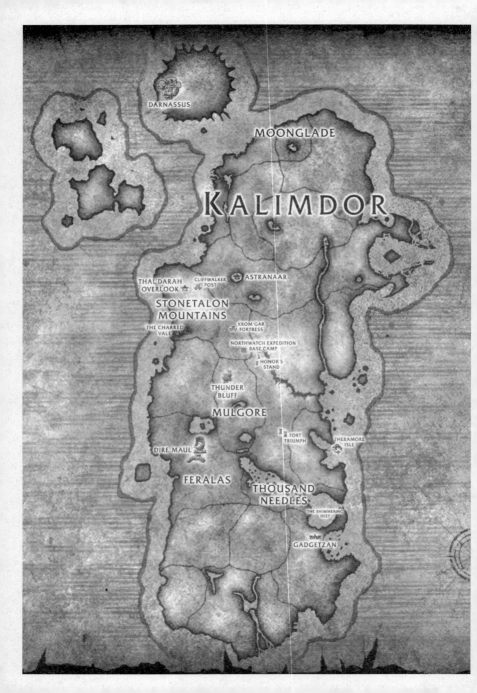

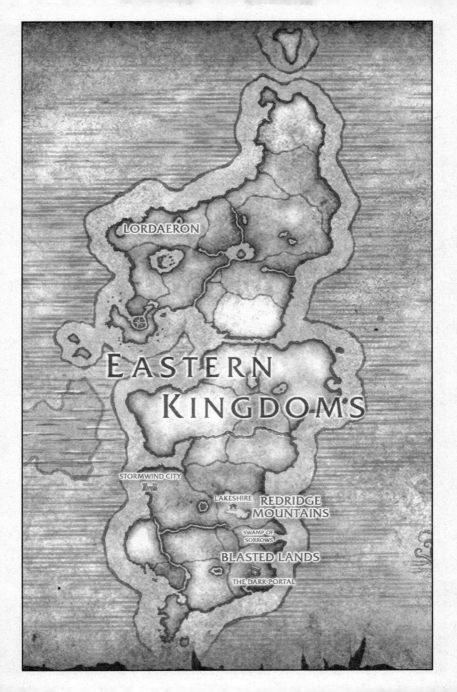

CHAPTER ONE
NEW SHORES

He had been dreaming of home, of Lakeshire—at least, he thought he was. One moment, he was in his stepfather's shop, watching the forge grow red and hot, the next he was on fire, burning up from grasping black tendrils that held his arms tight to his body.

If that wasn't bad enough, Aramar Thorne saw again the twisted, cruel face of his father's killer, the most hateful man in all of Azeroth: Malus, captain of the *Inevitable*. He growled at Aram, so close he could smell the sweat dripping off the man's brow. Aram's mother always told him that a bad person's innards would out, and the same had happened to Malus, contorting a once noble face into eyes and a mouth made only for sneering. Only for contempt.

He wanted the magical compass around Aram's neck and he would stop at nothing to get it, including, it seemed, bursting into Aram's dreams uninvited.

"I gave you every opportunity, boy. You brought this on your-self. Like father, like son," he said in a deadly whisper.

It was just like his memory of being back in Gadgetzan, back in Winifred's house, snared by horrid magic, unable to move, unable to breathe, friendless and desperate, knowing any moment could be his last. Aram struggled to reach for his cutlass, then remembered it had been useless against the dark energy, so instead he reached for the incomplete crystal sword hilt tucked in his belt. Reached for it and gasped. It was gone. But how? Now he truly had nothing . . .

There was no Light to save him this time, only Malus and his enormous hand slowly coming to rip away the one thing most precious to Aram, the thing he had sworn to protect for his father . . .

"Ticktock," Malus hissed. "Your time is up, boy."

And then, as quickly as the nightmare had taken him, it was gone. Malus exploded into thick, black smoke, the only lingering trace of him a pair of eyes in the darkness. Aram felt pressure on his shoulders, his chest, and shouted himself awake. He flailed while staring directly into the far more welcome eyes of his sister, Makasa Flintwill.

It was just like being back on the *Wavestrider*, when she would snap him awake with a steely, "Aramar Thorne, get your sorry bones out of that bunk!" He had heard the words so many times from Makasa, they were practically burned into his mind. But this time she wasn't yelling or impatient, just concerned, her dark brows knit with worry.

"Brother? We've touched down. It's time to go."

"Sure," Aram whispered. "Yeah, I'll be ready."

"Bad dream?" she asked as she left him, hefting her own pack and double-checking that she had her weapons and canteen.

"You have no idea," he said with a wince. The others had already gone ahead and left the goblin-made zeppelin, so Aram hurried to pack, though his hands were slick with nervous sweat. He couldn't shake the nightmare. Usually his dreams were of the Light, there to guide and protect him, but now? He hoped it was not an omen of things to come. It wasn't so strange, he decided, that the wild and sometimes scary events of the last few weeks would return to haunt him as he slept—most twelve-year-olds were worried about oversleeping for their studies or getting caught kissing behind the Boughmans' place. But Aram, dressed in his father's oversized captain's coat, wielding a cutlass and carrying an enchanted compass, was beginning to feel less like a boy and more like a young man.

Maybe he really *was* becoming a man. After all, they had come so far from where they began; for Aram, this long, winding adventure had started as a way to get to know his father better, but that simple plan imploded when the despicable Captain Malus sank their ship. Armed with his trusty sketchbook, Aram had followed the compass and visions from the Light, trying his best to fulfill his father's mission to find and then retrieve shards of the Diamond Blade scattered across Azeroth. This was of vital importance. Azeroth was a big place, hard for Aram to even fathom, just like the mission he had been tasked with. But he had managed so far—or rather, *they* had. For everywhere Aram went he seemed to pick up more and more allies to his cause, including the powerful druid Thalyss Greyoak, who had met an end he did not deserve. An end that Aram and more of his friends might face if he didn't rise to the challenges that lay before them.

And so he squared his shoulders and departed the zeppelin, feeling a pang of regret that there would be no more late-night chats about technique with his fellow artist, Charnas. Yet Aram felt optimistic that saying good-bye to the goblin did not mean good-bye forever.

The ladder was already lowered and Aram descended as steadily as he could, trying to balance all of his things and his dignity. When he landed, it was with the sea at his back and the blackened land spreading north and east into the vale, with mountains to the south. His optimism flagged a bit as he surveyed the landscape awaiting them.

The Charred Vale was, well, *charred*, and Aramar Thorne felt the smoke and ash sting his lungs the moment they departed Gazlowe's zeppelin, the *Cloudkicker*.

I don't know what I expected, he thought with a snort. The others didn't look pleased at the thought of traversing a burnt and darkened landscape, but Aram tried his best to see the luster in it. There was a severe, brutal beauty to the smoldering hills, a stark contrast between the embers still burning and the charred land. It would be difficult to capture it, he thought, to communicate the awe of it, but that was his job as an artist—he had to try.

He stood with his feet still on the otherwise untouched sand, the toes of his boots just barely brushing the blackened grass that carpeted the burning forest. An ashy wind ruffled his dark hair; it blew hot and dry, but still he shivered. Makasa, his taller, bolder counterpart and chosen sister, blew out a long, low whistle as she stood next to him. She fiddled idly with the chain crisscrossing her torso, then itched a new scab on her forearm.

"We're a long way from Feralas," she murmured.

And she was right. They might have been abandoned, hunted, and near-starving in that rain forest, but at least there *was* rain. Still, it might not be so bad. They would be able to see enemies coming from a mile away; that wasn't so easily done in a dense, misty jungle.

The airship puttered behind them, hovering, its pointed nose angling north. Gazlowe, the short, green goblin engineer whom Aram had come to greatly admire, sighed and strode across the beach to them, stretching his arms over his head. The remainder of the crew stayed aboard, a clear sign that they wouldn't be stopping there for long.

"All right, kid?" Gazlowe crowed, cheerful. Of course he was cheerful. *He* wasn't facing a two-day march through a burning forest. On tiptoes, he clapped Aramar on the back. "Here we are, the Charred Vale. Not bad, right?"

Drella, their eternally honest dryad companion, twirled a few strands of curling teal hair around her fingers and scrunched up her nose. "It is . . . actually very bad. The trees—the animals . . . Everything is in pain. I can hardly look at it."

"I thought everything dies," Makasa said with a smirk, throwing the dryad's frequent words back at her.

"It does," Drella replied with a quirk of her lips. "But not this *slowly.*"

"Oh yeah, forgot. You and your nature thing," Gazlowe said with a shrug, referring to her deep, druidic bond to Azeroth and all of its creatures, not just some *nature thing.* "I'm sure you'll get used to it. Hey! You won't freeze. And gettin' a fire started for supper will be a cinch."

Nobody indulged his jokes.

"Anyway." Gazlowe stretched again, ambling around the group until he stood facing them. He suddenly hissed, rubbing at his backside, which seemed to have been lightly singed by a falling cinder. "I told you this was as good as we could do. Sprocket and I gotta bounce outta here. The Mechanical Engineers' Guild of Azeroth won't stop the competition for any man . . . or engineer, or, uh, goblin, as the case may be." He winked, but only Drella winked back. Gazlowe coughed and thrust out his hand toward Aram, then pumped it hard when the boy took it. "Hey, kid, anytime you need me—and you got enough dough or a sufficiently sweet business proposal—gimme a call."

"Sure thing, Gazlowe," Aram replied with a weary smile. "I'm sure that will be any day now."

"All right, all right! Enough jokes already. You got some distance between you and Thal'darah Overlook," Gazlowe said, giving Aram's hand one last shake, then forcing his way through the travelers. They parted for him, and then turned to watch the goblin leave. Some of the crew, including Sprocket and Charnas, had gathered at the railings on the *Cloudkicker* and waved. Aram couldn't say if that was because they were being supportive or because they were just enthusiastic about leaving.

"Stay safe, kid!" Gazlowe called, all but leaping with joy onto the ladder that would take him up into the zeppelin. "Stick together. You got a good crew there."

Aramar Thorne waved him off, nodding. He did have a good crew. A solid crew. They had been through so much, surviving pirate attacks, gladiatorial combat, battles, races, *more* gladiatorial combat . . . He suddenly felt old and tired, then shook his head, forcing that thought away. They still had a long way to go—first, they needed to reach Thal'darah Overlook and see about fulfilling his promise to Drella. The *Cloudkicker* bathed them in a warm, sea-salted wind as it lifted off, machinery whirring and chugging.

Aram jogged over to Makasa, who was pretending to adjust her pack as she stared anxiously at the sky. "Are you all right?" Aram asked.

"I'm not sure we lost Malus," Makasa said, putting a hand up to shield her eyes as she watched their ride depart.

"With any luck he's off on his goose chase across the sea, and the *Crustacean* will buy us time." How much time, he couldn't say. Makasa, scratching her chin, seemed to read his mind.

"We got plenty of rest on the *Cloudkicker*. Time to put some miles on these boots." Spurred on, she put up both hands and mustered the group. Makasa stood before the half circle of them, Murky the murloc on the left, wearing his beloved new nets like a vest; then Hackle the gnoll, his club resting on his shoulder; Drella, a dryad of immense power, in the middle; and Aram at the other end, itching for his sister to get on with it.

"Excuse me!" Drella piped up. Her voice was harmonious, but commanding. She was transitioning into an older, more subdued version of her riotously colorful half-elven and half-fawn appearance. Spring was turning into summer for Drella, though it had been summer for everyone else for a long time. It was a dryad thing that Aram was only barely beginning to understand. Somehow, even in this desolate waste of smoldering wood, a butterfly had managed to find her and land gently on her head. Drella giggled and let it remain. "Oh! A friend."

"Is this important?" Makasa demanded, pinching the bridge of her nose.

"Yes, it is important! If only I could remember—hmm . . ." Makasa groaned.

"Give her a chance," Aram murmured, much to his sister's irritation. She had a firm rule against eye rolling, which she broke, demonstrating just what she thought of Aram's many indulgences toward the dryad.

"Oh yes, now I remember!" Drella mimed catching the thought and popping it back into her mouth. "When I was an acorn, Thalyss would whisper to me many stories about the great heroes of old, and how they each got good and true names to go with their good and true deeds. I believe it is time we each take our own true, *true* names."

Makasa groaned again. "Drella—"

"Just look how far we made it. We survived the Bone Pile and the Thunderdrome, where I became Taryndrella the Impressive, daughter of Cenarius, which you all know, of course! And you"— she pointed to Murky, who burbled up at her with a spit bubble growing from between his lips—"are Murky the Unstung! Impervious to scorpid venom! Ooh, good, right?"

"Mrgle, mrgle, Drhla," agreed the murloc.

"Drella." Makasa looked murderous.

"And you!" She pointed to Hackle, who tilted his furry head to the side. "You are Hackle the Revenged!"

That was in reference to the gnoll's feat of taking the head of Marjuk the ogre, a fearsome foe that had killed many of Hackle's kin in the Woodpaw clan.

"Aram will be Aramar Thorne, Wielder of Light!"

He couldn't help but nod, and was glad that Makasa had decided not to kill him before he got to hear his new "true, *true*" name. The name came from one of the stranger moments of their time in Gadgetzan, when Aram had narrowly escaped death at the hands of his sworn enemy, Malus. Caught in tendrils of black magic, Aram had wielded the hilt of the Diamond Blade to break the magic and flee to safety. The blade had serviced him then, but no such weapon of Light came to him in his nightmares. It had left him feeling so vulnerable . . .

"DRELLA." Makasa huffed, which was always a bad sign.

"You are Makasa the Binder!" Drella sang, undaunted and circling Makasa on her fawn-like legs. The butterfly in Drella's hair fluttered free and landed on Makasa's forearm, only to be smashed into colorful dust a second later. Drella, it seemed, hadn't noticed, bounding around, singing softly to herself.

"The Binder?" Makasa screwed up her face, the scars on her forehead and left cheek contorting. Hackle began one of his high, hysterical laughs but ended it quickly when Makasa shot him a look. "Aramar is *the Wielder of Light* and I'm the bloody Binder?"

"Yes! The Binder, because you are the stuff that holds us all together. Like paste! But stronger! Stronger even than paste."

That actually gave the young woman, tall and muscled and ferocious as she was, pause. Aramar knew that if there was one thing that might knock his sister for a loop, it was earnest sentiment. Whenever he dared wield the word "sister" aloud, she usually gave in to his demands.

"Fine, spectacular, I'm the Binder." Makasa wiped the butterfly's remains from her hand before the dryad could see it. "Will you listen now?"

Everyone was silent, even Drella, who was satisfied that she had spoken her piece and given them all their true, *true* names.

"We've had plenty of rest and food," she said. The *Cloudkicker* was already high above, the loud whir of its machinery growing softer as it carried Gazlowe, Charnas, and Sprocket on to their MEGA event. "I think it would be best if we marched through the vale with only one stop. It will be hard, and grueling, but I don't think any of us want to linger here longer than we have to."

"I agree," Aram said, nodding. He squinted out at the smoke rising behind Makasa and grimaced. "Tie something around your mouths; I don't think we want to breathe all that smoke."

"Aram's right." Hearing the older, more experienced girl say that always gave him a jolt of pride. For a long, long time, it was the kind of phrase he couldn't imagine her ever uttering. That was back in the days of him being shaken or kicked awake on the *Wavestrider*. Now, however, he and Makasa walked side by side as they pulled their shirts over their mouths and plunged into the blackened, steaming obstacle that lay between them and the Overlook.

Aram was surprised to find that Murky, small and green, dashed up right beside him and marched along with his flipper-like feet slapping the ashen ground.

"Mrgle, nk teergle, blurlem n Murky tilurgle-gurgle," Murky said, brandishing his small spear and pointing it hastily toward the depths of the vale.

The others and Aram all looked helplessly to Drella, who had managed to learn much of the little creature's language from her night elf druid mentor, Thalyss Greyoak.

"He says yes, we should hurry." Drella followed just behind the murloc, translating as she went. Then she leaned down and scooped up Murky, letting him ride on her back, sparing his bare, amphibious feet the scorch of the earth. "We should hurry, he says, or his true, *true* name will be Murky the Lightly Toasted."

CHAPTER TWO
LIGHTLY TOASTED

Makasa watched the heads of her compatriots bow dangerously low. Seven hours into their march through the bleak, black expanse of the Charred Vale and their morale, were it a thing she could hold, would be lodged somewhere in the smoking dirt at her feet. She trudged on, breathing only when she had to, eyes squinted against the stinging air, her hands looped around the chains on her chest as if she could pull herself along faster that way.

She glanced back at Aram, who was only a few feet behind. So far, he and Hackle managed best. Hackle's thickly padded feet and fur insulated him against the relentless heat. Flecks of ash like snow nestled in his mottled fur, and his ever-twitching nose made funny wheezing sounds. Aram's shoulders drooped, but he marched along without complaint. Makasa's vigilant eyes swept toward Drella, the dryad. She had cantered over to a withered tree, her eyes filmed with tears, but focused and concentrating. The dryad reached out with one hand, her slender fingers almost touching the blackened bark, and for a moment nothing happened, but then her entire body jolted, a connection of leafy green tendrils snaking between the dryad and the dead tree. Even Makasa was distracted as tiny, new shoots sprang up through the cracks in the bark. Drella shut her eyes suddenly, crying out and then rearing back, and Makasa groaned as she watched the littlest among them begin to tumble off the dryad's speckled back.

The new life growing on the tree stalled, already smoking in the cruel, hot air.

Makasa, still light enough on her feet, darted back and to the right, skidding through the fine layer of soft ash on the ground, stopping beside the dryad and catching Murky before he could hit the earth.

"Is he all right?" Aram trotted to her side, reaching over to wipe a smudge of dirt off the murloc's forehead.

"Murky nk blurg mlger." His huge eyes rolled back, and Drella gasped.

Then she coughed.

"Oh! I thought perhaps I could heal these trees, but my power . . . I am simply not strong enough yet. And Murky! He is so weak! He really is lightly toasted." She swept the murloc out of Makasa's arms. That was just fine with her. Murky, slimy and sticky, wasn't exactly a treat to hold. Even so, she couldn't help but share a frown with Aram.

"No," Makasa murmured while Drella tried to rouse the exhausted Murky. "We can't stop again." She turned north and shuddered. Dark clouds gathered, but too low to be rain. It was no natural storm, but some kind of strange, swirling dust formation. Worse, daylight fled, and the high, sharp ridges around them looked like scorched daggers spearing toward the sky. Far-off screeches that only Makasa had seemed to notice grew steadily closer.

Drakes, she thought. *Doom.*

Behind them, their tracks had vanished, swallowed by the shifting, hot winds that had crammed her eyes full of filth. Makasa wiped at her face and then sighed. After hours of dodging drake nests and fissures of flame, they were all of them caked in ash.

"We can't turn back," she addressed their troop. "The Overlook has to be closer than the shore. Besides, what would we do if we turned around?"

Aram shifted his pack, and Hackle tested the air, then gave a mighty snort.

"Hackle carry murloc," Hackle suggested. "Give break. Hackle strong, not tired yet."

But Makasa heard the strain in the gnoll's voice. Gods, they were all struggling. The map she consulted on the airship wouldn't change shapes no matter how much she wished it would—no, the distance remained the same: two horrid days to make it to the Overlook. The misery of the vale ought to break after the first day, but they still had to make it that far. Drella gently handed the limp and trembling murloc to Hackle, who did his best to pull a flap of leather armor over the poor little creature's face.

"We have to press on," Makasa said again. The others nodded, but didn't move. She looked again to Aram, and he fiddled nervously with the strap of his pack.

As if to prove Makasa right, a chorus of shrieks sliced through the eerie silence of the vale. The shadows grew longer the more they tarried, and Makasa yanked hard on the chain around her chest, pulling it free. She gave it a few experimental swings, swiveling in a circle. The smoldering fires in the vale flickered, playing tricks, but she knew a hungry cry when she heard one. The smaller dragon whelps might have been shy of them during the day, but that advantage would soon be lost when their larger kin took to the skies.

Black drakes. She could already imagine their massive silhouettes sweeping across the moon.

"I hate to say it," she said, marching to the head of their troop and adjusting the cloth over her mouth. "But that dust storm up ahead might be our best shot. Those drakes can't carry off what they can't see."

"Perhaps I could reason with the drakes!" Drella might have sounded her usual confident self, but even she looked wilted.

All the same, she dashed up next to Makasa, stirring the warm earth with her hooves, and Aram, predictably, squared up beside the dryad.

"I don't think that will work," Makasa warned. "I doubt drakes are big talkers."

"You cannot know that. And they have never spoken to someone like me!" Drella shot back.

"Now's not the time for risking that, Drella! Into the storm," Makasa called, and not a second too late. Another shrill cry flew across the dust toward them, and Makasa could swear it came with wind beat by cruel wings.

The path curved northeast, the hills crowding closer, the seething whirlwind of the storm hurrying down to meet them. It hit Hackle first, and he gave a gnoll's hiccupping laugh, not a merry sound, but one of shock. Makasa dropped her head down, spearing into the gritty wind that tore at her face and hands. She refused to drop the chain, convinced that the drakes would follow faster now that the sun dipped so low. Even with her face shielded, she felt her mouth fill with silt, her eyes burning, tears flowing freely down her cheeks. Aram was shouting something to her, but it couldn't be heard above the roar of the wind.

"What?" she thundered back. Her voice cut at her throat, gritty and dry.

It sounded like he was saying, "A dove!" But that couldn't be right.

Makasa threw herself to the side, dodging around Drella until she was shoulder to shoulder with her brother. "Say again?!"

"ABOVE!"

Aram ducked his head, grabbing Drella by her lean neck and pulling. The warning came an instant too late, and Makasa's eyes rolled skyward just in time to see a huge, ebony shadow dive down toward them.

Snarls and gnashing teeth, the acrid stink of sulfur, the drumlike beating of immense, leathery wings . . . The drakes had come.

She had been right about one thing—it was doom that those nearing screams signaled. But otherwise Makasa had been terribly wrong. The storm had not frightened away the drakes, but only made them bolder. That was the last thought she had before clawed feet tore into her jerkin, shredding her skin, and then, with a roar, she was hoisted into the air.

Makasa heard the others shouting and panicking, her heart hammering in her chest as she struggled to maintain a grip on her weapon. The wind nearly ripped the chain from her hands, but she refused to let go, flicking the end upward to try and startle her kidnapper. Her shoulders pulsed with pain, and she felt blood seeping into her shirt. Maybe that would make her too slick to hold, maybe the storm would win out and take her away from the drake, maybe, maybe, maybe . . .

The thing was just so bloody strong, and huge, the size of at least four horses. She could hardly think, hardly move, but she

tried to jerk the chain up toward the drake again, doing nothing but dislodging a few dry scales. The drake's wings beat hard, almost useless against the power of the dust storm, and Makasa dared to hope that it would keep them from climbing dangerously high. The flying monsters called to one another, shrill and alarmed, and an instant later Makasa heard a strange sound. A long, low horn echoed across the vale, certainly no roar of a dragon, but of something far more welcome.

She fought to hear anything above the din of the drakes and the whirlwinds churning around them, but after the horn came the sound of heavy feet. Many of them. It came from the north, from their destination, and while the monster hovered, trying in vain to break free of the storm, help came down the mountain. Three large blurs moved at great speed toward them, kicking up their own dust storm. She heard the other drakes and whelps scream and scatter, but her kidnapper hesitated, a fatal mistake.

Makasa flinched, listening to the whistle of arrows slicing the air, aimed toward them. More screams from below. Her friends. Another volley of arrows sang toward them, and these connected, peppering the drake carrying her. It shivered and jerked, roaring in sudden agony. Makasa found the strength for one last attempt with her chain, and spun it, arcing it upward. The end looped around one of the arrows sticking out of the drake's upper leg, hitting its target, and Makasa gave her own cry, pulling as hard as she could.

It worked! she thought, and immediately after: *oh no.*

Without warning, they were careening toward the ground. Makasa felt the storm slam into them again like a wall, and she closed her eyes, afraid of the impact, afraid of what would come when the winds let go altogether and she could do nothing but fall.

CHAPTER THREE
A RESPITE

"Can you hear me? Makasa? Makasa . . ."

This dream had come to her a hundred times before. Her mother called out to her in a voice like a lullaby. She chased after it through darkness so thick it felt like deep ocean. The salt of the sea hung in the air. The char of fire. Her mother's face, beautiful and blurred, waited just out of reach, receding into the shadows whenever she drew near. Makasa never gave up. She plunged into that clinging darkness, and when she at last broke through, it wasn't into her mother's embrace. Instead, she felt her heart plunge—a ghoulish face waited, grinning, a skeleton's rictus smile and the sweet rot of death draped around it.

"Can you hear me?" it said with its yellow-toothed grin. "Makasa?"

She threw up her hands against it, and sat up, then gasped, watching as Aram tumbled back, holding the spot where her fist had smashed into his cheek.

"Yeah," he muttered, shaking his head and chuckling in the dirt. "She can hear me."

Two strange faces stared down at her, both of them belonging to purple-skinned kaldorei. Night elves. Makasa groaned, clutching one shoulder and then the next, but that only brought another nauseating round of pain. She lowered herself back to the ground, finding that she had been deposited on a bed of leaves and soft boughs.

Her armored doublet had been stripped away, her shirt bloodied but not too badly torn. The sleeves had been pulled down to tend to her shoulders, and she sniffed at the greasy balm that had been applied to her wounds. There was a tang to it, almost like salt but not as sharp. That explained her dream. Glancing to her left, she could see the dark horizon of the vale still lingered to the south, which explained the char. But the dust storm had vanished, and the drakes circled far off, drifting back toward the distant shoreline.

"You are quite the fighter," the taller night elf mused. He had long silver hair, plaited and draped over one shoulder, his feathered helm in hand. He stood and regarded her with one faintly glowing lavender eye; the other was presumably injured, covered by a green leather strap.

"My chain!" Makasa jerked up into a sitting position again, and regretted it. But her pulse raced dangerously—had that damned beast escaped with her beloved weapon?

"It's here," Aram assured her, patting a bundle near her feet that included her jerkin. "Iyneath and Llaran brought the drake down. It didn't stand a chance!"

Makasa snorted at Aram's enthusiasm. Her young brother beamed up at the two night elves—Sentinels, they called themselves—whose matching longbows arced above their heads. The admiration wasn't exactly unwarranted, she decided, given that the kaldorei had managed to perfectly pin down a drake in the middle of a dust cloud without skewering her, too. Llaran, the female Sentinel, stood just a hair shorter than Iyneath. They had similarly refined features, long, slender noses and pursed lips that seemed to remain permanently bemused. Brother and sister, she considered, or even twins.

"Aiyell has sent her owl ahead," Llaran told her. "To alert the Overlook of your coming. They will want to send more guards to manage those drake swarms. They have grown bolder of late." She knelt and checked the wound on Makasa's shoulder. It didn't hurt as much as it ought to, she thought, meaning these night elves had helped them out of more than one bind. Still, Makasa wouldn't trust them, not while Aram carried that compass of his. Anybody, she knew, could be a spy.

"Thank you," Makasa said slowly. "We weren't getting out of that one alive."

"We weren't? *You* weren't," Aram teased. "We would've run out of that storm just fine."

She kicked at him, and he laughed.

"Rest now," Iyneath said in his pleasant and rumbling voice. "Aiyell will soon have a meal prepared, and when you are strong enough, we will strike out for Thal'darah."

The night elves departed, though there wasn't much to depart. They had made camp with her compatriots behind a small, hilly outcropping. She cast her gaze around, satisfied. It was a decent spot for a camp, defendable and sheltered. The crueler air of the Charred Vale lifted a little here, and she even saw fresh, green grass poking up among the cracks in the ground. To the west, a few cemetery stones gleamed, a feeble tree growing with a tangle of wild steelbloom at its roots. A fire crackled not far away, the popping sounds rising above the soft murmur of voices. The others. Makasa huddled back down on the makeshift cot, tired but something else. Something more.

"I almost got us all killed," she said, squeezing her eyes shut. "If those scouts hadn't found us—"

"You can't think that way," Aram replied. He took a dirty-looking rag from his captain's coat pocket and wiped at his face. She wasn't sure if it was any cleaner afterward. The soot of the vale had settled in the smile lines around his eyes, and it made him look significantly older than his scant twelve years. For a moment she saw their father, Greydon Thorne, staring back at her. "What choice did we have? If we went back, we would be stuck on the beach and easy pickings for those monsters.

The storm was a good decision, Makasa; it just didn't work out the way you planned."

"Yeah. And that's why it was foolish."

"It worked out, right?" He sighed. "You can't plan for luck, just hope for it. And now you can brag about surviving a drake. I can't wait to sketch it."

"I'd say we've earned some luck, too."

Aram nodded, tucking the rag away. She watched his hand drift near his collar, and she could see him trying not to reach for the compass. Maybe that was why he looked older, because he had that thing around his neck, the symbol of his mission to reconstruct the Diamond Blade, to save the Light, his father's parting gift to him, weighing him down like an anchor. It was his turn to look distraught, so Makasa shifted and tried not to bump her wounded shoulders.

She lowered her voice. "Do you believe the night elves, about who they are, where they're from?"

Aram's eyes glittered in the firelight, and he gazed off toward their troop. Or, more likely, toward Drella. Aram had gotten his first taste of responsibility in caring for the dryad, who, it seemed, was always getting into some form of trouble.

"You think me too trusting, but they didn't need to help us. They had no idea who we were in that storm. I was yelling at them not to hit you, but who knows if they heard me. I think we can trust them. We just need them to get us as far as the Overlook, then you can be as suspicious as you like."

She nodded. That suspicion wouldn't drop, not even if that stinky healing balm of theirs could magically disperse the dark cloud over her head.

"I'm glad you made it," Aram said, pushing up to his feet. "Don't worry about the storm, Makasa; you still made the right call. Who knows if we'd have made it here on our own. Now get some sleep. I can't see the back end of this place fast enough."

Makasa gave him a thin smile, watching him go, then settled down into her leafy bed. *Don't worry about the storm.* How? How could she not worry? How could she ignore the storm ahead of them, not one of dust and ash, but a storm of men and steel and cold, terrible vengeance? Malus might be off their back for the moment, but she had no doubt he would show his nasty face again. They could run from him, but he didn't seem the type to give up easily.

Sleep wouldn't come, but Makasa closed her eyes anyway and tried her hardest not to hear the distant drums of war.

CHAPTER FOUR
THE OVERLOOK

Aram's legs nearly gave out as they crested the final hill and reached their destination: Thal'darah Overlook. The second day's march had been less hot, surely, but not necessarily less arduous. The Charred Vale came with plenty of dangers, but once they broke away from the bleak, smoky ruin of the vale, the terrain rose steeply. The way around Battlescar Valley was almost entirely uphill. But there were trees, at least, living, not-on-fire trees with canopies the color of emerald jewels. The lushness stood in stark contrast to the clear-cut war zone of the valley itself, where the Alliance and Horde remained locked in conflict. Eagles looped overhead, crying to one another, the sound so sharp it could pierce straight through the mountains. Rams scattered at their approach, encouraging signs of life after so much brittle, black earth.

The Sentinels walked alongside their mounts—large, pearl-bright moonsabers that managed the steep hills with practiced ease. Murky relaxed on one of the saddles, comically tiny on such a giant creature. Makasa, of course, still injured, rode on Iyneath's striped saber, her mouth jammed shut in a firm and ungrateful line. She did smile a bit whenever the night elf scout loped up to walk beside her and inquire about her health.

Hackle, of course, stubbornly declined to ride, and Drella was already swift and steady with her fawn legs. Aram let Aiyell go on ahead, considering he felt good enough to make the journey on foot. And, if he were being completely honest, he wanted to spend the remainder of the march at Drella's side. Their journey to the Overlook was to undo the magical bond they had shared since her very recent birth, and Aram could admit to himself that he was nervous about the process. Would he feel different? What if it made her indifferent toward him, or even cold?

"There is something special about you two," Llaran had observed, her pale, violet eyes settling on them for a long time. "It is difficult to describe, but I sense . . . I sense—"

"A bond?" Drella provided. Her turquoise-colored curls bounced as she nodded at the Sentinel. "We do have a special bond. That is why we have come all this way. You see, I was born from an acorn, a beautiful, tiny little house. It was very cozy in there, but also cramped. And when I was born, the first thing I saw was Aramar Thorne, and now we are bonded for life! Is that not amazing?"

Drella closed her eyes and tossed back her head, clearly pleased with her explanation.

Llaran blinked back at them, then smiled what Aram was beginning to think of as her usual amused grin. "Surely there is more to it than that? Are you by some chance gifted with the knowledge of a druid, boy?"

"Not really," Aram said, helpless. "A druid tender sent us here, to undo the bond and, well, bond Drella to someone else. Someone more . . ." Competent? Wise? Knowledgeable? "Druidly."

He winced.

"Oh! A new word!" Drella marveled.

"Indeed." Llaran seemed lost in thought, but not about his new word. "I have heard tell of dryads being born, though I thought it required a druid tender, and a bond is formed with that druid so the dryad can be trained. I have never heard of a . . . human boy managing the task." She sounded bewildered. "And yet I cannot deny your bond. Odd."

Ahead of them, swaying back and forth on Iyneath's moonsaber, Makasa gave a conspicuously loud cough, one that was harsher given their recent smoke bath. Aram colored. Right. She didn't trust anyone, not even the elves who had saved her life, and now there he was, blabbing away to Llaran about their mission. But where was the harm? Eventually they would need to explain their reason for getting to the Overlook, and it wasn't like he had mentioned the compass or the shards . . .

"So yes," he concluded lamely. "We're here to see a druid called Thal'darah about the bond. To . . . to undo it." His heart sank at that. As much as he understood why the bond had to be changed, it didn't mean he had to like it. It was nice to be special, and to be special with Drella, who was the most fascinating creature he had ever laid eyes on. He snuck a glance at her, watching as she gently collected fallen wildflowers along the trail and linked them into a chain.

"When I shot that drake," Llaran mused softly, "I had no idea I was saving such an unusual band of travelers."

"Not that interesting," Aram insisted, aware that Makasa was still firing lightning bolts in his direction with her eyes. "Extremely average, to be honest. The bond was just an accident. I have a lot of those . . . accidents, I mean."

"Do not be silly." Drella lightly draped the crown over his sooty hair and giggled. "There are no accidents in this world."

His heart picked itself right back up and then began to beat wildly as he gazed into her bright, sweet eyes, her hands clasped under her chin. *There are no accidents in this world.* Did she mean that their bond was somehow fate? Was it that important to her? She gestured outward in every direction. "Everything is perfect. And you are perfect just the way you are."

He couldn't be certain, but up ahead it sounded like Makasa snorted. His heart stopped beating so quickly.

After that, he fell silent, trying not to huff too loudly as the path became steeper and steeper, until he was all but crawling his way up the switchback that led to Thal'darah Overlook.

They passed under a polished purple arch, glittery with ghost-like wisps, and Aram flapped his shirt, sweaty and exhausted. He watched Makasa being helped off her moonsaber and hoped dearly that she needed a rest, because by the Light, he needed one, too. To Aram, it seemed as if the outpost had been established as an antidote to the Charred Vale's bleak and smoky hills. Soft music, as mystical and beautiful as starlight, twinkled throughout the clearing. A ring of tall trees protected the smattering of buildings, including a well-built inn.

Aiyell spotted them first, and then the other Sentinels. Iyneath seemed to be the only male among them, and soon they were surrounded by curious, armored night elves. A brown owl sat preening itself on Aiyell's arm, its keen eyes pinned on the weary travelers even as it cleaned itself.

"You have arrived swiftly," she observed, coming forward to help the others dismount from their moonsabers.

"They are young," Llaran replied. "But stalwart."

Makasa backed away from the Sentinels, planting herself next to Aram. Despite having both shoulders bandaged, she stood tall, and gazed around at the gathering of elves before clearing her throat, saying loudly, "We're here to see Master Thal'darah. Please summon him."

Aram elbowed her, but only gently, mindful of her wounds.

"Or what?" Iyneath teased, placing Murky carefully on his feet. The murloc adjusted the spear and net on his back and promptly sat down, massive toes splayed out in front of him. Hackle looked equally exhausted, but stood his ground, rubbing his eyes with dirty paws.

"Slow down, young visitors," Iyneath continued. "Master Thal'darah will be summoned, but you must also find rest."

"Indeed. Find your comfort here, at least for a while. There will be time to speak of druidic spells and bonds and all sorts, but perhaps after you have eaten, yes?" It was Llaran's turn to chide them.

Aram preemptively nudged Makasa, knowing how much she hated being lectured.

But for once, she didn't put up a fuss, sighing and touching one of her new bandages with a grimace. "Sure. We're eager to continue on our journey. We didn't come all this way to—"

"And how far have you come?" Llaran asked.

She was interrupted, however, by a larger and considerably furrier face breaking through the crowd. Aram's initial instinct was to get out his sketchbook, and he saw Makasa reaching for her cutlass. He noticed that the tauren girl was smiling, or rather, she was gasping and throwing her three-fingered hands into the air. No Horde ambusher, then, as perhaps Makasa had expected, just another of the outpost's residents.

"Another dryad! Here! How exciting!" The tauren, taller than Makasa and with long, black braids flecked with brown, wore a long and flowing robe. Colorful feathers and beads were sewn

into the neck and sleeves. Her eyes were by far her most striking feature, glittery and round, sparkling with the kind of
friendly intensity that reminded Aram of Drella. "I've been
wanting to meet another dryad. By the Earth Mother, I have so
many questions!"

Drella stepped forward, dancing a little, as if they hadn't just
walked for two days and camped in an ash-covered cemetery.
The Sentinels around them seemed to regard the tauren with
veiled expressions.

"Hello, new friend! I am Taryndrella the Impressive, this is
Murky the Unstung. This shaggy fellow is Hackle the Revenged,
and the one with the really big coat is Aram, Wielder of Light.
The angry girl with the scary chain is Makasa the Binder. Do you
know Master Thal'darah?"

"Titles and questions, and so much youthful exuberance!"

Aram glanced away from the strange meeting taking place
before him. The voice boomed out of a tall, sturdy night elf, his
skin a milky blue, his face covered in a wispy beard, leaves and
feathers woven among the strands. He wore a robe much like the
tauren's, though it was more embellished and capped with tall,
elaborate armor pieces that pulsed with subtle magic.

He leaned heavily on a staff, and given the way the tauren
stepped back and demurred, Aram could only assume this was
the elf they had come to see.

"Titles and questions," he repeated, laughing, his bright eyes settling on each of them in turn. "You are safe now and welcome. Look how the wisps dance in the trees at your coming! Even my Sentinels are excited by your arrival."

Drella took one tiny step forward, a dainty hoof hovering in mid-air questioningly. "Are you Master Thal'darah?"

"I am," he said in that deep, warm voice of his. "It sounds as if you were looking for me. Well now, your journey is at an end."

Aram felt his shoulders ease, relief trickling over him like cool water. Even if the druid was wrong, even if their journey was nowhere near its end, he was glad to have that moment of peace, and to see Drella smiling brightly, as if they truly had not a care in the world.

CHAPTER FIVE
DINING WITH DRUIDS

Aram wiped a spot of kimchi off his sketchbook, cursing under his breath. He couldn't even wait until after supper to begin putting down on paper everything he had seen since leaving the *Cloudkicker*. After the first sip of fresh juice and a few bites of roasted sagefish smothered in spicy kimchi, his vigor returned. With that energy came his urge to sketch, and so he tried to manage shoveling food into his face, gulping down juice, and moving his pencil without making a mess.

He wasn't quite successful, but at least he had managed to draw a quick picture of the long trestle table at the inn and all of those gathered around it. Master Thal'darah sat at the head, with Drella and their new tauren acquaintance on either side of him.

"Galena," she had introduced herself breathlessly as they all walked to the inn to put down their packs and rest. "Galena Stormspear! I'm with the Cenarion Circle, well, with Master Thal'darah. He's teaching me everything he knows.

It's just . . . you can't know how exciting it is to meet you all. Life here can get a bit . . ."

She had trailed off, aware that her teacher was listening in, but Aram could fill in the blanks. Her excitement—her elation—was clear as Drella's pleasure at being so admired by the apprentice. Life at Thal'darah Overlook seemed tense for a young tauren, and Galena couldn't ask them questions fast enough. Aram got the distinct impression that most of the night elves were not willing to shirk their duties to converse with her, and that the travelers contained some of the first friendly faces she had encountered in a long while.

Where had they come from? How did they avoid the battle in the valley? Why did they need to see Master Thal'darah? Would she be allowed to help with this bond ceremony? It went on and on, a dizzying number of questions, all of which Drella was more than happy to field. And that was for the best; the others didn't have the patience for it, especially not Makasa, who positioned herself as far down the table as possible. They had been given water for baths and a light snack once they reached the inn, and then a short time later, as dusk deepened, Llaran summoned them from their rooms on the upper level of the inn. Everyone gathered downstairs, and Aram tucked into his food, half listening to Galena pepper Drella with questions, while Makasa brooded over her fish and stew.

After a time, Drella turned the tables, asking questions as they came to her, jumping to a new subject with little connection or logic while Galena, flustered, struggled to keep up. The tauren had left Mulgore at a young age, her druidic abilities obvious, and she was soon apprenticed to a Cenarion Circle acolyte in Feralas. She wasn't there long before a letter came, informing all Circle members that Master Thal'darah was taking on a new apprentice at last, and Galena jumped at the chance to go. Aram wondered if she regretted that now, given that, by her own admission, it was difficult to be the only tauren at the Overlook.

"Watch out," Makasa said, polishing off a third cup of juice. "I think you might have competition for the title of Drella's biggest admirer. Look at those moon eyes. I'll never understand it; she's exhausting."

"She's practically a newborn," Aram reminded his sister. The dryad had only been alive a short while, and though physically and mentally mature, still maintained the wide-eyed wonder of a human toddler. "I think it's nice, Makasa, don't you prefer this? Food and drink, a safe place to sleep . . . it sure beats running from ogres in Gadgetzan."

"Hackle miss home," the gnoll cut in. He, too, seemed mystified by the dryad and tauren fawning over each other. "Hackle miss real food."

The gnoll, much cleaner after a quick roll in a tub and a subsequent shake, picked up his plate of fish and sniffed, then growled.

"Why they ruin it with this?" He scooped up a bit of the kimchi with a claw and flung it, the blob of cabbage landing on Murky's plate. "Make nose itch. Hackle take raw fish next time. Aram tell them. Aram fix it."

"Mrgla, blurgly lurk-kelurk," Murky agreed, lips flapping in disgust at the splodge of kimchi.

"Raw for us," Hackle said with a sigh. He found a bit of the fish that had gone unsauced and tore it off with his teeth. "Aram tell them."

"I will," Aram said, amused. "I think it's rather good."

"Is no good, stink like ogre den."

Aram smirked. "I think it's just fermented."

"Then Aram eat ogre poop. Hackle have standard."

And with that, Aram took the portion of Hackle's food covered in the deliciously spicy kimchi and ate it himself. That he was now, without hesitation, sharing food off the plate of a gnoll did not go unnoticed.

"Hate to interrupt bonding time," Makasa cut in, "but don't forget why we're actually here. First thing in the morning you need to find out how to remove your bond with Drella. After that, we're not staying." She lowered her voice, glancing nervously down the table at Master Thal'darah, but he wasn't paying her any attention, instead engrossed in conversation with Drella and Galena. "Don't forget about the shards. We need a plan, and then we leave."

"I know," Aram insisted. His appetite vanished, and he shut his sketchbook with a grunt. He reached for his shirt, for the compass hidden underneath. Its needle remained fixed to the southeast, toward Lakeshire, and suddenly he sympathized with Hackle—he missed home. He missed the simplicity of life then, when he wasn't consumed with magical shards; the Voice of the Light; the death of his father, Greydon; the possibility of an even more mysterious uncle, Silverlaine; and a strange bond with a dryad.

Aram's gaze drifted down the table, and for a moment he watched Drella, her hair flying back over her shoulders as she laughed with Galena over some new topic.

"You're so different from Miri, the other dryad I know. You seem . . . special," the tauren was saying.

"I am," Drella replied, without a hint of shyness. "Entering my summer has made me feel *much* happier. But then, I am almost always happy."

"Sure," Galena said with a laugh. "Well, I wish Miri would find her summer; she is never, well, friendly. At least not to me."

Somehow, even with fawn's legs, the dryad made sitting at the table graceful and easy. The bond. He knew they had to break it, that Drella had a greater fate to fulfill, but part of him wanted to guard that connection fiercely. When it was gone, their friendship might change forever.

When eyes began to droop and the stars shone in earnest, Master Thal'darah insisted they all retire to bed.

"We will begin the process of removing your bond in the morning," the druid master promised them. "Galena and I will make preparations tonight, and now it is time you all had some much-deserved rest."

With that, Makasa pushed away from the table and disappeared up the stairs. The others followed, Aram leaving the table last. He wanted to talk to Drella before everyone went to sleep, but she trotted away from the stairs and out into the night.

"I want to sleep under the stars," she told him, waving happily as she dipped out of the inn. "The moonwell is so beautiful and so bright; it will be perfect company!"

"Goodnight," Aram called, surrounded by friends but suddenly lonely.

He and Makasa shared a space upstairs, and she dropped off to sleep at once, snoring away before he had even blown out his candle. Soon Hackle and Murky joined the chorus of snoozing, Murky's hiccups and Hackle's yips audible through the wall. Hackle was no doubt chasing ogres back in the forest, but Aram could imagine that Murky was dreaming about fishing and helping his friends.

Sitting up in bed, he found himself still wide-awake, and so he finished his sketch of the dinner table, taking more time with

Master Thal'darah and Galena. He wanted to put them down accurately, to learn the angles and quirks of their faces the way he had memorized those of his companions. Galena had such a youthful, gentle look, nothing like some of the fearsome tauren they had seen in the lower wilds. She had the same sturdy, bovine body of other tauren, of course, but she spoke with an almost night elven accent, her voice higher than others of her kind. He carefully re-created her long, intricate braids and the one tuft of black hair that stuck up roguishly from her part.

Master Thal'darah reminded him in some ways of his departed friend, Thalyss Greyoak, the patient and ancient druid who had sacrificed his life to save Aram. They both possessed the same long, flowing hair and well-kept beard, though Master Thal'darah filled his with decorations. Aram made sure to include the friendly smile lines around the master's mouth, and the many beads and feathers sewn to his Cenarion robes.

He sketched the moonwell, too, and the elven Sentinels—Iyneath with his moonsaber, Llaran with her bow drawn, and Aiyell with her trusty owl. After that, sleep eluded him still, and so he turned to a clean page and smoothed his palm over it. Hackle was already homesick, and so was Aram. Glancing at the candle, he decided he had more than enough flame to pen a letter home.

Mother, he wrote, pulling in a deep, steadying breath. Just thinking about her made tears sting behind his eyes.

He wasn't ashamed of it; a sailor on the *Wavestrider* had once told him that a man who didn't get teary-eyed over his mother was no man at all.

He scratched out *Mother*, writing instead: *Dear Mom.*

Where to begin? He wanted desperately to tell her everything, every truth, tiny and big, in his heart. He wanted to tell her the scary things they had seen, and the times they had laughed, and the moments when he felt hopeless and overwhelmed. But he thought of her reading all of that, and how it would frighten her. So, how to begin?

Dear Mom,

I'm writing to you from the Stonetalon Mountains, from a small outpost called Thal'darah Overlook. You wouldn't believe how beautiful it is here, and how different it is from Lakeshire! The trees are as big as mountains, but only after you cross a valley that's always on fire. I've come so far to get here, I don't even know where to start . . .

But he did start. Aram let it come pouring out, but only what he knew wouldn't frighten her too much or make her cry. He told her a lot about Hackle, and Murky, and how Makasa had started out as a foe and become a dear friend, a sister, even. And he described the *Wavestrider*, and Thalyss. He told her about taking the acorn into their care, and how, of course, even after Thalyss's clear warning, he still managed to get it wet. And that led to Drella. Aram babbled on and on about the dryad, about her smile and her laugh, and the way their travels in the sun had covered her face in freckles the color of spring grass. He knew he sounded foolish, but maybe, just maybe, that would make his worried mother smile.

Aram left out Greydon's death and their many brushes with danger. He didn't mention the arenas they had battled in, or the shards, or Thalyss's death, or Makasa nearly being carried off by a drake. Part of him wanted to avoid talking about Greydon, not just to spare his mother, but to spare himself. His hand shook over the page as he pictured his father's face. Time did not heal all wounds. Even if that one had begun to heal, just thinking too much about Greydon made the scab easy to break. Skirting around Greydon's whereabouts and death, he closed it with a promise.

I don't know when I'll be back, Mom, but I will return. Adventure is one thing, but Lakeshire is home. Tell Robertson and Selya I miss them, and Robb, too. Give Soot a big hug and an extra bone for me, all right? I love you, Mom, don't worry about me; I've got good friends by my side and I know they'll do everything they can to help me make it back to you.

That part was absolutely true. Aram tucked the letter back into his sketchbook, not knowing if or when he would send it. Then he glanced at his sister, Makasa, snoring away, her hands wrapped around her chain weapon even as she slept. He blew out the candle and settled down into the cozy mattress, listening to the wisps weave through the mountainous trees, their song like the whisper in the wind just before rain.

CHAPTER SIX
ILL OMENS

At first, it seemed as if Aram roamed the Charred Vale once more. Flames crept steadily at his feet, then grew, but soon the silence gave way to the shriek of splintering wood and the even harsher screams of men and women. Above him, a mast pierced through the smoke, the sail dancing with gouts of red flame. A ship. He was on a ship. Even feeling the tilted sway of a dream world around him, Aram's heart raced. The *Wavestrider* and the rhythm of its hull over the waves remained a vivid memory, but now it was being eaten alive by fire.

Aram plunged into the disarray, watching figures emerge as they sought to fight the blaze.

"Water here! A bucket now, man! I need water!"

"We're taking on too much water! We're going down . . ."

The voices soared above the crack and pop of the fire. Aram shielded his eyes, tumbling from the captain's quarters onto the main deck. He tried to make out faces of the crew, to see if this was a twisted vision of a memory or something more. Shadows flickered across the blaze that ate along the edges of the deck and then ignited the ropes secured to the mast. They snapped, whipping over Aram's head as the shadows resolved into bodies.

Cannons boomed, echoing across the water. He heard the sneering, haughty call he knew so well. *Malus.* Captain Malus and his vicious crew were attacking. But then Aram watched the sail above float down, still glowing with cinders, and he felt, even in the dream, his mouth run dry. Those were not the colors of the *Wavestrider.* Did he know this ship? The bodies moving fretfully about the deck were small, he realized, too small . . . *Goblins.*

This was not the *Wavestrider,* then, but the *Crustacean,* the ship that had departed Gadgetzan, believed by Baron Noggenfogger to hold Aram and his friends. The misinformation had tricked Malus, leading him on a fool's errand, chasing Aram on a ship he had never been aboard. But if this dream was real, if this was a true vision, then Malus had found the ship, and the *Crustacean* . . . Stars, it was *doomed.* Aram reached as a reflex for the crystal shard hilt he carried, forgetting that the blade was not yet complete. He was without a weapon. Helpless. Stunned. But the dream felt so real. He could all but taste the ash in his mouth . . .

The ship shuddered, thrown side to side by a sudden impact. The crew scrambled with buckets, and then, swords.

"To arms!" He heard the call go up. "We're being boarded! Cut their ropes! Don't let them take us!"

The *Crustacean*, prickly with still-burning fire arrows, lurched, beginning to sink, but not before Malus appeared, leaping aboard, jumping through the smoke and flames as if he were utterly impervious, a fire elemental made man. His vessel, a darkly menacing elven destroyer, must have found the *Crustacean* and set it ablaze to smoke out Aram and his friends. His cruel eyes gleamed, and he stroked the lapel of his coat, cutting down the nearest goblin with a casual swing of his sword. The boards under Aram's feet shook, a pair of ogre sailors stomping by, hammers raised in defense of the *Crustacean*. Crossbow bolts from the boarding ship stopped them short, and Malus took a large step over one of their bodies, heading toward Aram as if Malus sensed him through the hazy reality of the dream.

Aram took a step back, but found himself surrounded by the hot and licking flames.

"Malus, Throgg fight for Hidden. Fight trolls and elves and humans. Not fight ogres. Not after Dire Maul. Not again."

The voice, loud as the crack of the ships hitting together, sent Aram reeling back another few paces. Throgg, large as four men, with a gruesome horn jutting from his forehead and a spiked mace attached to his stump arm, batted aside a charging goblin as he stared down at the fallen ogres.

"Calm yourself," Malus told the seething ogre. "We just need the compass and the sword hilt, then we can leave this wreck at the bottom of the ocean and be about our way."

Aram watched Throgg toe one of the ogres onto her back and growl. He didn't look pleased.

Crew from the *Inevitable* swarmed, chaos darkening the deck. Aram could hardly see through the haze of gray and blinding flash of the flames. Malus stalked closer, headed toward the cabins, but a sudden burst of fire sent him tumbling backward. He recovered, putting up a hand against a shower of glowing wood splinters. One caught in his hair, and he extinguished it with a curse.

"Where are they?" he muttered, eyes sweeping the ship. "If I chased this forsaken ship halfway across the sea for nothing . . ."

His crew reemerged from the cabins below and the captain's quarters. The vision began to break apart, as if the fire had spread to Aram's mind, burning away the sight of it all. In the end, he heard Malus screaming his frustration as the *Crustacean* sank, its crew lost to ash and fire or the merciless blades of the attacking crew.

"Not here. Not here." Malus sounded half-mad, or perhaps completely mad.

But it wasn't long before Aram couldn't see him at all, and the red and gray of the massacre bled away, completely dark, and then unbearably bright. Light flashed so suddenly in front of Aram's eyes that he feared he would be completely blinded.

And then he heard a voice, a familiar voice, one that had

whispered into his dreams before. It filled him with warmth and resolve, but also a dread that couldn't be named. It was a force of power he couldn't quite understand, and so he couldn't help but fear it, too.

It was the Light. It called to him.

"Fate has other plans for you," the Voice of the Light said, gentle and resonant. "You have no need to fear."

Makasa Flintwill was not the kind to sleep in. Even wounded, exhausted, and confused, that morning was no exception. She ate a bit of hard rations from her own pack and greeted the sun as it rose, tending to her weapons by a fire in the middle of the protected hilltop outpost. As she oiled her jerkin and sharpened her blades, she didn't see any of it. Not really. Her mind was elsewhere, preoccupied with a dream of her own. One that had speared through her deep, dark sleep like a flashing blade.

A voice. A beautiful, terrible voice. In all her seventeen years, she had never heard anything like it. It was simultaneously as familiar and comforting as the way her hammock rocked on the *Makemba* when she was just a child and still sailing with the Blackwater Raiders. When her siblings still surrounded her. When she didn't think life was any more complicated than a sturdy set of boards under her feet and salt breeze in her hair. But the voice . . . it was also as cold as winter rain, as a sudden wound, as the crack of lightning over a stormy sea.

Above all, she didn't trust it, and she didn't like that it was speaking to her. Let Aram and Drella deal with all the upsetting mumbo jumbo of magic. It never appealed to her. There was power enough in a cunning eye and a trained sword arm. But now . . . Now she felt like the taint of magic had spread to her somehow. The voice wasn't natural, and it spoke to her of things that felt true but also, not yet real.

Turn toward the Light, Makasa. The Diamond Blade. Aram is on the path, though you walk it with him. The shards must be reunited. Seven must become One. Look, Makasa, look into the Light.

Makasa had resisted, as if there was any hope of struggling against the voice. She suspected it was the same voice that had visited Aram in his visions, the Voice of the Light. Anything called the Voice of the Light ought to be a good thing, she reasoned, but somehow her heart quavered whenever she thought of it. But she knew who it was. And she knew what the Diamond Blade and the shards meant. When she relented, when she indeed turned toward the Light, she saw images, one after another, places she didn't recognize and could barely even remember. Even as she sat by the fire, sharpening her blades, it gave her a raging headache to try and recall the places.

"Lot of help you are," she muttered. "Can't you just send me a map? A dream map?"

"Hi!"

Makasa started, dropping a small boot dagger and then

catching it, nimbly, by the blade with two fingers. She spun it, glaring at Drella, who had bounded toward the fire with her usual glee radiating like sunbeams from every pore. The young dryad swung her arms from side to side, then stuck her pinky between her lips.

"Good morning," Makasa finally bit out.

"You seem angry," Drella observed, trotting closer and examining her weapons. Something about the way Drella so clearly admired Makasa's chain and harpoon made her soften a little. Maybe it was time to trust, even just a little, since Drella had shown her ability to help the group and make them stronger. Makasa had worked on a ship crew, and trust—comradery—mattered.

"I am angry. I had . . . dreams. Bad ones. No, strange ones."

"Want to talk about it? Thalyss always said it was better to get your feelings out in the open than to leave them twisted up inside. We could talk." The dryad did a quick lap around the fire and then settled in beside her. "I am *very* good at talking."

We noticed.

"Not right now, Drella, but . . . thank you. For the offer."

It never hurt to be diplomatic, and while Drella certainly wasn't Makasa's favorite person on Azeroth, she knew it might not be long before they parted ways with her. Soon, Aram and Drella's bond would be broken, and Drella would remain with the druids while the rest of them journeyed on to find the shards and complete the Diamond Blade. Certainly, Makasa could slap on a smile for the dryad until then.

Commotion at the front of the inn drew her attention away from Drella, and Makasa swiveled to find the tauren, Galena, all but sprinting toward them, braids flying, her smile overtaking every other part of her face. Behind her, left behind in a dust cloud of enthusiasm, was Aram, stumbling down the steps, groggy, a pastry in one hand, the heel of his other rubbing at his eyes.

"Good morning, Galena!" Drella cried. "You look so beautiful today. Does she not look beautiful, Makasa?"

"Sure."

"You look lovely, too," Drella added, leaning down to pat Makasa on the shoulder, a gesture that would've earned anyone else a swift slash of the blade. Instead, Makasa just flinched and stood to collect Aram. "And your blades are lovely, also! You always keep them so shiny; it really is admirable."

"Good morning, Makasa," the tauren girl said, waving. "And good morning, Drella. Are you ready to start our chores? Master Thal'darah needs at least a full basket of wild steelbloom blossoms for the first ritual."

"Oh, how perfect! A morning spent in nature's glory, is there anything better?"

Galena and Drella subsided into laughter, and Makasa

sheathed her weapons, then not-so-gently took the tauren by the arm. Galena might have been taller, but she cowered, staring down into Makasa's eyes with a trembling lower lip.

"You keep a sharp eye on her," Makasa warned. "Wandering around in the woods? Just the two of you? I'll have your hide if anything happens to Drella before the rituals are completed."

"O-Of course," Galena stammered. "I'm with the Cenarion Circle, Makasa, and I'm sworn to protect her already. Dryads are sacred to us. I w-won't let anything happen to her. Besides, the guards will be close."

"Good," Makasa said. "That's good. You make sure they're close."

Looking haunted, Aram reached the fire pit just as Galena and Drella departed. The two girls didn't seem to notice him, but he definitely noticed them, his eyes trailing after Drella.

"I know you two are good friends," Makasa said. "But your bond will be broken soon. Maybe you should keep some distance, make it easier on yourself."

"And good morning to you, too," he replied, ruffling his own hair and trying to pat it down into a reasonable state.

"It could just be rough on you," Makasa said. "That's all I meant."

"Thanks. I mean, you're probably right."

She smiled wearily at that.

"You look tired. Bad night's sleep?" he asked. "Couldn't be worse than mine. My dreams lately have been so vivid. Too vivid."

"Me too." She nodded. "Dreams. Weird ones. Bad ones. Or . . . it was this voice, good and bad at the same time. It was like it made my teeth hurt or something, so powerful it was talking through me," she explained. Normally, she would never divulge that such a thing had happened, but she knew strange things happened around Aram all the time, and more often than not he woke from dreams in a panic, as if they were as real as the pastry she had just stolen from his hand.

Aram squinted, shuffling toward a log near the fire. Aiyell's owl soared overhead, calling out, then dipped to rip a field mouse off the dirt near the inn.

"What did the voice say?" he asked.

Makasa stood over him. "It spoke of the Diamond Blade. It tried to show me places, locations of the other shards perhaps, but it happened too quickly. It sounds like the visions you have."

"Yeah," Aram murmured. He looked . . . not afraid, but pouty. "It sounds like the Voice of the Light that talks to me, too. I didn't think—" He shook his head for a moment, then met Makasa's eyes. "I think it's great. It must mean we're on the right track. We just have to keep following the compass and find the remaining shards."

She shrugged. "Right now we need to focus on finishing

up here. Do you think we could go soon, leave Drella with them while they sever the bond?"

Aram shook his head, still working the inside of his cheek, put out. "No, Galena was telling me on the way down this morning they need both of us here for the ritual."

"Splendid." Makasa sighed. "Well, what can we do in the meantime, while they prepare the ritual?"

After a moment of staring into the fire, Aram pulled the sketchbook from the pack slung over his right shoulder and opened it. Makasa didn't normally snoop, but she noticed a letter tucked inside. A letter.

"Are you planning on sending a letter? You know that's dangerous, right? It could be intercepted, Aram."

"It's for my mother," he said with a sigh. "She has to be so worried about me. I can't leave her in the dark like this, Makasa; it just doesn't seem fair. Besides, this is an outpost on the edge of a war. They must have a safe way to send messages. And if they do . . ." Aram trailed off for a moment; then his eyes popped open. "Then maybe I could write to someone about my uncle. If he's really alive, he might be able to help us."

"That sounds risky." Makasa shook her head, running her hand nervously over the hilt of her cutlass.

"You're probably right, again. And where would I find him? I don't even know where to start looking," Aram finished the thought for her. Impressive, for a groggy twelve-year-old.

"Besides, how long would it take to get a response? If we want to be out of here as quickly as possible, then I don't think we can rely on some long shot like that."

"Definitely not worth the risk," Makasa said at once, feeling deflated by their lack of options. "Any advice on how to get that strange voice out of my head?"

Aram snorted and shook his head, then took up his pencil, turning to a clean page. "Sorry, sister, it's not always fun to be the chosen one."

CHAPTER SEVEN
UNEXPECTED VISIONS

Things were moving too fast. He already had enough on his mind with the unbinding ceremony approaching, and now he had to suffer visions of the *Crustacean*'s demise, and Makasa was receiving her own dream messages.

And then an idea, like a thorn, lodged itself in Aram's mind. *A thorn in a Thorne*, he thought, turning his sketchbook to a clean page. Why had the Light been talking to Makasa? Had it lost all faith in him? Was that also why it had shown him the horrible vision of the *Crustacean*, to show him his failure? Would it sever its bond with him the same way he was about to be cleaved from Drella?

As these thoughts and more swirled about, he lifted his pencil. He desperately needed a way to clear his head.

He let his torrent of reflections sit for a spell, listening to the comforting crackle of the fire while he decided what to draw. His initial inclination was to sketch the outside of the Overlook, but that didn't strike him as all that exciting. There was his copy of *Common Birds of Azeroth*, thanks to Charnas, and he briefly considered trying to re-create one of the many creatures within, but that idea fell flat, too.

Instead, he thought back to what Charnas had encouraged him to do, drawing not from what could be seen clearly with the eye but with the imagination. Drawing from a model required skill, of course, but Aram wanted to expand his abilities, and conjuring images from his mind to sketch seemed like the perfect exercise. At once, his pencil leapt into action, soaring across the parchment, the snarling jaws of a black drake coming to life, and then Makasa beneath it, her hand posed upward, swinging her chain.

Aram's view of the struggle had been obscured by the dust of the storm, but now he could see Makasa's openmouthed cry, her determination, the slight tightness by her eyes from the pain of the claws piercing her shoulders . . . Exhilarated, he tilted his pencil to the side, giving the whole scene a light gray wash to show the storm, then finished by adding a few incoming arrows flying toward the drake. It wasn't as accurate as some of his portraits, but he liked the tension and movement. Charnas was right: This had a different feeling to it, and Aram felt almost hypnotized, his breath short, his fingers moving as if by magic. A new page! He needed to try more.

Closing his eyes, he instantly pictured a deep cave and a figure emerging from it, a boy not much older than Aram, with a young blue dragon looming over him. Both the boy and the blue dragon had a scar over one cheek. For some reason the cave felt dark and cold to him, and wet, so Aram added small foot tracks along the floor. The young man's eyes felt alive when he saw them in his mind, and when Aram studied his drawing, he shivered, finding those eyes pierced through him from the page. It felt so *real*. Realer, he thought with another shudder, than some of his portraits of actual living people.

Aram flipped the page again but felt exhausted. Drawing from imagination took more out of him than the usual light sketching. He glanced up from his work, hearing a loud twinkle of laughter from the tauren and the dryad busy gathering flowers in the forest.

It was selfish and stupid to think of Drella as his, but his thoughts turned again to their special bond, a bond that Thal'darah's magic would soon unravel. Was that why he suddenly felt a pang of jealousy toward Galena? *Of course* a dryad would have so much more to talk about with a druid from the Cenarion Circle. Galena even knew other dryads, so it made perfect sense, but *still*. Feelings often didn't make sense; they just made problems. It wasn't a crush, he insisted to himself. They were just close friends. They had gone through so much, it was natural to feel close.

But before he could brood, he heard Murky and Hackle

arguing about what to eat from inside the inn. The gnoll seemed to be understanding the little murloc better and better, and Aram had to smile at the thought of what mischief those two might get up to if left unsupervised.

His knee slid, and the letter he had written to his mother slipped out of the book, fluttering to the ground. Aram bent quickly to retrieve it, his eyes lingering on the folded parchment. He still couldn't find the urge to send it. But another urge rose, one guided by that little thorn that had lodged in his mind after his discussion with Makasa.

Letters. What if he wrote to different places in Kalimdor enquiring after his uncle? Makasa was right about the risk, but he remained convinced he was also right that they could trust the Sentinels to send the messages safely for them. It seemed hopeless, but Aram would just have to be a grown-up about it and do something. And so he did, composing a brief letter introducing himself, and explaining that he was the son of Greydon Thorne, that he had urgent business with Silverlaine Thorne, and any information about his whereabouts would be appreciated. He toyed with the thought of adding a reward, but knew that would come back to bite him if he actually *did* hear something about his uncle.

Instead, he was honest and direct.

Please, he wrote. *Please help me find my uncle. It would mean the world to me.*

Aram copied out the letter several times, not knowing how many copies he might need, then tucked them all into his sketchbook and stood, stretching. Murky and Hackle emerged from the inn, each holding fish so fresh and raw they might have still been wriggling. The two trundled over to him, sat, then unceremoniously bit into their respective sagefish.

"Yuck." Aram shook his head, leaving them to their feast. "Warn someone before you do that."

"Hackle save you part," the gnoll offered, eyes glittering.

Before Aram could respond, Hackle and Murky dissolved into laughter, the murloc mostly burbling around a full mouth, the gnoll giving his tittering hyena laugh.

"Very funny. Have either of you seen Master Thal'darah? I wanted to ask him some questions about the ritual."

That was a lie, but a white one, he decided. He didn't want anyone to know about his plan to send off the letters; it would make it look as if he planned to leave before the bonding could be undone. Besides, Silverlaine was *his* uncle. Finding the man might help them recover more shards for the Diamond Blade, but that felt like a long shot. No, Aram was just as interested in finding him to know more about Greydon, and to know more about his place in the world as a Thorne. Greydon had been stolen from him so quickly, and the wound had never quite healed right. Still, he knew he needed to be careful.

Perhaps Makasa's suspicious nature was rubbing off on him,

he thought, watching Hackle swallow a giant mouthful of fish, scales and all.

"Hackle no see him today." The gnoll raised his nose into the air and gave a long sniff. "But he not far. Forest," he said. "North."

"Mrky nk blolger legl," the murloc added with a shrug of his tiny shoulders.

That was a no, then.

"Thanks," Aram told them, waving. "I'll check with the Sentinels, then. You two, uh, enjoy your breakfast."

The Sentinels were easy to find, patrolling slowly around the perimeter of the Overlook when they weren't out on the paths checking for stray Horde scouts. Aram left behind the campfire, heading east toward a small arch and a half-built glaive thrower, where Iyneath groomed his moonsaber. The giant cat wrinkled its nose at Aram's approach, but otherwise relaxed, nudging its furry muzzle into Iyneath's chest while he ran a bristly brush across the animal's back, raking out burrs and twigs.

"Cinderfoot, stop that," the one-eyed night elf chided. But the moonsaber, looking like nothing more than a big housecat, purred and pushed its nose against the Sentinel's chest again, then started pawing the ground.

Aram pointed. "Back in Lakeshire, they call that making biscuits."

"I call it a nuisance," Iyneath replied, but he was laughing. "He has not had a brushing in some time. I can forget that even creatures bred for war have a special bond with their masters. Much like your bond with the dryad, I would imagine. Have the rituals begun?"

"Not yet, I think Galena and Master Thal'darah are still making preparations. I've just been filling the time. Actually, I wrote a few letters, and I thought you might know the area well. I'm trying to find someone who was last seen in northern Kalimdor. A human man. Any ideas on where I might send inquiries?"

Iyneath paused, his one good eye flashing with interest as he glanced up at Aram. "Going somewhere?"

"N-No! No"—Aram scratched the back of his head nervously, scrambling for an excuse—"it's my uncle, actually. I just want to find him and make sure he's okay. He might be dead, for all I know."

"Oh. My condolences." Iyneath stood, dropping the brush before reaching into the pack on his belt and retrieving a small folded map. He beckoned Aram closer, then showed him the map, which was of nearby parts of Stonetalon and beyond. The night elf's finger moved swiftly across the various regions. "Now let me think. Astranaar, Fort Triumph, Honor's Stand, Theramore, and even the Northwatch Expedition Base have all received a swell of Alliance troops recently. If your uncle is a soldier, he might be there."

Aram nodded, doing his best to memorize the locations and the names. He had an artist's mind, one keen to remember

images, even subtle ones. His eyes followed the Sentinel's pointing, and his heart began to sink. Some of those places were far
away. It would take a long time to get there unless they could
magically conjure Gazlowe's airship again.

"Those seem like good places to try," Aram agreed. "If I gave
you the letters, could you see that they get to those outposts?
How long would it take?"

"Between our outrunners and the owls, not terribly long,"
Iyneath explained, scratching his chin. "We stay in regular contact with the other outposts nearby, to keep each other aware of
any Horde patrols on the move."

"It would mean a lot to me," Aram told him. "Here, I've
already copied out the letters. And . . . would you mind not telling anyone? It just feels like a fool's errand looking for him this
way, and it makes me feel, well, foolish."

Iyneath straightened to his full height, his smile turning down
slightly. "It is never a fool's errand to reach out to one's family.
You have my word, Aramar Thorne, it will be done discreetly."

CHAPTER EIGHT
SEVERING THE BOND

Taryndrella closed her eyes and cleared her mind. That was hard, of course, *really* hard. When they first began the ceremonies, she couldn't manage to do it at all. There were just so many things to think about! Like, why did butterflies only come in some colors and not *all* colors? And were red butterflies meaner than blue ones? That didn't seem fair to her if so, because red wasn't a mean or bad color at all. She found it perfectly lovely. Apples, for example, had become one of her favorite foods. And fire kept people warm! So many good, wholesome things were red that it really should not be considered an "angry" color, in fact—

"Taryndrella! Concentrate."

She screwed up her face and nodded. There was no need to open her eyes to see Master Thal'darah, already she was quite familiar with his Frustrated Face. He had many faces. Smiley Face at supper, because he so liked all the many new creatures at the Overlook. It was obvious he found everyone fascinating, but especially Murky, because he had never tried to communicate with a murloc before, especially one as brave and unique as Murky the Unstung. And, of course, she knew his Sleepy Face, which happened after they had been at the ceremonies for many hours, the smell of burnt steelbloom clinging to them all. Kind and Patient Face was her favorite because—

"TARYNDRELLA. By the blue hairs in my beard, I beg you: *focus*."

There he was again. Frustrated Face. She took in a deep breath and tried her best to banish the thoughts of butterflies and faces and beards. After a moment, the darkness returned in earnest. Taryndrella shivered, afraid. The smoke of the flower and incense filled her, and the visions came quickly. She stood at the edge of a cliff, surrounded by deep, cold shadows. That horrible darkness crept closer, the ends of it as long and spindly as spider's legs. The blessings of Cenarius kept her safe, and so she thought about those gifts, hard, for Master Thal'darah had promised her that if she just focused on good thoughts of a guiding presence, like Cenarius, then it would come to her in the vision. Only the beautiful warmth of his blessings could banish the icy darkness and clear her path to Aram. She would see him eventually in her visions, standing there right in the open, and when she finally did, then she could trot to him, pluck a single flower from his hair, and cast it into the wind, and the ritual would be complete.

The bond would be severed.

A tiny mote of light drifted down from above her. There was no sky, but the light had come from somewhere. Her heart, maybe, or it was her wishes made real. The little light danced and she smiled, following, reaching out to touch it. It shied away, leading her toward the scary, undulating darkness. Courage. She needed courage. Taryndrella did her best impression of Makasa Flintwill. Courageous, strong Makasa wouldn't be afraid of some stupid old shadows. Drella trotted toward the light, breathing deeply, telling herself that if she just watched that mote of happiness and hope, then the darkness couldn't get her.

It worked, for a time, and as she and the light neared the fringes of the shadows, the tendrils began to break apart. Farther and farther they traveled into the shadows, and it was terribly cold. Drella shivered, hugging herself, but she went on, refusing to give up. The vision ceremonies had never gone this well before, and that made her even more determined to press on! For a week, they had tried and failed to get her beyond the darkness, and now it was actually working. Drella forced herself not to look at the shadows, following the light, trusting it. But the tendrils of evil worked their way forward, encroaching on the light. They reached for her, snarling and cruel, tearing at her ankles until she screamed, arms outstretched once more, for the hope of the light.

But it was gone. Extinguished. She cried out, all alone.

Then the darkness won, swallowing her, a frigid embrace that left her teary and trembling.

"*Curses.*"

She opened her eyes, back in Thal'darah Overlook, to find the druid master with his Frustrated Face on. Galena looked no better. The tauren and the night elf exchanged a long look, the last wan strings of steelbloom smoke winding between them.

"I must have done something wrong," Drella murmured. "We can try again!"

"Peace, now, my dear, we are all too tired for another attempt." Master Thal'darah passed a shaking hand over his face, then pinched the bridge of his nose. "It should be working. Why is it not working?"

Galena chewed her lip, playing nervously with her braids. "I did every step just as you asked, Master. Maybe we have it all wrong. Maybe this isn't the right ritual . . ."

"There is something hindering us," he said, stroking his beard thoughtfully. "Something I cannot see. Tell me of the shadows again, dear."

Taryndrella shivered but did as he asked. "They are like ice all over me! They look like roots, but made all of shadow. Nothing gets through that darkness. This time, I saw a little beam of light. It fell right in front of me and I followed it, just like you told me to do. It cut through the shadows for a little while, but oh, it just was not enough!"

For a while, all three of them were silent. The sounds of the glade seemed far away. The wisps danced in the trees, Murky and Hackle chased each other around the fire, laughing, the moonwell shimmered with magic, crickets skimming quietly across its surface, but none of it gave her joy.

"I have failed you," she said, hanging her head.

"Nonsense," Master Thal'darah boomed. "If there is blame to be had, it should rest on our shoulders, not yours."

"But we did everything right! We followed every step set down by the Cenarion texts—"

Galena was silenced by a sharp look from the master. The mood of the ceremony had never fallen so low. At first, it had even been exciting, like making a new friend or discovering a fun human word, but now it just felt like chores. Chores was something Aram had taught her about, and everyone hated them but for some reason did them anyway. Drella did not *hate* the rituals, but she was beginning to think it was a lost cause. Tucking one hand under her chin, she let herself feel the disappointment. Usually, it was simple enough for her to banish bad thoughts, especially now that it was her summer, but maybe it was time to consider that this wasn't going well and might never work.

"I just think maybe Aram should be part of all this," she murmured.

Master Thal'darah, moving with his usual slow grace, stood and brushed off his robes. "I have told you, he does not need to be here, only close by. He does not possess the proper abilities to complete the ritual. *You* are unique, my dear. You are special."

"That is it!" The thoughts tumbled into her mind all at once, so quickly it made her giddy. She popped up, turning a circle, balling up her fists and dancing. "You are right, Master! I *am* special!"

"Well, humility is also an important characteristic, Taryndrella, and you should take care to—"

"No, not like that, silly! I am *different.* You told me so yourself after our first ceremony, I have powers you have never seen before in a dryad! Is that not neat? It is neat, but also important. Important because if I am different and special, then maybe these rituals are not for me. Oh, good! You are here!"

Aramar Thorne had wandered into their portion of the glade, his hair neatly combed and tied off, his too-big jacket sagging with all the things he had jammed in the pockets. His eyes widened at her greeting, a sweet, sleepy grin spreading across his face. Drella very much liked his grin, because it always reminded her of a tired kitten's. So endearing. The boy came closer, standing next to Galena and before the small altar where the incense and steelbloom smoked.

"How is it going?" he asked. "Did it . . . did it work? Because I don't feel any different."

"No! It did not work at all," Drella informed him. "In fact, it has been going badly! But that is all right. I know why now."

"And why is that?" Master Thal'darah sounded strange, like he didn't believe her but also wanted to laugh.

Drella trotted over to Aram, linking her arm with his and beaming around at the three of them. "Because our bond is completely, unbelievably unique to us! I am special, and so is the bond. Aramar has cared for me since I was just an acorn. Not a night elf, not a druid, but a human boy! Can you believe it? That is something so big, so important and beautiful that we should not forget it."

Master Thal'darah stroked his beard again and nodded. "Say more."

"Well! I think because our bond is so special, that it must have different rules. These rituals are for someone else. Aramar gave me a gift, the gift of life and then kindness, risked his life and the lives of his friends to keep me safe. Gifts are special, and gifts should be given in kind."

Galena hopped up to her hooves, nodding much faster than Master Thal'darah, sending her braids all over the place. "That might be right! The bonds we learned about didn't sound that deep. They were made with magic . . . What if their bond was made by *fate*?"

"Ooh! I like that word. *Fate*. It gives me chills. Fate!" Drella shivered from her pointed ears to her tail, to demonstrate.

"This is worth considering, certainly," Master Thal'darah murmured, pacing. "We may be encountering a kind of bond the

Cenarion Circle never recorded or tried to undo. If this is a bond created by fate, then nothing we three try here will change it. How did you say it, Drella? Gifts should be given in kind. Perhaps the service young Aramar Thorne has performed for you must be performed back, to complete a sort of circle."

Aramar had said nothing, scratching at his neck and shuffling from foot to foot. She could feel through the air and through their bond that he was confused, and nervous. Drella smiled at him, hoping that would help.

"So . . . the bond can't be broken yet?" Aram said slowly. He didn't look upset about it, and that made Drella very happy. She had worried, just for an instant, that the news would make him sad. After all, they had come all this way to undo the bond, and now that just didn't seem possible.

"The two of you have an intense connection, more intense than I anticipated," Master Thal'darah explained. "The thread between you is strong, so strong that none of our magic can break it, apparently."

"Yes," Drella agreed, beaming at Aramar. His cheeks had gone unbelievably red. *See?* she thought. *Red really is a nice color!* "I can feel how strong it is between us. Do you, Aramar? Do you feel as strongly about me as I do about you?"

For a long time he just blinked at her, still red, his lips parting as if he might sigh or burp. Then he moved his head, gradually at first, then swiftly. His arm linked tighter with hers, and he took a big swallow, then said, "Of course, Drella, I—I feel the same way. About the bond, I mean. It's . . . strong. Really strong."

Master Thal'darah regarded them both, chuckling, a few leaves falling out of his beard as he clapped his hands together and shrugged. "Then our work here is complete, and I shall write to the Moonglade at once. Still, Aramar, I think it would be best if the two of you stayed for a while longer. We should study this strange phenomenon as best we can. This is *quite* the development. Quite the development indeed."

CHAPTER NINE
SILVERLAINE

*Q*uite *the development* didn't describe or encompass the mental quake Aram was experiencing. He left the glade with his head spinning and the skin under his collar hot enough to scorch.

I can feel how strong it is between us. Do you, Aramar? Do you feel as strongly about me as I do about you?

Why did those words make him feel so . . . so . . . itchy? Itchy everywhere. He thought he might sing or vomit, or maybe both at the same time. His feelings for Drella, once an annoying little voice in the back of his head, swelled to a screaming chorus. Had she just admitted that she liked him? It didn't make sense. Drella liked everyone. This was just more of her characteristic friendliness, surely. But he couldn't get the sensation of her arm linked in his out of his mind, or the way she smiled down at him with such force, as if all the contentment and bliss in the world shone out through her teeth.

"What happened to you?"

Makasa. He stopped dead in his tracks. Their courses clashed as she left the inn and he sprinted toward it. The other sounds of the Overlook were far away, as if he had been left completely alone with his thoughts. And now, Makasa. Both of her dark brows leapt to her hairline.

"Brother, why are you sweating like that? Do you have a fever—"

Aram shook his head, trying to collect his senses. "N-No, I'm fine. Where were you going in such a hurry?"

"To find you. We need to come up with a plan. A better plan than 'wait and see.' But you should get some rest if you're feeling sick." She strode up to him, pressing her hand against his forehead.

"Stop it"—he pushed her off—"I'm just . . . flustered."

Makasa snorted, crossing both arms over her chest. For the most part, her wounds had healed, thanks to the tending of the Sentinels, and she moved much more freely. Aram tried to dodge around her so he could disappear into the inn and soak his head, but Makasa caught him by the elbow, swinging him around. Never before had she looked more sisterly. Or more menacing.

"Wait. What happened? Your face is all red. Spill it."

"The rituals aren't working," he said, hoping the diversion would work. Makasa squinted, and he hurried to deepen the story. "There's some kind of . . . block? I don't know. Do I look like a druid?"

"You *look* like a cooked hen. Your cheeks are going to explode if they get any redder."

"The point is," Aram half shouted, "we *do* need a plan. I just don't know what we should do next. Drella and I can't undo the bond, but Master Thal'darah wants me to stay put. He wants to study us or something. For the Circle."

Makasa rolled her eyes. "Oh, that is *not* happening. If this bond stuff is over with, then we need to get moving. The *Crustacean*'s diversion won't last forever, and Malus will be spitting mad once he realizes we fooled him. He'll put all of his effort into finding us, and when he does? Well." She drew her hand like a blade across her throat.

"He already knows."

Her brown eyes widened like an owl's, and even her jaw went slack. "What?"

"Malus. They caught up to the *Crustacean*. That voice in your head? It showed me all of it. The crew, everyone, they're gone. Gone because of us. *Me.* It's a debt I can never repay, Makasa; they gave their lives to buy us time. Since you're having visions now, too, you can look forward to the terrible ones, the ones that make you realize you're failing your father and your destiny and the world. Miserably. I should know, the Light's been talking to me for a lot longer than you."

Makasa looked ashen, but she didn't say anything in response to his outburst. She immediately turned back to the inn.

Aram hurried to catch up with her longer strides. "Where are you going?"

"To pack. Look, we need to hurry if Malus is already wise to our ruse." Sighing, she brushed by him.

"I know, Makasa. Don't you think I know?"

Aramar hung his head, defeated. Guilt swiftly replaced confusion. Drella and her feelings for him were shoved far, far away. He felt just as feverish, but also ill. All those people had died for them and he had been content to sit there, collecting moss, while Drella and Galena at least *did* something. Even if it didn't work, they had tried. What had he done?

"There you are, Aramar. I was hoping to find you."

Not now, Iyneath.

He wrangled his temper under control and put on a thin smile, turning to face the one-eyed night elf, who looked, surprisingly, excited. His smile soothed Aram for a moment, and then the boy saw the letter in the elf's hand. Was it possible?

"The owl I sent to Northwatch Expedition Base returned this evening," he said, holding out the folded parchment to Aram. It was still sealed, and more thrilling, he could see that it was addressed to him. "It is the nearest outpost from here, but I will let you know if the others respond, too."

"Thank you," Aram breathed, taking the letter.

"It could mean nothing," Iyneath warned him. "But I do hope you hear what you want to hear."

The Sentinel gave a half bow and turned, disappearing into the trees at the edges of the outpost. Aram glanced around, completely alone, and then scurried inside, up the stairs, and into the room he shared with Makasa. Even from there, he could hear Makasa shouting at Murky and Hackle to prepare their things. At least he would have a bit of time alone, and know to hide the evidence once the panic died down.

Heart beating wildly, Aram tore at the letter, reading as quickly as he could, a lump growing bigger and bigger in his throat as he did.

To Master Aramar Thorne,

I received your inquiry with great pleasure, young sir, and it is with equal delight that I can inform you that I know your uncle, Silverlaine Thorne, very well. My name is Morris Wheeler, and I am an Alliance infantry officer serving at Northwatch Expedition Base. Silverlaine and I both served for a time in Stormwind, and then later as a detachment in Westfall. He is a man of great quality, loyal and honest. Since our last meeting, we have kept in regular contact, and he is, at present, not far from here, his last letter posted from Ashenvale. I have already dispatched a messenger to his last known whereabouts, and I urge you to meet me here, at the base, where it will be my great honor to make an introduction.

Yours in friendship,

Morris Wheeler

Aram stared down at the letter, his hands shaking. His uncle was alive, then, and only a few days from his current location. It almost seemed too good to be true, and for a moment, he remained convinced it was. According to Iyneath, the area near the expedition base was swarming with Horde. Ashenvale had been hit hard recently by forces from the Barrens, and his uncle could easily be killed before going south. Still, it filled Aram with a spark of hope, one that almost banished the guilty cloud over his head.

But the relief was short-lived. He closed his eyes, folding the letter and holding it to his chest. Makasa's shouting in the next room brought with it the horrible reminder that they had dawdled too long, and now it was all for nothing. He and Drella hadn't accomplished their goal, and an entire crew of men and women had perished, burned alive or cut down by Malus and his minions. This was his fault, he knew; he was the source of all this suffering. He set down the letter and then pulled out the compass around his neck and the hilt of the Diamond Blade. Side by side, compass and blade, he put his hands over the cherished items and felt, deep in his heart, what he must do.

Nobody else need suffer on his account. Those same doubting thoughts from earlier now took a firm hold in his mind. Maybe they were right; maybe he had already failed. If the Light was speaking to Makasa, too, then that could be proof that he was no longer some important chosen one. With her strength and her courage, maybe she was the better choice. But he could still play a part.

They needed to know more of the blade and his father's mission. Greydon Thorne was dead, and while Aram trusted and admired his companions, they were, after all, just children like him. Uncle Silverlaine would know what to do. It would hurt—Aram would be lonely and full of doubts—but at least it would be action. And if he failed? Well, he would be the one to go down, not anyone volunteering on his behalf.

Fate has other plans for you, the voice had said in his dream. *You have no need to fear.*

That voice had never let him down before. And so he would go, he thought, and he would try not to fear. Aram put his compass and blade hilt away, deciding, then and there, that his own heart, and not a compass, would choose the right path.

Something was horribly, terribly wrong. All wrong. Taryndrella bolted upright, a few stray blades of grass and leaves floating down from her hair as she shook herself awake. Pain. She sensed pain. And panic.

But how could that be? She felt calm, at peace, in fact, resolved. Master Thal'darah and Galena could study her and Aram, grow to learn more about their bond, and then once they were satisfied, she and the others could continue helping Aram on his quest. But now he was in turmoil. *Turmoil.* That was a new word, one Galena had taught her. She found it strange, but it did fit what she sensed now bubbling up in Aram. Never before had their bond alerted her in such a way. It felt like a dozen bells were ringing all at once in her head, and she would never sleep at all if that kept happening. The clearing was still, peaceful. Night had fallen hours ago, and besides some faint snoring from inside the inn, everything was silent. The dark comfort of a warm night settled over all, draping it in the lullaby of frogs and crickets, of the wisps weaving softly through the wood.

Galena slept not far from where Drella liked to sleep, under the trees and moons, on a heap of boughs and leaves next to the moonwell. The tauren slept deeply, no doubt exhausted from their trying ritual that day. Master Thal'darah was somewhere inside the inn, and a handful of guards roamed the periphery of the clearing. Standing carefully, Drella blinked up at the stars. It was a cloudless night, and she could see well by the moons and starlight.

The panic and pain in her mind had a clear direction, and

Drella knew she had to follow it. Galena would fret if she woke, and so Drella went as quietly as she could. The guards would be a problem. They would alert the outpost the moment they spotted someone fleeing the area. But Aram was somewhere outside the boundaries of the Overlook. How had he gone unnoticed?

It wouldn't do. She had to follow. Oh, but Galena would be furious when she found out Drella had left. The druids wanted to study their bond much more closely, and it was rude to just run away with no explanation! How could Aramar leave his friends behind? How could he leave *her*?

The solution occurred to her as she slid silently across the clearing, reaching the less guarded pathway leading north. Most of the attacks from the Horde and the drakes emanated from the south, and so the way north saw less attention. Aramar must have slipped out that way. Drella would find him, convince him to return to the Overlook, and then everything would be right and good again. Galena would not fret, Master Thal'darah would not be offended, and their little fellowship would remain united.

Simple enough, she decided, then froze, one hoof snapping a twig clean in half. It seemed deafening, the crack, and she cast her gaze around nervously, expecting to hear a guard bursting through the tree line. Footsteps. Soft. Curious. Someone was coming. Drella made a soft squeak of defiance and sprinted under the arch on the northern path, then swerved at once into the woods and picked her way through the dense trees.

The footsteps continued, though they sounded more distant, and so she continued on, following the pain that radiated on the horizon like a broken heart.

Aramar was in immense anguish. She hoped that it wouldn't last, and that seeing her, seeing a kindly friend, would ease his torment. This was what their fate bond was all about, she thought—nobody could do absolutely everything on their own. Everyone needed a loyal friend.

The footsteps drew near again and Drella forced herself not to call out. It was ever so hard not to just explain what was going on! But she could solve it, of course, before dawn broke and everyone began to worry. Why raise even a single brow in concern when she could simply retrieve Aramar on her own? They were bonded; he wouldn't run away from her without good reason. This was just a misunderstanding, one she would soon put right.

Whatever followed her wasn't giving up. The Overlook's guards were keen and well-trained, and Drella began to vary her steps, trying to shake the pursuer. Faster and faster she ran, hearing those dreaded footsteps match her pace. There was a low growl then and it did not sound friendly.

Oh dear.

Drella crashed through the woods, forgetting her silent steps, breaking through to a narrow path that wound into a set of tumbled ruins. The leaves and bushes rattled behind her, the night air cooler as she ran and ran. That growl came again, louder, and then a snarl, and Drella gave a shriek of fear, turning finally to look at what had chased her into the road.

"Look out!"

It was too late. She had swiveled to look at precisely the wrong time, sending her careening blindly into a body. They smacked together with twin cries of surprise, and then they went down, hard to the ground. Drella didn't know what was more urgent to confront, whatever she had just landed on or the thing snapping at her hooves! She pushed herself up quickly, and gasped, finding a blade swinging in front of her face.

Aramar.

He was covered in bits of dried leaves and mud, no doubt from their fall, but already he had leapt to his feet, brandishing his cutlass at . . .

A young twilight runner. No murderous beast, just a tiny but fast pursuer. Drella giggled, watching as the feline, which had lost all its vinegar the moment it was faced with two defiant creatures, gave a startled "mrr-owl" before hunching up and slinking away.

"What are you doing here?" Aram knelt, helping her up. She pulled a twig out of his hair and flicked it away. She was excessively glad to see him, and also glad to have made it onto the road unscathed.

"Finding you, of course. Hello!"

"Sh-hh," he hissed. "Keep it down. Do you want to wake the entire outpost?"

"Sure! I will let them know that I have found you, and now you will be coming back," she chirped, taking him by the hand.

"No, Drella, it doesn't work like that. I'm leaving." He carefully worked his hand out of her grip, sheathing the cutlass and hefting his pack before turning toward the northern road. The road to unknown things.

"Do you not like us anymore?" she asked, taking a single step after him.

"That's not the— Of course I like you," he said. Then softly, "I—I happen to like you a lot. But there's something I have to do on my own. I keep messing this up, keep getting all of you and other people caught up in my problems. It shouldn't be that way. That's why I have to go. How did you find me, anyway?"

Drella trotted up beside him, studying his face closely in the moonlight. There was no smile there, not any she could see, and his brows arced down toward his eyes. "Our bond, I could sense you leaving. I do not want you to go."

"I have to," he insisted.

"Then I will go with you!"

"Drella, no. I don't want you to get hurt. I'm flattered that you want to join me, but it's too dangerous. Listen, the ship, the *Crustacean*?"

She nodded.

"The one that was meant to trick Malus? Well, it did, for a little while. But he figured it out. He tracked them down and he killed everyone on board. Everyone. That blood? It's on my hands."

Drella frowned, concerned, and swiftly reached out, grabbing him by the hands.

"Your hands are dirty, yes, but I can see no blood."

"It's a figure of speech," Aram said, sounding tired. "It means they're dead because of me. I don't want to let anyone else get hurt like that. Do you understand? I want to protect you. All of you."

Drella watched him walk through the starlight away from her, his steps more resolute and steady than she had seen them in a long time. His shoulders and back, straight as a healthy tree, were unbowed, his head tall and proud. He meant it. Drella's lower lip quivered, and she hurried after him, feeling the pain in his heart as keenly as if it were her own.

"We protect each other," she told him. "We have a bond, Aram; it is special! You have known me since before I was me. Whatever you have to do, we can do it together."

He glanced at her briefly, a small smile tugging at his lips.

"You really mean that?" he asked. "It's—it's not going to be easy. You can still turn back. Won't Galena miss you?"

"Everyone will miss me," Drella assured him. "I am very missable. Galena may be my friend, and it will be bad to hurt her feelings, but you and I share a bond. That is different; that is one of a kind. Irreplaceable."

Aram gave a soft laugh, leading them deeper down the road, past sleeping stags and rams, past the toppled stones of ruins long forgotten. "Irreplaceable? That's a big word for someone your age."

"Galena taught it to me; she taught me many words," Drella explained. "But I know all sorts of things, too much for my age. But I am older now, can you not tell? Summer is here."

It was his turn to study her intently. "You do look . . . different. Some of your foliage is turning brighter, greener, and some of it is yellow. Will you change like that when all your seasons come?"

She nodded, serene, feeling less pain in his heart as they walked and traded their amiable whispers among the ruins. Reaching out, she glided one hand across an ancient, graying pillar. "I will change with all my seasons," she said. "And I will know more with each one, too. These stones, I can hear their stories. Echoes of echoes, the cries of those lost so long ago that there is nobody with even a memory of their passing. It is sad, Aram, but I will remember them now. Can I tell you all about them? You could sketch them! Then they would not be so lost at all."

"Sure," Aram said, nodding, his eyes gleaming in the moonlight. "Tell me everything you know."

CHAPTER TEN
COMPANIONS

Once, when Galena Stormspear was knee-high to a kodo, she took her mother's favorite water jug to the well, the decorative jug they only used for special occasions. Her mother had made her promise to be careful, that the pottery was precious, an heirloom belonging to her mother, and her mother's mother, and so on and so on into a history that made young Galena's head spin.

Rain the night before had made the paths to the well slippery, and Galena rushed, even though she knew it was wiser not to. Her grandpa Otue had made the journey from Bloodhoof Village, and for a tauren his age that was a long, long way to go. While she fetched water in the special jug, Grandpa Otue spun tales of his days as a brave for the young ones, and Galena hated to miss out. Nobody told a story like Grandpa Otue. Her fondest memories of Thunder Bluff all included him, sitting next to him on the floor, wood smoke winding through the tent while he puffed his stained pipe and told another tall tale, gray beard twining down to his belt.

Be swift but careful, Mother had warned. Galena was swift but not careful, slipping on her return trip to the tent, falling with the heavy jug weighted down by the water, the pottery shattering into a million pieces as she and it fell to the ground. A passing tradesman offered to help her collect the shards, but Galena wouldn't have it. She ran home, crying, cowering at Grandpa Otue's hooves.

"I broke it," she wailed, clinging to his leg. "Mother warned me, and I broke it! I will be cursed forever. The ancestors will never forgive me."

Grandpa Otue patted her head, smoothing down her braids. The others, her brother and her cousins, snorted at her tantrum, teasing her for being a big, clumsy baby.

"The lesson is to always consider time," Otue told her, firm but not unkind. "Your haste brought only regrets."

"I only wanted to hurry back to hear your stories!"

"Well, we will have no more stories now. Someone must fetch the water, and someone must tell your mother about the broken jug."

Galena had never been hasty or sloppy again, always methodical, listening, *careful*. When other Cenarion Circle apprentices dashed off their studies the morning the master wanted them, Galena had prepared long before, practicing the assignments twice, or sometimes three times, then taking notes, then memorizing her notes. It was why she had come to apprentice for Master Thal'darah at such a young age. Galena prided herself on her attentive ways, giving credit always to dear Grandpa Otue and her mother.

But now she stood in an empty clearing, the boughs where Taryndrella the dryad once slept tamped down but empty. Empty. Where had she gone? Galena had searched the obvious places in the Overlook right away, but the dryad was not to be found. Nobody knew of her absence yet, but that wouldn't last, and soon Galena would have to confess her negligence to Master Thal'darah, and then he would be furious, dismiss her, and send her back to Thunder Bluff to cook smelly strider steaks in her mother's tavern for the rest of time!

Galena gulped down a few breaths, squeezing her fingers into fists before turning away from the inn and back toward the moonwell. The same thorough nature that had gotten her to this post would also take her to the dryad. She had sworn to Master Thal'darah that she would protect and watch over Taryndrella, and that was precisely what Galena meant to do.

Dawn was breaking, and only the fresh guards on watch stirred. Their failure to stop the dryad could be addressed later; first she had to find their lost charge. She made a clear spot in the dirt, wiping it into a circle, then scrounged for fallen acorns among the leaves and around the well. Acorns were more than sacred to dryads, and with the right spell, Galena would have a trace on Taryndrella in no time.

The druidic magic flowed through her hands as she dug a small hole, dropping in a few acorns before covering them with her palms. A hum emerged from the earth, then a smooth, emerald light, swirling between her fingers and the acorns, growing in power and color until it surged up into Galena's hands, traveling along her forearms and up, up, until she could breathe in the potent magic. The energies of the soil, the song of it, seemed to be winding north.

North.

Where could the dryad be going? It didn't matter. Galena's only mission was to find the dryad and bring her back to the Overlook. They were nowhere near done studying the unusual bond between her and the boy, and the Cenarion Circle would want to know just how the connection had been made. Galena was beginning to doubt it could be severed at all, but in her extensive studies, she had found more obscure methods that might be tried.

And they could only be attempted if the dryad was brought back safely. She had probably just gone wandering, enchanted by a passing insect or swirl of leaves caught on the breeze. The same things that made Drella charming also made her difficult to handle. Flighty. Easily fixated. With all of nature and Azeroth her playground, it was no wonder the dryad had disappeared from the clearing. Galena could hardly blame her. Life at the Overlook had been unsettling with the war so near; why would a dryad want to linger around so much pain?

Right. The dryad. North. Galena had her plan, but not much else. Quiet as a mouse, she snuck into the inn, borrowed a handful of nuts and dried fish from the larder, and took one of Master Thal'darah's walking sticks in case the path had unsteady spots. He wouldn't miss it, not when she would be back before breakfast.

Galena ran back out into the warming glow of morning, calling to Aiyell as she went, promising to be back shortly, just after she collected something she had dropped in the woods.

Somehow, spending so much time with Drella made it impossible to know what to do with his hands. They were never quite natural or at ease. Aram tried folding them over his belt buckle, but that looked stupid, so he stuck them instead in his pockets, but his pockets were already full of junk.

Words unsaid lingered between them thick as smoke, and Aram wondered if the dryad could feel it, too. She was so young, so sweet, but he had no idea if she had any conception of, well, *feelings*. Their bond was one thing, and he was secretly overjoyed that she had cared enough to sneak out of the Overlook and follow him, but that didn't mean it was for anything more than friendship. In hindsight, it seemed easier to decide to leave his friends behind and strike out on his own than it was to say the right things to a girl.

If Makasa could see him, she would be half-mad with laughter.

"Do you know where to go?" Drella asked. She never walked a straight line, always weaving here and there to brush her fingers across a flower or greet a sunning turtle.

"My uncle is supposed to meet me—us—at the Northwatch Expedition Base. If the weather holds and we don't run into any trouble, then it will only be a few days."

"Will your human legs not get tired?" She left the dirt path once more to study an outcropping carved with childishly unsteady letters. *THRAGMO BE HERE.*

"Probably," Aram admitted, a little sheepish. "Eventually we will have to make camp."

"I could find you a ram and tame it," she offered, batting her eyelashes in thought. "Or a stag. It will be much faster that way. Or you could climb on my back. It made carrying Murky much faster in the Charred Vale."

Aram coughed, feeling that awful, itchy heat blaze across his neck. "Maybe the ram. Yeah. That could work. Will it take long?"

"Oh, no!" She laughed.

The ruins on either side of the road became sparser, the surrounding clumps of green trees less dense. They were heading downhill, and if his memory held from the map Iyneath had showed him, then they were nearing the fork to Cliffwalker Post. Aram decided to give that area a wide berth, afraid that tauren scouts would spot them as they passed in broad daylight.

"After we get a little farther down the mountain, then you should give it a try. I don't want to be caught out by Horde scouts; they could be anywhere in this part of the pass," he explained. "I know you think everyone is kind, but those tauren won't be friendly."

Drella jutted out her lip. "I do not think everyone is kind, Aram. I have been kidnapped, remember? They had good hearts, of course, good hearts twisted by darkness. We all begin with nothing but light, but shadows have a way of creeping in." Twining a few flower stems together, she held them up to the sun to admire her work. "I am not stupid, you know."

"I didn't say—"

"I know you think that sometimes I am foolish, that I do not see things the right way, but that is not so. And I know Makasa thinks I am dull as a dirty rock, but she is also wrong." Drella scooped up another wildflower along the roadside and added it to her growing crown. "Gentle does not always mean weak. Hard does not always mean strong. In fact, hard things become brittle, and brittle things often snap."

Aram nodded, peeling off his jacket and flopping it over one shoulder. The day was growing hot, and he had no intention of sweating and being putrid around her. "We just see things differently, and that's okay. But we're doing this together, remember? That means we both have to use our strengths. I know where we're going, that's all, so try to trust me on that."

"I will!" she crowed, and then dropped her finished flower crown on her head.

It matched the changing colors of her hair, and the flowers that seemed to bloom naturally among the strands. Her tail, too, looked like it was transitioning into a bright emerald shade.

"That's the outpost," Aram cautioned, pointing to a rising path to their right. Tauren totems dotted the way, and even from a distance, Aram could see figures moving among the trees at the top of the rise. "Hurry now, we need to get back into the forest."

Drella obeyed, for once, silent. They scampered down the dusty path, steadying each other, loose rocks and pebbles shooting out from under their feet. It was treacherous going, and Aram nearly stumbled once or twice, but they made it at last to the grassier edge of the woods below, and then to the safety of the trees. They paused, and Aram peered around a sturdy trunk, watching as a heavily armed tauren brave emerged down the path that led to the post. He gazed around, shielding his eyes, then gave up and climbed the hill.

"Close one," he murmured, wiping at the sweat on his brow. "We should be careful and quiet."

"Yes," Drella said, galloping down the hill and deeper into the trees. "Oh, look! A ram! He looks sprightly . . ."

Aram ran to keep up, then stopped short, watching Drella work her magic as she put out her hands, as if in surrender, and approached the skittish animal. Big and woolly, the ram had horns at least the size of his arms spread wide. Aram couldn't make out the creature's eyes, hidden as they were behind so much dirty fur. Swirls of golden brown and white colored his back, and at Drella's approach, the ram backed up, then reared, bleating in alarm.

"I am a friend," she said with a musical laugh. "There's no need for all of that! Could a meanie do this?"

She wrinkled her nose a few times and wagged her stubby fawn tail, and that seemed to amuse or calm the animal. He gave a soft bleat, then lowered his head, butting his massive curled horns into her arm.

"Now that is much more polite," she told the ram, beckoning Aram to come closer. "He is our friend now, and his name is Blossom."

"Blossom?" Aram shook his head, easing up to the ram with wide, slow steps.

"Yes, Blossom. I think it is a wonderful, wondrous name!"

"Sure. Blossom. Will he let me ride him?"

Drella tapped her chin a few times, then leaned down and looked into the ram's eyes for a moment. They seemed to be communicating silently, and Aram had to admit, it was very impressive. Not that she hadn't impressed him before, but it still caught him off guard. "As far as the expedition, I told him. That is our deal."

"Great." Aram breathed a sigh of relief. "Perfect! Thank you. And, um, thank him for me, too."

"Happily!"

Aram had just gotten up the courage to swing up onto the beast when a shout came from the way behind them. Cliffwalker Post. The ram bucked, knocking Aram to the ground. Someone screamed. There was a terrible commotion, the earth churning as if shaken by a sudden rockslide. A horn, brassier and louder than that of the night elves, sounded from the peak above them. Dust drifted down toward the forest, and one figure ran toward them, screaming for help, a force of four furious tauren behind her.

"Galena! We have to help her!" And Drella was off, galloping toward the spears and shouts, directly into the path of the enemy.

CHAPTER ELEVEN
OUT IN THE OPEN

Galena had never taken to kodo travel, and in similar fashion, being swept onto a speeding ram was no better. It didn't help that she was just a little too large to ride the ram. But the Cliffwalker tauren were relentless, chasing them down into the trees, shouting and brandishing their spears. And were it not for Aram and Taryndrella intervening when they did, Galena would have easily succumbed to their charge.

"Keep going!" the dryad called, splitting away from them.

"No! We have to protect her," Galena screamed. No, no, no! This wasn't happening. Her awkward grip on Aram loosened even more as she swiveled to watch the dryad run back toward the tauren. "I swore to protect her! Turn this thing around!"

"She knows what she's doing," Aram shouted over the thunder of hooves and whip of the wind.

"She's sacred, she's—"

But Galena's next words were stolen out of her mouth.

She watched, entranced, as the dryad flung her arms up toward the sky, and every tree around her shuddered, then creaked, their branches bending in unison, forming a solid, intertwined wall between their pursuers and Taryndrella. The dryad gave a whoop of delight and danced in a circle, listening to the tauren crash into the barrier and call out in confusion. Then she returned, a spring in her step as she easily matched the stride of the ram, and together they plunged down into the valley, only stopping when they could find a good vantage point among the trees.

Aramar hopped down first, then helped Galena gain her hooves.

"Thank you," Galena began. "But what I was—"

Aram cut in, meeting Galena's eyes. "We aren't going back, if that's what you've come to tell us."

"It is really kind of you to come for us, but I am going with Aram to find his uncle," Taryndrella explained, gently brushing some leaves and pebbles from Galena's shoulders.

"Everyone in the Overlook will be in a panic," Galena said. She couldn't believe what she was hearing. This wasn't the dryad wandering away, caught by a whim; this was an escape. She blamed the human instantly. Drella had been listening to her and Master Thal'darah—she was cooperative and interested— but Aramar had been bored and absent from the start. He could never be bothered to show up and give a single care about what they were trying to accomplish.

"You're selfish!" Galena said to the boy. She had never been in a shouting match, but this was serious. "I'm sworn to protect her. Do you understand that? She's sacred to us. Special. You can't just run off with her because you fancy seeing your family!"

"And you have no idea what you're talking about!" Aramar rounded on her. "She doesn't even know you; she knows me! The bond means she wants to follow where I go. We don't have time to wait for the rituals anymore. You all said it yourselves, the bond can't be changed, so we have to keep moving. Or else—"

Taryndrella yelped, falling to the ground. She covered both of her eyes, and at once, both Galena and Aramar went to her.

"No more fighting," Taryndrella wailed, tears streaming down her face. "No more shouting!"

Aramar sighed and stood, raking both hands through his unruly long hair. "She's right. This is pointless. Listen, you can come with us if you want. Once we reach the expedition base we can send word back to the Overlook and let them know we're safe. I didn't mean for her to follow me, all right? I tried to do it alone."

"He is right," Taryndrella said softly, wiping at her wet cheeks. "He would have done it alone, but I cannot let him do that. We cannot be apart, not with the way things are between us. Master Thal'darah said it himself, what we have is too strong."

Galena and Aramar both fell silent at that. The human boy shifted; suddenly blushing, he dropped the coat that had been resting over his shoulder and nodded, his jaw working back and forth before he blurted out, "Yes. What she said. What we have is strong, and what I feel is . . . Well, it's also strong. I didn't want to admit it to myself or anyone else but it's probably obvious."

The tauren helped Taryndrella to her feet, and let the dryad lean on her for support while she finished drying her tears. With the arguing stopped, she seemed much calmer.

"What's obvious?" Galena barely paid attention to the boy, more worried about the sacred creature she had sworn to protect.

"That—that I have a crush on her."

Taryndrella gasped as if struck. "Aramar! You would not! You would never hurt me!"

"What? I— Oh. I . . ."

Galena snorted softly, bewildered. Were all human boys this ridiculous? She patted Drella lightly on the back. "It means he likes you, you know, *romantically*. Like when his people marry."

"I didn't say that!" Aramar shouted, now so red it looked as if his head might burst.

"Love," Galena said, wise. "He means love."

"I didn't say that, either!" He tossed his hands in the air, all but feral with frustration. Then he emerged from his tantrum, smoothing back his hair, taking a deep breath before saying, "I just feel strongly for her. And yes, in a . . . in a more-than-friends way. Is that so weird? We have this connection, I mean, I don't even know what to call it."

At that, the dryad pushed Galena away with a soft smile as she glided toward the boy. She took his shoulders in her hands and squeezed, then leaned down and bumped her forehead with his. He went completely still, and Galena wished she could disappear rather than watch their exchange.

"Of course I love you, Aramar. Nothing will ever change that. But it is not married people kind of love. It is . . . Well, it is like when you see the most perfect duck in the world, and you just want to hold that duck forever, and tell it how wonderful and glossy and good it is. But that duck is not yours, and it will thrive on its own, so you let the duck go and love it from afar, loving the way it glides and grows. Does that make sense?"

The boy groaned. "Not really."

Taryndrella pulled back from him, touching him gently on the cheek. "How I was born, when I was born, it made me choose you, but now I choose you every day, as my friend, as my companion, as my equal. We are on a journey together, but it will not end the way you want it to. I do not even know if it could. I am just . . . me! Drella! And I do not know if me—Drella—can even *know* romance."

"I get it," Aramar said, nodding. "It's . . . fine. Really. It was a stupid thing to say, anyway."

"No, it was not," Drella said seriously. "It was honest! And Thalyss always told me that being honest is never bad."

The boy ambled away, back to the ram, picking up his coat and his pack and sighing. Galena had no idea what to say, and the dryad simply smiled, no doubt certain she had said all the right things, but Galena wasn't so sure. She almost wished she might have known the boy sooner, and told him, when it became obvious, that a dryad would never have that kind of connection to anyone, human or otherwise. But that was a thing only druids could know, and not a boy who saw only a kind, lovely girl with bright eyes and flowers in her hair.

"Are you . . ." But she had no idea what to say.

Aramar pulled on his coat and gave them both a chuckling half smile. "Yes. I'm fine, I promise. Now can we push on? By the Light, I'd rather be speared to death by tauren scouts than go through that again."

"Do not charge off," Galena said to his back. "The path ahead is choked with webs; there could be spiders lurking."

"Great." Aram sighed. "Spiders. My favorite." He shuddered, already thinking he could feel spindly legs crawling up his arms. Why did it have to be spiders? Well, he thought, anything was better than staying there and dwelling on that rejection a moment longer.

CHAPTER TWELVE
WEBWINDER PATH

"ARAMAR THORNE, I SWEAR BY EVERY FISH IN THE SEA, WHEN I FIND YOU, I WILL GUT YOU MYSELF."

The timbers of the inn shook from Makasa's rage. She had torn the little room she shared with Aramar apart, but not a single trace of him remained.

Hackle, timid for once, shuffled into the doorway, paws knitted together. "Aram, Drella, druid gone. Hackle sniff. North smell right."

"Then we go north"—Makasa grunted, pulling on her doublet—"and we go north now. Find Murky. I don't want to waste another second."

The old druid complained, of course, as if her brother leaving in the middle of the night with nary a word was her fault. And maybe it was—maybe she should've heard him sneaking away—but it was still his dumb idea and not hers. Hackle and Murky had her back, flanking her as they stalked through the outpost and toward the northern archway leading into the hills.

"Galena is gone, too," Master Thal'darah was saying, following them, his hair and beard disheveled. "Please . . . If you find her, make certain she is safe, that she makes it back to us!"

The tauren was the last thing on Makasa's mind, but she puffed out a sigh, pausing briefly before leaving. "I'll tell her what you said. Maybe if we get lucky, they're just having a picnic somewhere."

"Hackle no think so."

"Yeah," she muttered, hefting her harpoon and setting out north. "Makasa no think so, either."

There were no drakes or gouts of fire to contend with, and they made good time. Hackle proved invaluable, his nose taking them on the path north that turned east and then back south, heading toward the Northwatch Expedition Base. Makasa could only imagine what Aram was thinking, and a twinge in her gut told her to leave room for mercy, that maybe, just maybe, he had a good reason. Or maybe something nefarious had happened. Maybe they hadn't left of their own accord, but had been kidnapped.

They picked up the trail once more in the forest outside Webwinder Path, after discovering the remains of a strange barrier of tree limbs all knit together. A few broken spearheads and carve marks told her that tauren braves had tried to cut through.

"They're not much for climbing," she said, launching up onto the barrier with ease, "but these feet and hands have gone up and down masts too many times to count. Here!"

When Makasa reached the top, she swung one leg over, steadying herself, then lowered her chain, giving something for Hackle to grab on to. Murky climbed readily onto his back, and then she helped hoist them up, Hackle using his feet to claw into the wood and make it an easier ascent. On the other side, the gnoll again found the signs of the dryad, human, and tauren. Makasa didn't like the look of the path ahead, the trees denser, thick with shadows, and worse, Hackle smelled something more than just their friends.

"Spider," he said with a grunt. "Many spiders. Be ready for fight, or end up dinner for big bug. *Big*, big bug."

"Mrky prrgle tk, nk kerlug!" The little murloc took out his spear, jabbing it at the air.

"Eyes open. I don't want any surprises. We're losing daylight and I don't imagine our chances against spiders will be any better in the dark. Come on."

Makasa didn't expect to hand over leadership duties to Hackle, but the gnoll raced ahead, nose in the air, choosing a path through the increasingly webby forest, zigging and zagging so much that it was almost dizzying. Daylight indeed began to dwindle. Through the forest and above the jagged tops of the hills, Makasa watched the sky turn dark blue and then purple, livid orange streaks stretching over the mountains until she had to squint to see the way ahead.

Hackle slowed, his paws clenching as he glanced this way and that.

"Lrkna murg?" Murky whispered.

Makasa looked down at the murloc, who stared back with his head tipped to the side in inquiry.

"No, no stop," Hackle replied sharply. "You tired? We carry. No stop. No look up, either."

"What?" Makasa swept down and picked up the exhausted murloc. His little legs were far shorter than theirs, and it was no surprise that he tired out before the others.

"No look up," Hackle said again, picking his way through the trees. Somehow, Makasa could sense that they were far off the well-traveled road.

To their right, she spotted something white and shiny hanging between two large branches. By then, she had grown accustomed to the unsettling sight of the cobwebs slung between rocks and over cave mouths, but this looked different. The white object, as large as a human child, twisted in the faint breeze.

"What is that?" she hissed.

"No look." Hackle grunted. "No ask. Fast now, we go."

They ran, Murky bouncing on her shoulders, his spear banging into her arm as they raced through the densely clustered trees. Makasa noted more of those odd white oblong shapes dangling on webs as thick as rope, and each one made another hair stand up on her neck. One seemed to pulse as they went by, and she could swear she heard a strangled sound coming from inside. What if Aramar and the others had gone this same way and met with a gruesome end? She shivered. There could be rabbits or birds or even bigger things in those hanging cocoons. She considered going back, slicing one open, just in case Aramar really was hidden inside, suffocating and helpless.

"Wait," Makasa said softly, trying to catch up to Hackle. He had the build and feet made for quick forest travel, and it was a challenge to meet his swift pace.

"No stop. Only run!"

"Hackle! What if our friends are inside those things? We should check—"

"No!"

But Makasa slowed down, trying to see one of the cocoons in the darkness, glancing behind to make sure they hadn't amassed any followers. There was nothing there, just the light wind rattling the trees and the quickly fading sunlight. She aimed her harpoon and swung, slicing open one of the thick, slimy coverings on the nearest cocoon. It was more difficult to cut than she expected, and the feeling of it made her want to gag. A slight gap opened up in the covering, and inside she saw

nothing but the gleaming bone of a skull, an empty eye socket staring back.

"Hackle no smell friends! Run! Run! No look up!"

The gnoll had circled back to collect her, stealing her away before the shriek of surprise could escape her lips. She hadn't expected to find a skeleton inside, and a cold, horrible chill ran down her spine.

She had to trust Hackle. If the gnoll said he didn't smell Aram and Drella, then she would just have to put her faith in his snout. Not her first choice, but they were down to few options. Run and never look back seemed suddenly like the wisest plan.

"Urka! Urka urka urka!"

Murky started to whisper in a panic, smacking the top of Makasa's head harder and harder, as if her skull was his own personal bongo.

"Stop! Stop that! What is he saying, Hackle?"

A fine strand of web touched her face, and she gasped, pawing at it blindly, feeling it grasp at her fingers, unbelievably sticky.

"He say *up*. Lots of time he say *up*. No listen, only run."

Hackle grabbed her arm again, pulling, but the murloc continued hitting her on the head until she cursed and reached up to smack him back.

"Urka urka urka urka!"

Makasa gave in, ignoring Hackle and glancing skyward to see what had the murloc in such a frenzy. The ice running down her spine froze her into place, sheer terror rooting her to the spot. The forest around them was nothing compared to the intricate forest above, a labyrinth of webs formed into tunnels and loops, a veritable fortress of glittering ivory strands. On silent feet, hundreds of spiders waited, eyes glowing red in the coming darkness. And closer, just above them, descended the biggest, hairiest spider Makasa had ever seen. It was the size of a horse, and plunging swiftly toward their heads.

"Murky!" She called out to him just as the spider's pulsing belly came into striking distance. The close, grasping legs were near enough for her to feel the bristly hairs.

Murky screamed, and Makasa ducked, but it was too late. They were going to be pulled up into the horror of webs and hungry spiders above.

Not again, she thought. *I am not being picked up by another bloody monster.*

The murloc must have read her mind, reacting in a flash, taking his little spear and shoving it up into the spider's abdomen. It gave a deafening shriek, eyes brighter, a furious crimson, its legs flailing hard.

Murky stabbed it over and over, but its scream of pain had alerted the others.

Makasa clamped her hands down on the murloc's tiny legs, holding him fast, and ran, bolting across the sticky forest floor, listening to the sound of a thousand hungry spiders hurrying to make them their feast.

"Good job, Murky!" she called, amazed at what she'd just said. *Who'd have ever thought I'd be relying on a murloc to save us from a monster?* "Now hold on tight, and don't look up!"

CHAPTER THIRTEEN
CCAMP

The sun had come out to shine its light on the banners of the Northwatch Expedition Base Camp, and they glowed as brightly as beacons cutting through a storm. The pennants planted there snapped and bounced, a strong wind starting from the south.

"It'll rain soon," Galena said, raising her short muzzle into the air. They had diverted off the road, going east off the main path to avoid a tauren patrol. Galena told them the Krom'gar tauren might give her a chance to pass but would certainly give a human and a dryad trouble. Krom'gar was the Horde's stronghold in the area, after all.

"Those are Northwatch banners," Aram replied, pointing. "See? It will be a climb, but maybe we can outrun the storm."

Drella took up the rear, taking her time, collecting flowers and herbs as she went to make crowns for both him and Galena. As much as Aram would have preferred to travel alone or just with the dryad, he couldn't deny that the tauren druid was useful. She used her druid abilities to reach out to nature and find the safest places when they camped overnight, keeping the creepy-crawlies in the dark at bay, and her sense for weather was so keen it was almost magical. Drella, while sweet and powerful in her own way, was also easily distracted.

It was a relief that she had not brought up his crush again. The benefit, he realized, of fancying a dryad was that they did not react in predictable ways. She did not seem shy or embarrassed, but her same happy, confident self. Maybe he should have expected that. For his part, Aram still felt his face grow hot whenever she glanced at him, but the mortifying feeling was passing, and he even managed to hold her gaze now and then. Life would move on, he thought, and eventually he would understand the duck thing she had said. It was tempting to grasp onto the idea of being "a perfect duck" to her, but he knew she hadn't meant it in the way he wanted.

He distracted himself by watching Galena work her druidic magic.

"How do you know how to do all of this?" Aram asked. "I thought you were mostly just an apprentice, stuck in Feralas and then at the Overlook."

She shot him a steely glance. "I may be just an apprentice, human, but I've trained for this all my life." Here she indicated the dryad behind them. "Nature is to be protected, cherished, and creatures like Taryndrella are to be guarded at all costs.

I might not have been sailing the high seas or fighting ogres, but the CCAMP is invaluable. The combined wisdom of centuries of druid knowledge about the wilds!"

Aram frowned. "The cee-cee-ay-em-pee?" he asked.

"The Cenarion Circle Advanced Mountaineering Pamphlet. Every acolyte and apprentice is issued a pamphlet when they join the Circle." Galena unhitched the small, weathered pack from her furry shoulder and dug inside, bringing up a tattered and water-stained volume. "I would let you look, but it's only for us druids."

"Right," Aram murmured.

"It teaches you how to anticipate the weather and sense dangerous animals and dark entities. There's an entire section on shielding a fire from the rain, and guides for edible plants and poisonous ones!" Galena began pointing at the various shrubs clustered under the trees as they passed. "That's edible if you boil it. That one? No. And that one? That will make you vomit for days."

He had never heard anyone sound so giddy about throwing up.

"You're enjoying this," he said with a snort. "You've been waiting for something like this, haven't you?"

The tauren glanced away, shoving the pamphlet back into her bag. "I admit, it beats powdering dried berries all day. Most druids will never meet someone like Taryndrella. It's exciting, yes, but it's also a big responsibility."

"I'll protect her, too, you know."

Galena nodded, pausing to lick her finger and stick it up in the air, testing the wind. "I know. I can tell you really care about her."

Groaning, Aram shook his head. "We've been over this—"

"I'm not teasing you," Galena said, solemn. Her smile faded more as her pointed ears twitched and she leaned into the breeze. "Something is strange . . ."

"Hello again, friends!" Taryndrella caught up to them, giving them each a flower crown fragrant with herbs. "Is it not a beautiful day? And so thrilling! We are going to meet Aram's uncle! We are *so* lucky."

Aram normally would have thanked her for the gift, but he concentrated on Galena, watching as the tauren's ears flicked again. "What is it?" he asked.

"Another Krom'gar patrol, and they're not far," she replied. "We should hurry. If the rain starts, it will slow us down on an uphill climb, and I doubt they're friendly with the Alliance posted at the base."

"We could try talking to them," the dryad suggested, linking arms with Galena.

"Not this time. I mean, I know I didn't let you do it with the drakes, either, but I promise it will be the right time eventually," Aram said, keeping close to the shallow caves pocking the mountainside. "We shouldn't waste more time in the valley."

Or in general, he thought. The night before as they made

camp, Aram could not sleep, not just because he could swear he heard skittering in the trees, but because his head was so stuffed with worries he thought it might pop. He should've sent word to his mother saying that he was safe. He shouldn't have run off, leaving Makasa and his friends behind. He should've realized sooner that nothing could ever happen between a human and a dryad. He needed to hurry and find the remaining shards, complete the Diamond Blade, and save the Light. On and on it went, his eyes snapping open whenever he thought of another thing he had forgotten or wasn't doing quickly enough.

And then there was Silverlaine. That, more than anything else, kept him wide-awake. As much as Aram respected Greydon Thorne, he had no idea what to expect from his brother. He had tried sketching him so many times, but it never quite came together. It was like there was a huge blur over the man's face whenever Aram tried to imagine him. Maybe that was fear, fear that he wouldn't be able to help, or that he would reject Aram and not take his mission seriously.

Soon he would know. Soon he would find out if Silverlaine Thorne was the hero he needed him to be, or just another disappointment.

The first drops of rain hit them as they slipped by the barricades set up by the Krom'gar tauren. Galena had been right—they were not friendly, and whenever they spotted a soldier through the trees, Aram could see their backs bristling with sharp spears.

Yet the valley remained quiet, and as soon as they found a clear crossing on the road, the travelers tested their luck, running across and hiding in the bushes on the other side. A hill rose sharply upward, a steep path cut into it that, much like at the Overlook, swept its way back and forth up the sandy path. At the bottom of the hill, two war-stained banners greeted them, charred with fire and yellowed by exposure to the sun. Still, they were the gold anchors of the Northwatch livery, and even as the rain beat down harder, Aram felt his spirits lift.

Two hard days of travel, but they had made it, helped by the ram Drella had tamed. The dryad insisted on setting him free with a kiss on his nose when they reached their destination, as was her deal with the creature.

"Where are the guards?" Galena asked as they started up the path. She glanced nervously behind them. Aram couldn't blame her—they were exposed to anyone in the valley with eyes. A well-aimed arrow from the Krom'gar could end their adventure in a blink.

"It's about noon, isn't it?" He glanced up to find the position of the sun, but it was rapidly being covered up by clouds. "Might be the end of a shift."

Even as he said it, he had to admit that it was very quiet for an outpost. They continued up the steep road, Drella humming softly to them, occasionally making up words to a song she had been composing all day as she picked flowers.

"Can you even believe it?" she said, giving a little spin. "We are going to meet your uncle! Oh! Oh no! I do not have a crown for him. Will he hate me forever?"

"He can have mine," Aram said with a chuckle, taking off his own elaborate gift from her and handing it across. "I won't tell him it's a hand-me-down."

"That is so generous of you," she said with a beaming smile. Then she paused her trot to fling her arms around him, squeezing tight. Aram appreciated the gesture, but they needed to get a move on before the cursed rain drowned them. "It will be even more special this way, almost like it is from us both!"

As Drella clutched the crown to her chest, the clouds opened up in earnest, rain pouring down so hard it hurt Aram's eyes. He blinked rapidly, hurrying up the hill, his boots churning the mud as they picked up the pace, eager to finish the climb and seek shelter. The wind banked, throwing the rain sideways, so dense that Aram could hardly see the way forward. Out of breath, he staggered to the top of the hill with Galena wheezing hard beside him. The climb hadn't bothered Drella, though her bright, colorful hair was now sodden and stuck to her shoulders.

The Northwatch banners, soaked, hung lifeless on their poles. Not a single fire burned in the camp. The tents, what Aram could see of them, were empty, the rain drumming loudly on the canvas. A crack of lightning split the sky, and for an instant, the Northwatch Expedition Base could be seen in its entirety, abandoned but for a few soldiers gathered near the tents. No, not soldiers . . . He gasped and reached for Drella, another flash of lightning revealing the cruel, glittering eyes and beak of an arak-koa. *Ssarbik.*

Aram's heart stopped. The Alliance must be off fighting nearby, the camp abandoned in the chaos. Perfect timing to set a trap. They had come all this way, drummed up all that hope, and for a *trap.*

"Aramar!" Drella called out as the crushed, wet flower crown slid out of her hands and into the mud. The next bang came not from the sky, but from Ssarbik, a bolt of purple energy shooting across the camp, aimed at Aram and his friends. Too swift to dodge, too cunningly cast to withstand.

A trap. Did they have Silverlaine? How did they know to come there? None of it made any sense! His temper flared, and as the magic hissed toward them, he reached for the hilt of the Diamond Blade. But his rage was not enough, and the shadow magic surged around them, Galena falling in a heap at his feet.

The glow of the Diamond Blade's hilt lit a small pool of golden Light around them, and by that glow, the remainder of his ene-mies emerged. First Throgg, massive and snarling, a mace slung over his shoulder, his other hand, a stump, protected by an enor-mous wooden shield carved into a hideously roaring war pig. There was no sign of Valdread, but that didn't matter; Aram knew the Forsaken mercenary could be lurking anywhere in the rain-darkened shadows. Ssavra and Zathra, both in oiled leather hoods, emerged from the tents on either side of Ssarbik. Zathra, the orange-skinned Sandfury troll, guarded something in her arms that moved, swiftly, crawling up her shoulder and then curling around her arm. Aram shuddered at the sight of it— Skitter, her trusty scorpid and living weapon.

Aram raised his cutlass, ready to charge, knowing that it was up to him to be brave now that they were already down to just the two of them. He had never missed Makasa more in his life— it would be so much easier to dash into battle with even a hint of confidence if his sister were there, letting loose a war cry and raising her harpoon.

But Drella didn't fail him. She was there at his side as they raced toward Ssarbik. The others were dangerous, of course, but the arakkoa's magic could reach them from the farthest distance. He watched as Zathra pulled two small crossbows from inside her cloak and Throgg hefted his deadly mace, but it wouldn't matter. Ssarbik cackled, throwing his birdlike head back in glee as more tendrils of purplish black magic shot from his feathered hands.

Aram shouted, the breath forced out of his lungs as he fell at once to the ground, using what little strength he had left to keep the cutlass from flying out of his grasp. He tried to gulp down air, tried to flail, but the shadow magic kept him in place, squeezing hard, as if the tentacle of a great beast had wrapped around him. Blinking through the rain, he saw that same long horrible magic flowing from Ssarbik's robes to Galena. She lived, but she could not move.

"Be careful!" he whispered, still fighting for air. With both Aram and the tauren frozen in place, Drella remained their last hope. But that hope quickly withered, and Aram cursed, watching Throgg dodge the roots that Drella was summoning from the ground, knocking her down with one precise jab of his shield.

"NO!" Aram twisted in the mud, but it was no use. Drella crumpled, falling to her side, but not before she covered her head with both arms protectively. "Leave her alone! Fight me! Fight me, you cowards!"

"Foolissssh boy." Ssarbik chuckled again, clearly enjoying himself. "There will be no essscape thiss time."

Throgg bent down and scooped up Drella as if she were no more than a leaf, her slender fawn's legs dangling as she hung dazed in his arms.

"Throgg smash now, one hit, she go to sleep."

"No, Throgg. Not yet."

Aram shivered. He knew that voice. Of course, the Hidden wouldn't just appear like this without their callous, sneering leader. *Malus.* The tall, dark, heavily armed murderer ducked out from one of the tents, cleaning his teeth with the point of a dagger. His left hand was covered in a heavy iron gauntlet. He pulled up his collar against the rain, glancing first at Aram, and then Drella, and finally the subdued druid behind them.

"Well, well, if it isn't little Aramar Thorne and his traveling zoo." His lackeys ate that up, laughing, Ssarbik a little too enthusiastically, to the point that Malus had to shoot him a look to get the arakkoa to shut up. "Where are the rest of your friends? Don't tell me the Krom'gar got them. I wanted to finish off your whole band of fools myself, just like I finished your father's."

Aram gritted his teeth. It was tempting to bite back with something smart, but he didn't want to give Malus anything.

Malus stomped over to him through the mud, kneeling, bringing the sailor's scent of tobacco, salt, and rum with him. Reaching for Aram's chin, he forced the boy's head upward, until he had no choice but to stare into the man's cold, black eyes.

"Go on," Malus said softly, almost kindly. "It's all right."

Don't fall for it; don't forget who he is.

"Go on. Ask what you want to ask. I know you're just dying to spit it out."

Aram seethed, but Malus was right. Twisting, Aram tried to move his hands enough to free the crystal shard hilt, but there was no way to move, not with Ssarbik's magic holding him so tightly in place.

"Where is he?" Aram muttered. The shadow magic squeezed him harder and he coughed, feeling as if his rib cage would shatter at any moment. "Where's my uncle? What did you do with him?"

Ssarbik gave another shrill cackle, and the others followed his lead, laughing in Aram's face. But Malus didn't even crack a smile. He let go of Aram's face and clucked his tongue, then stood, leaving Aram with a cold swipe of mud across his chin.

"How did you manage to slip my net so many times when you're this stupid?" Malus sighed, wiping the mud on his gloved hand onto his trousers. "Aggravating, is what that is."

"Tell him!" Ssavra clapped her feathered hands, the arakkoa's head tipping to the side. "Say it."

"Yeah, boss, tell da boy," Zathra chimed in.

Malus silenced them with a single glance. "Why, Aram, I'm disappointed. You ought to be thrilled, boy, you ought to be giving me a nice, big hug."

"If I touched you, it would only be to shove my cutlass through your guts!" Aram shouted. But he didn't like the look on Malus's face, the quiet, easy smile, the expression of a man who had won and won big. Aram didn't want to give him the satisfaction of his panic, but he could feel cold nausea spreading through his stomach the longer he stayed frozen there in the mud. There was more here that he didn't see, not just the trap, not just the ambush . . .

"Now, now," Malus chided, again gentle and calm. "Is that any way to speak to your uncle?"

CHAPTER FOURTEEN
AMBUSHED·

Reigol Valdread had to feel sorry for the boy.

He himself knew despair. He knew anguish. And now, crouched in the protective boughs of a nearby tree, Valdread watched the young man experience the deepest kind of betrayal. The wail Aramar Thorne gave stirred his sympathy, even if he had no real opinion on the kid one way or another . . . It was hard to watch someone so young suffer that way. It would have been less painful if Malus had stuck a knife in his back and ended this for good.

The rain muffled their voices, but Valdread bent his ear to hear them better, a sick, icy feeling spreading across his chest.

Just have done with it. No sense dragging it out.

But this was Malus he was looking at, a man who had become increasingly self-obsessed and erratic. He watched as Throgg, the immense, horned ogre, almost dropped the stunned dryad he held. The big oaf shifted from foot to foot, impatient, about as uncomfortable as Valdread himself. Ssavra and Ssarbik seemed to be enjoying themselves, which only made Valdread despise them more. This was a child, not some all-powerful foe they had brought low. The gloating was just vulgar.

"You're a liar!" the boy shouted, thrashing.

Malus indulged in yet another laugh with his compatriots, crouching again to get in the boy's face and really rub it in. "Did you really think nobody would notice those letters you sent? I have eyes and ears everywhere, fool."

Like up a tree, for example. Valdread winced, being the one to spearhead and manage Malus's network of spies. Malus had already gotten wise to the boy's ruse with the *Crustacean*. After that, Valdread merely had to pay off enough weak-willed goblins in Gadgetzan to pick up the real trail. It led to the Stonetalon Mountains, then went cold, but Aramar Thorne had been thoughtful enough to send missives to every corner of northern Kalimdor, giving Valdread an easy solution.

"I don't believe you. I'll never believe you!"

The boy was covered in mud, still struggling against the black tendrils of magic pinning him to the ground. The tauren girl stirred, awake, tossing furiously against her magical bonds. He would watch that one closely, for her robes gave away her connection to the Cenarion Circle. A druid. She would be formidable in a fight. But where was the young woman he traveled with, who carried the chain and the harpoon? Surely everyone here knew she was the real threat.

"What have you done with my uncle?"

Malus stood and slicked the rain back off his dark hair. "I *am* your uncle. I'm sure you can see the family resemblance, even if you don't want to. Listen, Aramar, it won't give me any pleasure to kill you and your friends, but the Diamond Blade is mine, and you've given me too much trouble. I know better than to let you roam free; you'll just keep sticking your nose into my business."

Cold. Dreadfully cold. Valdread had wondered, idly, how Malus planned to spring the news on Aramar Thorne. Malus had told them all his approach and his intentions as they sailed up the coast toward the Stonetalon Mountains. The others, of course, found it riotously funny.

"Perhapss I missssjudged you, Maluss," Ssarbik had hissed, giddy, apparently, at the thought of a young boy's life being turned upside down. "Thiss plot of yourss is cruelty itssself. Marvelousss."

Zathra was for it, too, and even her pet scorpid picked up on the excitement in the ship's cabin, clacking and chattering its spiny tail.

Throgg had been in a foul mood since the *Crustacean*, sulking in the shadows, drinking far too much and then clumsily muttering about his growing dislike of Malus. Malus paid him no attention, underestimating whomever he considered stupid, which was a grave weakness in Valdread's eyes.

As the rain slowed to a more bearable dribble, Aramar Thorne seemed to be struggling in the dark grip of belief. He clenched his jaw, obviously holding back tears, shaking his head constantly. Sometimes his lips moved, but no sound came out. Malus pulled out his broadsword, examining it, taunting the boy with his imminent demise.

"You would kill your own nephew," Aramar shouted. "If you're Silverlaine Thorne, you don't deserve the name!"

"Watch it." Malus swept his broadsword low, the blade flashing dangerously close to the boy's cheek. "What would you know about the Thorne name? Why even care about it? Your father abandoned you; he only ever saw you as a nuisance. A burden."

Aramar thrashed. "That's not true! In the end, he tried. He tried to save me. He wanted me to carry on his work, and it's only because *you* took him from me that I won't know him better!"

Valdread winced. Ah, yes. He had told the boy he would not see Greydon Thorne on this world again, and that was the truth. Greydon Thorne lived, imprisoned on Outland, but the boy had no idea. The arakkoa and troll behind Malus fidgeted. They wanted blood, and they wanted it soon. Malus was dragging this out, and Valdread read plainly the hesitation in the man's stance. The broadsword inched away from Aramar Thorne, and Ssarbik made a disgusted noise.

"Let me go, Malus. This is wrong. There must be some part of you . . . some small part that knows this is wrong." Aram bit out most of his words, then took a deep breath, trying his best to crane his neck and look Malus in the eye. Valdread wondered what the boy saw. Did he, like Valdread, see a man who was losing control of himself, or did he truly see a man capable of redemption?

Was it possible that Malus might really listen to the boy? After all, fighting a man of one's own age was fair, but cutting down one's own nephew while restrained . . . that took a different degree of viciousness.

"Malusssss!" Ssarbik half screamed. "I cannot hold them forever. Do it!"

But Malus shook his head, running one hand thoughtfully over his stubble-darkened chin. There was a resemblance there, between man and boy, more so than Valdread had noticed between Greydon and Aramar. For Aramar, it might have been like looking into a twisted mirror of time, seeing a future version of himself weathered by age and unkind choices. They had the same dark hair and arresting eyes, the same strong chin and noble nose.

"You can't be my uncle," Aram sputtered, pale with denial.

"He is." It was the dryad. Still held by Throgg, she looked suddenly calm. "He is your blood, Aram. And there is something . . .

Conflict! So, so much conflict. It must be painful inside his heart—"

"Shut up," Malus spat, shooting her a glance. "This is nonsense."

"No. I can sense it, Aram, through our bond. Through the blood you share. There is still a man in there, twisting from his true nature. Corrupt and set on a path he feels he must see through, but in so much pain! A creature in pain can be healed, Aram. A creature in pain can change!"

"Change," he echoed her in a whisper. He went still for a moment, then gave Malus a steadier look. "Listen to her. Listen to me! It doesn't have to be like this," Aramar said, soft but determined. "She's right. You can change. You can always change. That's what Greydon taught me. Maybe he wasn't always the best father, but he tried, and in my eyes he changed."

Valdread had to give the young man and the dryad credit—it was a stirring speech, and one that seemed to ring all too true of Malus.

And Malus's hesitation had the effect of a spell being cast over his minions. Throgg almost dropped the dryad girl, turning toward Malus, his attention no longer trained on the children, but on Malus himself. There was a charge like the scent of the air before lightning, and even Valdread sat up a little straighter in the tree, his ravaged and exposed spine clacking audibly as he did so.

Malus wouldn't really turn on them, would he? It wasn't possible . . . But then, his leadership had been failing recently, there were whispers of mutiny, discontent among Ssarbik and Ssavra, and as for Valdread? Well. He was a mercenary. His loyalty was bought and paid for.

"Hey, what you doin'?" Zathra took a daring step toward Malus, her crossbows at the ready.

"Don't listen to them," Aramar said, straining against the magic tendrils holding him down. "Listen to me! Listen to your family."

Malus stared down at his nephew, silent in the stilling rain. Perhaps this really was the line, asking a man to execute his own flesh and blood, defenseless and vulnerable, heartbroken in the mud.

In a strange way, it made Valdread respect him more.

"Then you accept that I am your uncle?" he pressed. "That though our paths differ so greatly, Greydon is my brother?"

"Yes," Aramar whispered. "I believe you. Drella wouldn't lie to me, and she wouldn't lie about the man you could be."

Throgg lifted his mace; whether he intended to aim for Malus or Aramar, Valdread couldn't rightly say.

"You accept that I'm family," Malus went on, his voice almost lost to Valdread in the tree. "And you . . . you really accept that I can change? After everything I've done. After everything I've become. The pain I've caused. The *death*."

That one was harder for the boy to swallow, but either he was a convincing liar or he had a forgiving nature, for he nodded, once. The dryad in Throgg's arms strained against his hold, and the tauren girl was looking more coherent by the second. Malus needed to make a decision, and so did Valdread. Who would he side with? Or was it better to simply disappear, and leave this sordid mess to sort itself out?

"Weaknessss!" Ssarbik shrieked. "Betrayal! Your true nature exposssssed!"

Well. That settled it. Valdread hated that bird and his annoying voice. He would be Team Whoever-Let-Him-Stab-Ssarbik.

"Silence," Malus thundered. "I said: Silence!"

The hilltop clearing went utterly still but for the drip-drip-drip off the tree branches and tents. Aramar stared up hopefully at his uncle, no longer struggling against his bonds.

"You don't have to hurt anyone again," Aramar told him, painfully sincere. "You can live up to the Thorne name. I'll help you. I'll . . . I'll forgive you."

Malus held up his broadsword, examining the blade, his eyes fogged, lost in thought. He then slowly, carefully, sheathed the weapon. "I can live up to the Thorne name," he repeated. Then, in a voice so gentle it almost didn't sound like him, added, "I will."

Throgg began to swing his mace, enraged, but not before Malus put up a hand to still him, grabbing his broadsword again and slicing it toward Aramar Thorne's neck. The warmth Valdread had seen in the man's eyes was gone, replaced with nothingness, the cold, black stare of a man unencumbered by shame or regret.

"Just kidding. Kill them. Kill them all."

Several things happened at once, and so quickly that even Valdread scrambled to understand the field. Throgg swung wide of Malus, burying his mace into the mud. Then, without warning, Malus pulled back his sword and prepared to swing it down fully on the boy's head. Ssarbik squealed with delight, and his sister preened and cackled. Zathra aimed her crossbows not at Malus's back, but toward the tauren still restrained near the edge of the hill. And strangest of all, a blinding, dizzying light burst from where Aramar Thorne had scrabbled in the mud.

The black shadow tendrils holding the boy and the tauren dispersed, evaporating, shards of golden Light streaming out in every direction, vanquishing the arakkoa's magic. A flash of pure, gleaming Light made Malus stagger, the boy's scream of effort mingling with the battle cries of the ogre and arakkoa.

Now, Valdread thought, *things are getting interesting.*

CHAPTER FIFTEEN
BLOOD AND REGRET

Ablast of Light met them as they crested the hill, and for a moment, Makasa was left stunned and blind until she rubbed her eyes and the chaos became clearer. Galena, covered head to foot in filth, turned toward them, waving her arms. They made their way to her as she collected herself.

"By Cenarius's left antler, you're here!" She pointed frantically back toward the battle. "Okay, what do we do? Oh, what do we do? I should be prepared for this; I should be prepared but I'm not! The CCAMP says to avoid outright conflict if at all possible, t-to always use diversionary tactics unless trained in the feral or natural arts, but there's no section on *arakkoa dark magic ambushes*!"

Makasa shook her head, almost speechless. "What? Slow down. Look, just stay out of the way, all right? Don't get yourself killed."

Galena nodded, then gasped. "Taryndrella! Quickly! We must protect her!"

"And *Aram*," Makasa said, gritting her teeth. She had expected to arrive and give him the verbal beating of his life, but all of her anger fled at the sight of Malus trying to decapitate him. What a coward, waiting until Aram was bound and helpless to strike that blow. He would pay for that, she vowed silently, charging with the others toward the mayhem.

"You will not hurt him!" Drella had wriggled her way free of the ogre who had been trying to keep her still. Makasa watched as the dryad summoned roots from the earth itself, twining them around Aram, pulling him away from a cascade of dark energy bolts hurled by the two arakkoa.

They were holding their own, but another blade—or harpoon—wouldn't hurt.

"Urka, urka, frund!" Murky was screaming about "up" again, but this time it had nothing to do with giant spiders. Instead, she watched Hackle catch the little murloc as he hurled himself into the gnoll's arms, and then was tossed like a cannonball into the fray. Spear raised, he crashed headlong into the troll, Zathra, knocking the crossbows out of her hands and sending her pet scorpid crashing into the mountain. Skitter fell to the ground on its back, legs clawing helplessly at the air. It only stunned the troll for an instant, and soon she had spun away, kicking into the air and then landing nimbly with a short dagger drawn.

Hackle, hyena-laughing with the bloodthirsty glee of a

warrior gnoll, took hold of his beloved war club and charged in after Murky, narrowly avoiding a bolt of magic from Ssarbik.

Makasa watched the purple blob of magic vanish over the edge of the hill, swinging the chain, looking for the right way in to the fight. Throgg might be the biggest threat to Drella, and so she changed course, running full-on toward the ogre, hoping to catch him off guard.

"Oh, hi, friends! We are so glad you came!" Drella greeted, shielding Aram with thick roots that burst artfully from the ground, roots that were soon shredded by Malus's broadsword slicing through them. Aram parried with his cutlass, but he was losing ground.

"Hang on!" Makasa called. "I'm coming!"

"Not so fast, young lady."

She felt the chain dangling near her left elbow stop short. Someone had grabbed it and pulled, and the force of it ruined her balance, sending her crashing into the mud. She landed with a thud on her rear, wincing, but she leapt back to her feet at once, ignoring the pain shooting up her back as she spun.

The Forsaken. The overpowering combination of sickly sweet jasmine water and rotting flesh hit her like a slap to the face. She took a few cautious steps back, glancing from his stance to his blade and then to his face. Smiling, he flourished his blade experimentally, then took a practice lunge toward her. It wasn't an attack in earnest; he was taunting her.

"Stay out of this," Makasa said with a sneer. "Don't make me embarrass you in front of your friends."

"Ooh. *Ouch*." He chuckled. His hood was drawn up over his head, but she could see that yellow-toothed smile and the depressing remnants of a once-handsome face now reduced to rot and bone. "Pity, girl, you missed quite the show. Your little friend discovered Malus is indeed his uncle. It was the most heartwarming reunion. But that's all right; it's time for another sort of show, the kind where I teach you a harsh lesson about dueling your betters."

"Are you going to fight me or just run your mouth?" Makasa watched him stab toward her again, judging his left side to be the weaker, specifically his leg near the knee. He favored that leg, and it didn't look quite balanced. She grunted, swinging her harpoon, landing a weak blow against his knee.

Valdread compensated expertly, though she didn't miss his hiss of pain. If she had another chance, that was the spot to hit.

"Not bad," he chided playfully, slashing toward her, the blade whistling next to her ear. Close. Too close. "Not bad at all. You're quite the little fighter. You remind me of another spitfire I once had the pleasure of dueling. In fact, I haven't enjoyed myself so much since I sparred with the captain of the pirate ship *Makemba*!"

The *Makemba*. Her ship. Her *mother's* ship. Home.

The mere mention of that ship was like setting fire to tinder, igniting a blaze in Makasa's heart that she didn't expect. It exploded out of her with a shout, and she swung harder, harder . . . What did this creep know of her mother? What right did he have to even utter the name of that ship in front of her? Every punishing swing of her harpoon might as well have been punctuating the phrase *How. Dare. You.*

"Dear me, touched a nerve, have I?" Valdread chuckled, but his smile faded as quickly as his laughter, for he had lit something dangerous in Makasa, something that made her fight with more strength and determination than she had felt in a long time. It was like the bottom dropping out on her life when the *Wavestrider* sank, that sudden, sickening emptiness that came before the pain and fury filled in the space.

Behind them, the arakkoa Ssarbik noticed Valdread and Makasa circling each other. The birdlike creature gave a squawk, one of his shadowy bolts hurling toward them. It seemed, strangely enough, to veer much closer to Valdread than to her.

The undead swore under his breath.

"Not again. I'll deal with that nuisance presently," he muttered. "After I defeat you, girl."

She saw an opening again for his leg and took it, giving an all or nothing swing, the power of it sending her forward too quickly. Her boot slid through the mud and she surged forward, flailing, just one moment's carelessness, but that was more than enough.

Makasa gasped, watching the blade come down, feeling, all at once, the darkness, the shock, and then? Nothing.

There was truly no mistaking it now, not after that duel. Valdread knew the stance and the swing well. It was a unique rhythm, a warrior's dance, and few possessed the grace or physical prowess to use it effectively. The girl had bloody well smashed up his knee, and one more hit from that harpoon of hers and he would have been in real trouble. As it was, she had gone down like a sack of potatoes, crumpled in the mud with her chest still rising and falling. That would have to suffice; there was no time to dally, as his woefully incompetent co-henchmen were already losing to a bunch of children and a frog.

Granted, the frog did have spirit, using his net and spear with surprising ability, already disabling Zathra's scorpid, rendering it useless as it scrabbled under the murloc's tightened net.

Valdread took one last look at Makasa in the mud, wondering if perhaps it would be prudent to move her to a safer spot. He decided against it, but not before hearing a curious sound whistling toward him. Not whistling, *whooshing*. He knew that sound. Magic. Dark magic. It came with a preemptive tightening of the guts, a premonition-like feeling of unease. Out of the corner of his eye, as he turned, he watched the dark bolt, hurled by Ssarbik, speed toward him. But the magic would never touch him, never satisfy Ssarbik's deceptive intent, for the dryad girl, light as a hare, leapt in front of it, deflecting the magic, nullifying it at once.

He closed the distance between them, watching as the last remnants of the shadowy bolt turned to no more than ash at her hooves. While his body turned toward the dryad, his eyes remained fixed on the cowardly arakkoa. The nerve of that creature, waiting until he was completely vulnerable to take advantage of the chaos and do a bit of light *murder.*

"Awfully generous of you," Valdread told the dryad, sweeping her a gallant bow. "I'm not sure I deserved that, but I thank you all the same."

He had not the slightest interest in using his weapon against her, and when he did not raise his blade, she gave a swift nod and then surrounded them both in a brief shield of leafy emerald magic.

"You should not be," she told him plainly, not meanly, just as if it were fact. Valdread wasn't exactly disagreeing. "But there is good in you. You helped me, helped *us*, when you could have turned your back. And good things should be protected! Besides. That was just mean! Mean and not fair! Bye!"

Valdread pieced together the "good" that the dryad referred to—when he fought her abductors in the Bone Pile, allowing her and her party to escape foul villains who were seeking to raise a powerful Scourge into Azeroth. *I did it more to hurt the Scourge than to help her*, Valdread mused, but he wasn't going to correct her.

And then the dryad was gone, hopping away, blithely deflecting a large mass of shadow magic aimed at her by Ssarbik.

Ssarbik, whom Valdread would need to deal with directly, but not before intervening on Zathra's behalf. The troll was not getting along well, and without her scorpid to help, she seemed unhinged. She flailed her knife blindly at the murloc and gnoll, who had cornered her against one of the Alliance tents. Valdread dashed toward her, using his silent speed to his advantage, careening into the gnoll and murloc duo so unexpectedly that both of them yelped, tumbling into the mud.

"I owe you one, brudda. Now you be helpin' me wid Skitter, eh?"

He could indeed help her with Skitter, because the murloc and gnoll were no longer of any concern. Ssarbik, perhaps because he had been caught, rededicated himself to fighting on the correct side, binding the nuisance children with more black, shadowy tendrils of his magic. That took a bit of the pressure off, and Zathra and Valdread knelt together, cutting through the sturdy nets trapping the scorpid, who clacked gratefully and scuttled up Zathra's leg to her shoulder, perching there with its tail ready to lash out. The murloc blabbered at them, frantic as his nets were shredded and left useless.

"If you don't mind, Ssarbik, perhaps you could mind our actual enemies and do your job," Valdread drawled, watching as the arakkoa puffed up his feathers indignantly.

"An accident, I assssure you," the creature hissed.

"Of course." Valdread rolled his eyes, but couldn't find fault with the caster's effectiveness. The fight had turned quickly in their favor. Aramar Thorne had been slashing bravely on with his sword, but he was fatiguing, and falling back, and it had taken little effort for Ssarbik to intervene, catching him and the others up in his shadow magic. But not the dryad. That child remained irritatingly immune to such things, her affinity with nature making her totally impervious to the shadows that fell in useless tatters at her hooves as she bounced away.

"Her!" Valdread shouted. It was instinct, no, practice. A fighter of his age and caliber was a well-honed machine, one part connected to the other. And so he shouted it without thought, more as an immediate and given response. Her. She was the problem. The tauren, while perhaps a druid, had already been conquered by Ssarbik's magic and subdued again. Aramar was exhausted, his strongest ally unconscious, the murloc and gnoll no longer a threat . . . It was the dryad that they need worry about. She and she alone needed to be brought down.

And yet . . . And yet . . . And yet she had just saved him.

Regret, as keen as the regret he felt when remembering his

humanity, his real and mortal lifeblood, swept over him like a winter chill.

"Yes, her!" Ssavra and Throgg turned their full attention on the dryad. She was swift and skilled with her magic, but the colorful little fawn girl was soon overwhelmed. Zathra joined in, swinging her blade, Skitter stabbing toward the dryad with its barbed tail.

"Crowd her toward the mountain's edge!" Malus shouted. He hung back, apparently regaining his strength, but his minions obliged.

"Leave her alone!" Aramar called, struggling once more against bonds too strong to fight. "It isn't fair! Leave her alone!"

Valdread was forced to agree. It proved a pitiful sight—Ssavra, Ssarbik, the immense Throgg, and the darting troll all cornering the dryad, pushing her away from her friends and the tents and toward the perilous edge of the overlook. The way down was long, and nobody would survive it. With the rocks and ground so slick from the rain, she could easily slip and fall even before the Hidden reached her.

And it was all Valdread's fault. He had turned the full force of the Hidden against her, and now she was doomed for it.

Zathra, perhaps shamed by being so humiliated by the murloc and gnoll, lashed out first. The dryad, her back to the open plunge of the cliff's edge behind her, put up her hands, conjuring but a weak wisp of roots toward her. Ssavra was relentless, hurling dark bolts of energy at the girl, distracting her. The dryad cried out, eyes wide with fear and shock, as Zathra surged forward, long, wet hair streaming down her back, both she and the scorpid clinging to her screaming in fury.

The knife, keenly wielded, found its target, drawing a scream of pain and then, blood.

CHAPTER SIXTEEN
THE SACRIFICE

Aramar Thorne felt time slow to a strange state, freezing and then reversing. He was six again, playing by the lake's edge, when nasty Darren Boyle pushed him down into the sand and took his wooden horse. A girl his own age from the village ran over and elbowed Darren in the back, and got the horse back for him. It was the first time a stranger had stuck up for him. Then time flew forward again, and he was on the *Wavestrider*, and for once he had actually tied off a main mast rope correctly; that had earned him a single approving nod from Makasa, and he felt his heart grow with pride. Forward again, to just the night before, when he and Drella and Galena all sat around the fire, companions on this strange and winding journey.

"I don't think I'll be able to sleep," Aram had mused aloud. "Not with all those spiders nearby. Did you see the size of the webs? Awful."

"But you must sleep!" Drella looked scandalized, braiding

flowers into her hair over one shoulder, sitting in her curious sideways manner to accommodate her fawn legs. Her skin glowed orange in the firelight. "Lie down, both of you, and I will sing you a lullaby."

"I'm not a kid," Aram protested, but laid down anyway.

"Sh-hh! I want to hear a dryad lullaby," Galena had whispered. "Don't ruin this for me."

And so Drella sang to them, quietly at first, and then with more confidence. That wasn't anything new. Drella sang all the time, and for any reason, but this was different. Aram could tell it meant something to her, that it wasn't just some random bits of thoughts she had strung together with a melody, but a genuine song she had learned somewhere. Had Thalyss taught it to her when she was still just an acorn?

There I was
In the wood
With sunshine so bright.
There I was,
Not alone but alive.
There I walked in my grove
With hope and pride.
There I shall stay
When I fear the rising tide.

Stuck there on the hilltop of the base camp, his arms pinned to his sides, his chest throbbing with pain, Aram could swear he heard a soft whisper of the song again. Should it comfort him? Should it frighten him? He couldn't move, paralyzed, watching in mute horror as Zathra's blade sank into Drella's side.

Galena screamed. Zathra howled with glee. And Aramar felt the blade go in as if it had been stuck between his own ribs and not Drella's. Their bond. He had never doubted it, but also never given it too much thought. Now he knew it was real and personal and vital, and his eyes filled with tears as he watched Drella grasp the knife and pull it from her side, blood soaking through the flowers and leaves covering her midsection.

Rage. Sadness. Fear. Clarity.

There I shall stay
When I fear the rising tide.

Clarity. He would stay in that clarity, that singular focus that overtook him and made the crystal shard hilt pinned to his side glow suddenly white-hot with energy. Just as Drella was bound to him, the hilt seemed bound to his state, and the Diamond Blade exploded to life, a ripple of Light and heat blasting out from it in every direction. Aramar hardly felt the impact, but everyone else on the hilltop was not so lucky. The burst rocked the others to the ground, even Throgg and Malus toppling into the mud as Aramar broke free of the magic holding him, the shadow once more dissolved by the power of the Light.

"To me! Hurry!" Aramar shouted, and Drella listened without hesitation, galloping over the stunned bodies of Ssarbik and Ssavra, who had edged her toward the cliff's face but now lay prone on the ground. Malus was the first to regain his feet, and the nearest, having stayed near the tents and not crowded Drella like the others.

He leapt toward Aram, snarling and swinging, his broadsword reflecting the last of the Light that had flattened everyone to the mud.

"No more!" Malus bellowed, his black eyes bristling with anger. His face had gone red with rage, spit dribbling down his chin as he grunted and swung his sword with reckless abandon. "I'm *done* with mercy."

Aram, foolishly, let his attention be drawn by Drella. She was taking too long to reach him, slowed by the grievous wound in her side. He had to protect her, and yet he couldn't, not when Malus descended on him. He was a tornado of violence, blade flashing relentlessly, Aram doing his best to deflect the heavy blows. But Malus was, in the end, not only a trained swordsman but a grown man of incredible strength, and Aram felt his wrists begin to ache from the effort of parrying the broadsword.

"At last," Malus hissed, winding up for one last overhead

swing. Aram braced, feeling his whole body shudder from the force of the blow as their swords clashed, and Aram slumped to his knees, overwhelmed and defeated. "Ssarbik! Get up, you useless peacock, and get us a portal out of here. NOW."

Malus knocked the cutlass out of Aram's shaking hands, then reached down, grabbing Aram by the collar of his father's coat.

"You've won," Aram muttered, trying to pry at the man's far stronger hands. "Just kill me. Don't hurt the others; they don't deserve this."

"You're right." Laughing, Malus slammed the rounded hilt of his broadsword into Aram's temple, dazing him. The world tilted and Aram fell over onto his side, gasping, feeling the compass around his neck break under the weight of his elbow. The glass shattered, but Aram didn't have time to mourn for it. The sense had been knocked from him, but he could still see a blur coming toward them at speed.

Drella.

No, he thought. *Go away. Flee. This is all my doing, all my fault—*

"Drella." He groaned, weak. The others were rallying, the Hidden and his friends, and he could see Makasa shaking her head as she crawled up onto all fours. Aram's head pounded, his vision failing. But Drella . . . He could see her, bounding toward them. Malus had heard him say her name, and he spun, broadsword in hand, intercepting her before Murky or Hackle could come to her aid.

His hand lashed out once, precisely, cuffing her across the face the same way he had hit Aram. Drella reeled, going up onto her hind legs, her eyes huge with fear as she went down into the mud.

"Nature preserve me, nature guide me," she was saying, over and over again, but she was weak and wounded, and nothing but a flicker of emerald magic danced on the ends of her fingertips.

Time slowed again. Aram felt as if he might vomit from the pain coursing through his head and side. He watched Malus, his uncle, round on the dryad, preparing to raise his sword and strike the killing blow.

"Stop."

It wasn't Makasa who said it, or Galena, but Valdread. The Forsaken, mud-flecked and hunched, placed himself between Malus and the dryad, his blade ready as if to challenge.

"Get out of my way, corpse," Malus said with a snarl.

"No." Valdread stood his ground.

"You mercenaries are all the same. Never worth the price." Malus sliced his broadsword through the air and huffed. "I don't pay you for your opinions, and I don't pay you to challenge my authority. Now shut up and move."

"The boy is down; he's defenseless; you have him now. You have the compass, man. You have what you want. Come to your senses. This isn't a clean kill. Look at her; she's hardly more than a child. Come now, Malus, this isn't necessary. It would be murder."

"No," Malus said, shaking his head, and for a moment, Aram thought he might see reason and show mercy. Instead, he gave a strange flick of his head. Behind him, near the cliff, Ssarbik and his evil magics had been waiting. The blackened tendril wrapped around Valdread's middle, catching him by surprise, which registered at once on his desiccated face. His mouth fell open as if to let out a scream, but it was lost to the wind as Ssarbik's magic wrapped around him, whipped him across the camp and over the cliff's edge, sending him plummeting to his doom.

"*That* would be murder. Ah. A little peace at last. Now"— Malus sighed and raised his broadsword again—"where was I?"

Aramar knew what would come next. He tried to crawl, tried to scream out a warning, but it was too late. Murky and Hackle would never reach her in time, and Makasa and Galena trailed well behind. All was suddenly quiet, except for Drella's strained gasp of surprise, the broadsword striking true, striking deep, deeper than any wound that could be healed.

The roar that came after didn't sound like Aram to his own ears, but it was, and Malus let him come, let him gather the dryad in his arms. Malus didn't seem to care, or notice, going calmly to retrieve the crystal shard hilt and the broken compass in the mud. His work was done, and Aram's heart was shattered.

Distantly, around the perimeter of his grief, Aram could see more black shadows rising from the ground, bending around his friends, holding them fast. A dark purple-and-black light flickered in the middle of the camp, then reality tore open, an oblong portal shimmering into view.

"You're all right," Aram whispered, gathering Drella close to his chest. She was so light, like she was already gone, disappearing. There was warmth left in her shoulders, in her cheeks, and he brushed at the mud there. "You have to be all right."

"I am not afraid, Aram," she murmured, smiling, not even a sad smile, but a true one, the only way she could smile. "Do not be afraid. Please do not be afraid for me."

Malus's shadow darkened them, the crystal shard hilt tucked into his belt, the shattered compass sticking out of his vest pocket. Why couldn't he just go? Why couldn't he just leave them?

"Haven't you done enough?!" Aram shouted, holding Drella. Rocking her. "Just leave us alone. You got what you came for. Leave us alone. Leave us . . . please."

"Oh no, nephew, I'm afraid my master has other plans for you. Get up, or I'll make you."

"But . . . but Throgg thought you want him dead," Throgg said, scratching his head.

Malus rolled his eyes. "Just something to frighten the boy. I have orders."

Unmoving, Aram refused to look up at his cursed uncle. Instead, he watched the last sweet light in Drella's eyes shine up at him, watched the smile on her lips quaver.

"Listen, Aram," Drella murmured, her eyelashes fluttering, a tear cascading down her perfectly round cheek. She pressed something soft and delicate into his hand, closing his fingers around it. "You must listen, Aram, when nature speaks to you."

Then he was ripped away, Malus dragging him, kicking and screaming, by his coat. Aram wouldn't give up. He fought. He fought hard. And he watched, hopeless and heartbroken, as Drella's small, still form grew farther and farther away.

One by one, the Hidden disappeared into the portal. Aram felt its terrible power humming as Malus dragged him toward it. He searched out his friends, each of them struggling against Ssarbik's binding shadows.

"Aram!" Makasa called out to him, her face stricken, eyes wild. "Aram! I'll find you! We'll find you! Aram, I promise you, we'll—"

Her last words were swallowed up by the portal closing, and then he was sucked into darkness, his only sense that something had changed. He closed his eyes and felt the loss like an arrow to his chest. Their bond. It was *leaving*. He'd never realized the magic that coursed through him—the connection he'd felt to her—until it was suddenly and irrevocably severed.

A hungry pit opened inside Aram's chest, consuming all feeling until he felt nothing but cold.

CHAPTER SEVENTEEN
FAREWELLS TO A FRIEND

The silence kept in the camp for only a moment. Then Makasa heard Murky's webbed feet slapping against the mud as he hurtled toward the fallen Drella. Hackle came, too, but more gradually. Then Galena wailed behind them, falling to her knees in the mud.

"I failed her," she said, fingers grasping desperately at the earth. "I had one mission, one purpose . . . To protect her. I vowed to protect her, and in her moment of greatest need I . . . I failed."

"Come on," Makasa said, reaching out her hand.

Galena sniffed, taking it. "What do we do now?"

"She is our friend, and she deserves to die with her friends around her."

The dryad stirred at their approach. Murky was already draped across her stomach, head buried in his arms as he slobbered and burbled, inconsolable.

"Hackle sorry," the gnoll mumbled, wiping at his snout and

crouching. One huge paw smoothed over the dryad's mud-streaked hair. "Hackle try, but not fast enough. Not strong enough."

Drella managed to lift her head, just a little, and Makasa raced over, kneeling and letting the dryad rest her head on her legs. Smiling weakly, Drella gazed up at her and gave a nod. "I am so lucky," she whispered, her breathing shallow, "to have such good friends."

Makasa bit back her anger, her fear, while she waved Galena closer. She felt utterly helpless. The wounds the dryad had suffered were not survivable, Makasa knew that much, but she didn't want to frighten the girl. Although . . . Drella seemed calm. Peaceful. There was no panic in her voice as she put a gentle hand on Murky's head.

"Do not be afraid, friends," she said, looking at each of them in turn. "All things die."

Nobody spoke. Murky sniffled, lifting his head enough to blink up at Drella with glossy eyes. "Nrk gllrgg," he bubbled.

"Oh, Murky, I think I *have* to go. But do not be afraid. All of this, all of it was our destiny together. There is a harmony to nature, a way and a flow. Like the path of a river, like the path through the soil that a stem takes to find the sun. A river may be dammed. A stem may be chewed away by aphids or grasshoppers. And a traveler may be diverted in any number of ways. But the flow exists, and we are without a doubt a part of its whole."

Makasa took the dryad's hand and felt her heart twinge. She had heard those words before, spoken by Thalyss, who had sacrificed his life for Aram, too. Drella's fingers were growing very cold.

"Makasa," Drella murmured. Speaking was becoming difficult, each word labored, each taking a deep breath to get out. "You are so strong, friend; do not forget to be soft sometimes, too. Soft things can bend and mend and *grow*. They need you. We all need you. Seven must become One. Depend . . . on each other. *Stay together.*"

She smiled then, and was still, and Makasa felt her little hand go limp against her palm.

Wind shimmered through the wet trees, fluttering the flowers growing among Drella's colorful curls. Galena reached over, carefully, and closed the dryad's eyes.

"Earth Mother grant you swift passage," Galena whispered, and then something in a language Makasa did not understand.

They sat in silence around the dryad's body for a long time, and Makasa suspected, like her, nobody had any idea what to do. Drella was gone. Aram taken and likely to follow their friend into an early grave. The compass—the only way to locate the other shards of the Diamond Blade—was in the hands of the enemy, on the march to gods knew what end.

Makasa shifted, laying Drella's head gently on the soft earth.

"We need to make camp, find something to eat, regroup." She

wouldn't let the dryad's sacrifice be in vain. Makasa had to lead now; she had to be strong and sure, and not let them all go to pieces. Not that it was easy, not that she wanted to start barking orders, but someone had to pull them all back together. What was it her brothers had once said? *If you keep on a path, if you just move forward, it keeps things from catching up with you.*

"And we need to . . . We need to bury her."

"I'll find a place," Galena murmured, rising slowly. She drifted solemnly away, and Makasa could hear her crying softly as she went.

"Hackle no understand," the gnoll said, taking in a deep breath and watching the tauren go. "Galena not know Drella like us."

"She's a druid, Hackle. Dryads are sacred to them. I don't pretend to understand it, but I think Master Thal'darah wanted her to protect Taryndrella. Just . . . leave her be. She's going to take it hard."

"We all take hard," Hackle added. "Drella protect us. Drella make crowns, make music. Drella friend."

Murky stayed with Drella the longest, refusing to leave her side. Makasa let him, patrolling through the battle-torn camp. A few weapons had been left behind, and so she gathered those up, and found the most weatherproof tent, then decided against it. What if the Hidden just took a portal back and finished them off? No, they would have to move, and move soon. Her bones ached with exhaustion, her hands jittery. Aram . . . How could they even begin to find him?

The last of the day's sun bled across the horizon, illuminating the camp briefly, the dying rays touching on something shiny in the mud. Makasa squinted, thinking maybe it was just a bit of blade that had broken off in the scuffle. But she knelt, examining it, digging around it in the muck until she could pry it loose.

She gasped, holding it up to the dwindling sunlight, turning it back and forth. A bit of brass, a tiny gear. It must have been part of Aram's compass, falling out after he broke it in the fight. But there was no sign of the rest of it, and Makasa nearly chucked the find over the cliff. Instead, she pocketed it. That was all there was to find. Just a useless scrap. Otherwise, they were down to just a little bit of food and fresh water, a camp they couldn't use for fear of reprisal, and Aram's abandoned pack. Makasa took one last look around, just to be sure she hadn't missed anything, and rounded up their things, carrying the packs and weapons to the edge of the cliff, where the path cut into the hillside dipped down.

Galena was just coming up from the valley below, her shaggy brows knit with worry.

"I—I think I found a nice place to bury Taryndrella," she said.

"That's fine," Makasa replied. "That's good, but what's wrong? You look like you've seen a ghost."

The tauren gulped and pointed downward, and then Makasa

heard it, a strange, low groan, like someone waking up from a tremendously long nap. What in the world . . . ?

"There's something you should see," Galena whimpered. "*Someone* you should see."

Makasa had to laugh. A dry, humorless laugh, but one nonetheless. The fall from the top of Northwatch Expedition Base to the valley below had not been kind to Valdread. The Forsaken had shattered like an egg, fragments of his body strewn about the bowled-out base of the mountain: a hand there, a booted foot here, and nestled against a shrub, the mercenary's head, still somehow attached to his torso. Someone might call it a miracle, but Makasa only felt it was a curse. Sure, it had been cold and cruel of Malus to have Ssarbik send him spinning off the cliff, but she hadn't anticipated grieving over it; Valdread and every single one of the Hidden had to be dealt with eventually, and the mercenary's early demise might have been a win for them.

But no. He had survived, watching her with his unsettling, faintly glowing eyes, a bemused smile pulling at the remaining flesh on his cheeks. His hood had fallen back, revealing a surprisingly robust mop of dark hair. But that was about all of him that could be described as robust.

"Thanks for popping by," he said with a deepening smirk. "In a spot of trouble."

Makasa crossed her arms over her chest, sticking out one hip.

Galena cowered behind her, half covering her eyes. "You're gonna stay in that spot, too."

Valdread sighed, glancing about, perhaps trying to locate the parts of him that had landed farthest from the site of impact.

"Go back up the hill," Makasa told the tauren. "I can deal with this alone."

But Galena took a step right up next to Makasa and squared her shoulders, taking her hands away from her face, looking down at Valdread with clear eyes. "N-No. I was too afraid to do much of anything in the fight. I have to be braver now. I'll stay with you."

A little impressed, Makasa nodded, and down on the ground, still tangled in a bush, Valdread groaned and rolled his eyes. "Yes, yes, this is all very touching, but I am, as you can see, in pieces. Tragic. And inconvenient. Oddly itchy, too. Would you mind lending a hand?" He chuckled, nodding toward his forearm, heaped in a puddle a few feet away. "Or two?"

Could he be serious? Makasa hardly believed the nerve of the man.

"No. Not today, Valdread; you're not going anywhere," she said.

Galena cleared her throat softly, drawing Makasa's attention. "He *did* try to stop Malus from killing Taryndrella, did he not?"

Makasa squinted.

"And look what he got for his trouble," Galena went on. "He didn't need to say anything."

It was Valdread's turn to clear his throat. His eyes flicked away from them, and then back up to Makasa. His stare made her go cold all over. "And there is the small matter of me having one of the *crystal shards*. It fell out of your boy's compass after it broke."

Growling, Makasa darted forward, putting a foot over one of Valdread's detached bones, threatening to snap it with her boot. "Where is it?"

"Wouldn't you like to know? Go ahead, break it. Or you could take your foot off my femur, and we could be civilized. You know, come to an understanding."

"Where. Is. The. Shard? Where is my brother?"

"Makasa . . ." Galena shook her head, slowly. But what did the druid know? She hadn't been part of the group for very long, and even if she showed a real dedication to Drella, what did it matter? It hadn't saved the dryad. Makasa wasn't beholden to the tauren; she wasn't really beholden to anyone but her brother. And she *would* be getting Aram back, no matter what.

"If you have a weak stomach, you can go back up the hill," Makasa said icily.

Galena took a few steps toward the path, hands knit together with worry. Her eyes were so glossy, so nervous . . . *Not strong enough for what has to be done*, Makasa thought. They weren't dealing with some weak-willed henchman. Valdread was dangerous, and treating him like a wounded bird just because he had taken a bad tumble was risky. Too risky.

"You fancy yourself a real tough one, right?" Valdread piped up. He no longer smiled, but regarded Makasa coolly, observing her like one might a butterfly pinned to a collector's table. "Everyone else is just a little weaker, a little more naïve. They don't see the world like you do. No, no, you're the real deal, mmm? A real leader? Well, let me let you in on a secret I learned in SI:7. Assets are assets. No matter the unexpected places they come from. A good leader knows that."

"A lecture? Bold choice." But Makasa was more interested than she let on. SI:7 in particular was interesting. It wasn't just Stormwind's most elite covert force, but part of a memory that shimmered up to meet her from the long-ago past. Her mother had told her tales of the agents, told her that she had even gotten to know someone in the force, befriended him.

Valdread continued studying her, and now his sly way with words made even more sense. He was indeed dangerous, and no doubt calculating just what to say to change her mind. Curse him. It was working.

"Go ahead, girl," he drawled, shrugging armless shoulders. "Walk away. Turn your back on an advantage and make the chances of failure just that much greater. Someone else will be along eventually, and they can put me back together. I've got nothing but time."

His knowing smile turned her stomach.

"Unless I kill you," she replied.

"Good luck with that. Truly. Come, this display is getting tiresome. Accept my help, and the shard, or walk away. Malus has the boy. I don't know where he will take Aramar, but I do know how to fight him. And while you waste your time with me, the Hidden will not be so slow to act."

Damn him. Makasa tossed up her hands, knowing she needed that shard. Knowing, deep in her gut, that Valdread *was* an asset. If nothing else, he knew the Hidden inside and out, and his insights could prove invaluable. Then there was his old SI:7 training. And his near invulnerability. It all stacked up in one direction, and Makasa swallowed her pride, and her disgust, bending down to pick up the femur she had been so ready to snap.

"Galena, help me gather these pieces up. Don't let them touch. We'll accept your help, Valdread, but on *our* terms."

CHAPTER EIGHTEEN
MURKY'S LAMENT

Vrum should have been there, but they needed to put Drhla under the big tree in the valley, and soon. So said Mrksa, and everyone listened to her. Murky followed them down the long and winding path as the afternoon changed into evening. They had to move quickly, because Mrksa wanted to be back on the road to the Overlook before night came on. Murky wanted to help carry Drhla, but he wasn't strong enough, and so he walked alongside the big piece of tent they had used to make a kind of bed, and he put one hand on it as they brought it down the hill to the pretty tree in the valley.

They all stood in a shape like the moon while Ukle and Mrksa lowered Drhla into the ground. It had taken Mrksa and Gluna almost two hours to make the hole, and they were dirty and tired, but still helped carry Drhla all that way. They were strong, he thought, and good frunds. Only good frunds would do something like that, work all day at making a big hole and still find the strength to do more.

For a while, nobody said anything. They all looked at one another, and Murky wondered what his frunds were thinking. In a way, he didn't even know what *he* was thinking. Confusing. There was another hole, a hole in his heart, a space that he didn't know how to fill. In his village, there were losses all the time. Nasty birds swooped in and carried off tadpoles. Sometimes humans attacked, or gnolls. That sadness was different. Looking at Drhla in the ground, watching as they poured dirt over her, Murky felt his eyes well with tears again.

Drhla had always been kind. Always listened. Not everyone listened to Murky. He was small and probably sounded strange to them, but he ought to be listened to. He ought to be . . .

Gluna stepped forward, then knelt. She took in a shaky breath and then put her big hands on the fresh mound of turned earth.

"I did not know you long, Taryndrella, daughter of Cenarius, but I'll never forget you. You were my friend and my teacher. Earth Mother light your path." She sprinkled something on the dirt and then stood, rubbing at her face.

Again, nobody spoke. Night was coming. Murky glanced around at his frunds and then took a long step forward, puffing out his chest.

"Drhla was one of the first dry skins to understand me,"

Murky began, wishing it was easier to get it all out. "She always listened. I know I make some of you laugh, even when I don't mean to, but Drhla didn't laugh at me that way. She shared her fruit with me, even if I hated it. She sang me songs. She even knew murloc songs, but I'm not sure how. 'Fish in the Stream,' she sang that to me, and 'My Favorite Pearl.' Now who will talk to Murky?" He couldn't say much more. He was going to cry again. "Now who will listen?"

Mrksa prodded Ukle, and the gnoll quickly nodded. "He say Drella good friend, always listen and never laugh at him. He say she sing him special songs and he miss her. Hackle miss her, too."

Close enough. Murky joined the others, and then felt Gluna put her big furry hand on his shoulder. He let it stay there; it even felt nice. Maybe Gluna would listen. Maybe Murky was not so alone after all.

Mrksa went to kneel by the mound of dirt, putting her palms on it. She didn't say anything that Murky could hear, but he knew she was thinking hard, and that was just like saying something, only it was just for Drhla to hear. Murky hoped Drhla, no doubt mending her nets and eating a fish feast at the feet of the great tide gods, would hear what Mrksa wanted to tell her. It was only good things, he decided, because nobody could think bad things about their frund Drhla. Not even the strange dry skin in bits, who was their frund now, too, apparently.

When the afternoon was well and truly gone, and the air

turned moist and the ground turned cold, they collected their things and started on the road toward the Overlook. The tauren dry skin had to wear the man in bits, Vldrrd, on her back, and that made Murky happy. He had never seen a dry skin adult carried that way, the way murloc tadpoles were transported when they were very young and useless.

Murky collected his mangled nets, determined to fix them at the Overlook. A murloc was nobody without their trusty nets.

He walked next to Mrksa, who was their leader, and sometimes mean. Maybe, he thought, if he was brave enough and protected her from the spiders on the path, then he would get to lead, too. Or at least, she would listen. They walked in silence away from the sight of so much terrible loss and pain, but it was hard to go. It was hardest to leave Drhla behind. When they were rounding the corner, about to lose sight of the camp and the grave, he paused, turning to look once more.

"Mrksa! Mrksa!"

She stopped, looking down at Murky as he grabbed her shirt and pulled, pointing and pointing with his spear. A beautiful tree grew, a new one, taller and more beautiful than the one just next to it, where they had buried Drhla.

"She heard us," Murky told her. "She heard us speaking to her in her home among the tides!"

Ukle translated without being asked. "He say she hear us."

They stood in a moon shape again, all of them in wonder,

watching the stunning pink-and-purple tree grow and spread before their very eyes. Murky would never forget it, or the way those new, shimmering leaves started to fill the big hole in his heart.

Mrksa touched his shoulder this time, giving him a strange smile that he didn't quite understand. "Mrgle, mrgle," she told him. "I think she heard us, too."

CHAPTER NINETEEN
FRIEND OR FOE

Traveling in a cramped leather pack on the back of a tauren druid was not exactly what Reigol Valdread had in mind when he bargained with the Flintwill girl. *Humiliating. Untenable.*

"Would you mind not bumping me so much? Blast, it's worse than riding a kodo."

"When did you chance to ride a kodo?" she asked, glancing over her shoulder at him.

Valdread snorted. "I served with Stormwind's finest. I've done and seen much. Why, there was the time I came upon a tauren patrol in the moonlight . . ."

The druid listened intently while he launched into a story. Much of it was fabricated for her benefit, intentionally so—she was an easy target. Wide-eyed and desperate to make herself useful. He had heard her wailing over the dead dryad from his spot down in the valley, and listened to her berate herself for not doing more. It was almost moving, as was the quaint little ceremony they had done for the dryad, and the frog creature speechifying with as much pride as any priest of the Light. He had to admit, the vast tree that sprang like magic from her grave was rather impressive, a sight he would not soon forget.

He did truly regret the dryad's passing. His intervention had not been mere theater. Even if she found him unnatural and dreadful (and really, who could blame her?), he enjoyed the chaos she brought to things. The unpredictability. There was no reason for her to throw herself in front of Ssarbik's magic and save him, but she had. If nothing else, she amused him, and the world was darker and more cynical without her. A pity.

The druid, carrying him like some ridiculous baby, proved intriguing, too. She meditated by night to sense the best campsite, and feverishly consulted a pamphlet that hitched a ride in the same pack as him. Yet her slavish devotion to the book paid off. Their fire that night when they camped was warm and unwavering, and no creatures dared come near. Valdread, having no need for sleep or food, had decided to keep watch all night long.

The next morning, they continued toward Thal'darah Overlook unharmed, the roads mercifully clear, the weather sunny and dry. That was good. The last thing he wanted was to be humiliated *and* sopping wet. Or attached to a sopping wet tauren, of all things. Thankfully, the druid was far less pungent than other horned and furred tauren he had the displeasure of knowing.

"Is this to be my fate forever?" he asked the Flintwill girl as they climbed the hill east of Cliffwalker Post. "To be . . . luggage?"

"Patience," she chided, smilingly smug. She was enjoying his predicament a little too much, he decided. "You gave us the shard, sure, but that's just one step."

"Difficult to take another step without legs."

The shard, as it happened, had been lodged in the tread of his boot. It was a stroke of luck, or, if he were a more sentimental type, fate, that had led the glowing treasure to become stuck in the mud on his shoe as he tried to dissuade Malus from killing the dryad. Once Flintwill's troop had collected up all of his parts, he told them to check the muddy tread of his right shoe, and like magic, the shard was there. The Flintwill girl kept it in her pocket, and he noticed her compulsively checking on it every few steps of their journey.

"We can regroup at the Overlook," Makasa told him. "And we'll figure out what to do with you there."

"Splendid. I'll just relax and enjoy the view until then."

"Don't be annoying," she muttered.

"I'm far better company when I'm more man and less puzzle."

The girl just rolled her eyes. "Yeah. I doubt that."

Everything about her was irritatingly familiar. From her confident bearing to her deadly way with weapons. It reminded him of a woman he had dueled on the *Makemba*, that much he had told the girl, but it was more than that. He hadn't just admired the woman for her skill in battle; she was also beautiful. Apparently the fierce woman had found him charming, too, though their companionship had lasted no more than a fortnight before she had moved on and he was forced to return to his duties.

He told the girl nothing. Trust was a two-way street, and he would need to play his cards carefully to get his parts back and attached to his body. He was under no obligation to remain with this motley assortment of adventurers, though he felt certain they would lead him to Captain Malus and Ssarbik, to the revenge that he so desperately craved.

Makasa hadn't realized how exhausted she was until they reached Thal'darah Overlook. Galena would have to explain to the druid master what had happened at the base camp, and why they had returned in the company of a dismembered, sentient corpse. It was a task she didn't envy, and even alone in the room she had shared with Aramar at the inn, Makasa could feel the change that settled over the place once the news was heard. The march back from the base to the Overlook had taken days. Long, hard days. Makasa drew a bath and kept to herself, trusting that Murky and Hackle would keep watch over their prisoner—or, new traveler—while she got a quick rest in.

"Hackle club," the gnoll had told her when she had Galena put Valdread down in his sack, resting him against a bench in the inn. "Dead man tell us all. Hackle club until he talk. No trust. He no friend. Hackle make talk."

"No, Hackle," Makasa had explained, waving her hands. "He gave us the shard. He's not our friend, sure, but he's . . . Well, he's valuable. Don't just club him over the head; he might be useful."

And a small, stupid voice in the back of her head insisted that there was much more than that. *Personally* much more. How had he known about the *Makemba*? Had he really dueled her mother? If so, Valdread *would* be interrogated, but not by Hackle and not with a war club.

"We need him alive," Makasa told him finally. "For now."

"Mrgle, mrgle!" The murloc had heard her loud and clear, taking his spear and standing guard, much to the amusement of Valdread, who eyed the frog creature with open curiosity and a wrinkled nose, perhaps due to the light fishy scent that followed Murky wherever he went.

Not that Makasa smelled any better after constant travel and conflict. An hour later, after settling her companions at the inn, she sat in the hot water of a bathtub, eyes closed, listening to the guards set their watch. As dusk fell, they began singing an eerie dirge that made the hairs on her arms stand up. Their sad, high voices filled the air, mourning Drella's passing as wisps and fire-flies filled the clearing. Makasa watched the glow bugs flicker outside the window, then dropped her head into her hands.

What should they do now? Everyone was waiting on her to decide. But all she wanted to do was go to Master Thal'darah and beg him to fix everything. She couldn't, of course, and what, really, could he do? They didn't have the means to re-form the Diamond Blade, and they didn't have Aram, or even Drella. The scope of what they had to do, the vastness of it, made her want to crumble.

All the impossible decisions fell to her now. Not that it had been any different before—she was the oldest and most experienced of the group—but there was more pressure now. They were running out of time. How long would Malus keep Aram alive? What did he plan to do with him and the hilt of the Diamond Blade?

A light flickering on her bed drew Makasa's eye. The shard. She left the tub and dried herself off, sitting on her cot in a warm sheet, holding the shard in her palm. It was warm to the touch, glowing faintly. That and Aram's bag were all that remained of him. She set down the shard and picked up his things, riffling through until she found his beloved sketchbook. Opening it, a folded piece of parchment immediately tumbled into her lap. She read it, hands shaking with frustration as she reached the conclusion.

Aram had written to his mother in Lakeshire, recalling their adventures, well, the not-so-scary ones, anyway, and promising her he would be all right. He was safe, he said, because he had his good friends with him. She glanced between the letter and the shard. The compass had been pointing to Lakeshire all that time, telling Aramar that the next shard they needed was there. And now she had found a letter, a letter that needed to go to Lakeshire.

That was enough for Makasa. Sometimes, she thought, it was better to just do the obvious and right thing. But how would they get there? Thal'darah Overlook was far, far from Aram's home, on an entirely different continent! Makasa couldn't even fathom the distance, or the proper way to get there. A journey back to the coast, naturally, and then a ship, but how would they find a vessel large enough to survive a sea journey that long and dangerous? Unless . . .

Unless.

They hadn't gotten to the Stonetalon Mountains by sea, but by air. Would Gazlowe come to their aid once more if she asked? And how would she find him? She searched Aram's sketchbook, finding fond sketches of all their MEGA friends, including a lively scene of Gazlowe, Sprocket, Daisy, and Hotfix. Sprocket. The MEGA event, that was where they and the zeppelin *Cloudkicker* would be. Saying a silent apology to Aram for using his sketchbook, Makasa began composing a letter, hoping that a bird sent by the Sentinels would reach Gazlowe in time and give them, at last, just one meager dash of good luck.

"Here goes nothing," she murmured, sealing up the letter. She waited until the mournful singing in the glade dissipated, and then she dressed, going in search of a bird to take the letter, and with it, all their hopes.

CHAPTER TWENTY
PARADISE LOST

Life was good. No, life was great, for Gazlowe and Sprocket. Charnas couldn't stop drawing every insignificant little thing he saw at the MEGA event, but for Gazlowe and Sprocket? Things couldn't be better.

"Now this?" Gazlowe kicked up his heels, sipping a fruity drink and admiring the trophy they had won, a trophy nearly as tall as Charnas, and much, much better to look at. "This is paradise."

Paradise was maybe a stretch, considering the event was in the smoldering remains of the Charred Vale, the stink of it palpable, but still . . . A cold drink in his hand, the waves lapping at the edges of the deck, a trophy to kiss and admire, a substantial cash prize to enjoy, the adoration of so many fans—*Paradise.* Gazlowe sighed, adjusting a pair of sun-blocking spectacles and shimmying down into his cushioned lounger.

Their winning inventions, a fleet of DLVR-E drones, whirred

above them, floating metal disks kept aloft by an ingeniously rigged fan blade and a propelling system harnessed to the bottom. The obstacle course was on the water, a series of detachable and moveable flotillas floating off the coast of the Charred Vale. The waters there were smooth and easy, the perfect place for a pop-up competition. It was a challenge just getting there and docking a vessel, so even entering the event required a measure of genius.

For days, Gazlowe had watched the other competitors fussing over their inventions. The obstacle course was rumored to be a real doozy that year, but Sprocket was ready. In the end, they had cleaned up, their little drone machines speeding past the competition, zigging and zagging through the hoops suspended over the water, and dropping off colored balls into coordinating goals spaced throughout the course. It was seamless. Magnificent. Poetic. Their machines performed so well, in fact, that there were already goblins muttering about cheating.

Let 'em grouse, Gazlowe thought, slurping his drink. They had won fair and square.

"Charnas!" Gazlowe shouted. His cousin sat on the edge of their private cabana on the winner's flotilla, his legs dangling over the edge, feet just above the water line. "Get over here! Drink your drink! Gah, look at that. All the ice has melted! Leave the birds alone; they'll be there later."

"Not this one," Charnas called over his shoulder. He was dressed all formally, trying to impress everyone with his style.

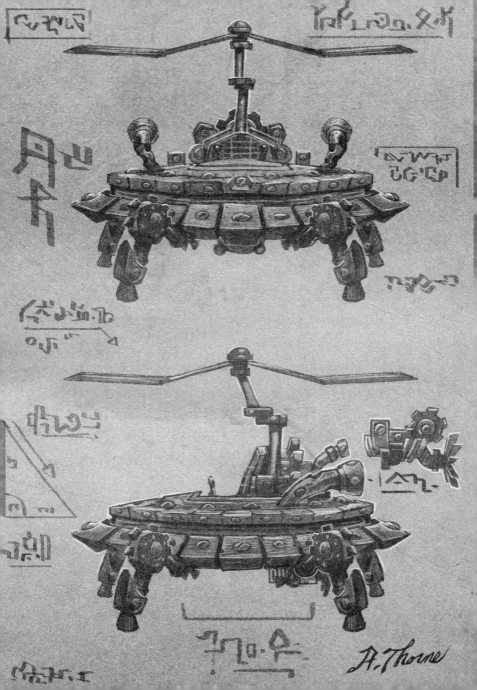

And blast it all, but he wouldn't shut up for one second about being the official MEGA event artist. Whatever. Sprocket's brains had won them the day, the trophy, and the prize.

Paradise.

"Look." Charnas set down his pencil for half a second, pointing at a small dark shape in the sky. It was growing bigger, getting closer, diving down toward the MEGA flotilla. Music on steel drums still played on the main party barge. Now that the competition was over, everyone relaxed, and the music and merrymaking would last long into the night. Gazlowe took one glance at the bird and shrugged. He didn't want it to mean anything.

"What about it?" Sprocket asked. The leper gnome had nicely jazzed up his mechanical containment suit, managing to wedge a pair of swim trunks over the long, metal legs. Itching at his nose, but really just tapping the jar around his head, Sprocket snapped at the barman to refresh his drink. "Gaz is right. Get up here and relax. You work too much."

Instead of waiting for him, Sprocket reached for the remote controlling the DLVR-E devices. One of the disks whirred louder, lowering, and Sprocket dropped a fresh drink on it for Charnas, sending it speeding over to him at the edge of the barge.

But Charnas just waved it away. "That isn't a seagull. What do you think it's doing out here?"

"Sightseeing? Who knows?" Gazlowe sighed. His cousin was a lost cause. "Who cares?"

Charnas climbed to his feet, sketching furiously, probably capturing eighteen different poses of the stupid bird as it dove down and down, then flattened out its course, sailing toward them. Wait? Toward *them*? Gazlowe sat up straighter, watching as a brown owl glided to a stop, perching right on their trophy.

"Hey! Get off that! It's ours!" Sprocket tried to shoo the owl away, but it nipped at his gloved fingers and shook out its wings.

"It's carrying something!" Charnas tucked his sketchbook into his belt and trotted forward, carefully unhooking a message tied to the owl's leg.

"Think it's for us?" Gazlowe muttered, finishing his drink.

"Who else?" His cousin unfolded the note, then handed it across to Gazlowe.

So much for paradise.

"Maybe it's for someone who doesn't want to be bothered," Gazlowe said. But he took the note. It might be urgent, and after all, the important bit was done. They had won the contest, the trophy and purse were theirs, and soon the MEGA event organizers would pack up the flotilla until the next year. He wiped his hands on his shorts and scanned the letter, feeling paradise slip farther and farther away with each word. It was bad. No, it was a mess.

"Oof," he murmured. Sprocket and Charnas gathered close, waiting. "It's from the Flintwill girl. The kid—Aramar's been kidnapped. That dryad friend of theirs is . . . gone. Dead."

"We have to do something," Charnas said at once. Gazlowe wasn't so sure. He liked Aram fine, he was a good kid, but where was the profit in it? They had a good thing going on the beach, and trouble, particularly violence, could get expensive.

"She wants us to take the *Cloudkicker* to the Overlook, then to Lakeshire," Gazlowe said, then gave Charnas the letter to peruse. "Well, *that's* not happening."

"Is Aramar being held there?" Charnas tilted his head to the side, scratching his chin. "That doesn't seem right . . ."

"Nah, but it sounds like she has a plan. Can you believe how needy these kids are? Let's see, yadda yadda, Malus is really Silverlaine, he tricked us, etcetera . . ."

"Gazlowe . . ."

"What?" He glared at Charnas.

Charnas shifted toward him, and he hadn't seen the goblin look that serious or disappointed in a long time. He felt a lecture coming on. "Do you not want to do the right thing? I thought you were fond of Aram."

"I am," Gazlowe conceded. "And?"

"And I . . . might be somewhat responsible for the predicament they find themselves in." At that, Charnas glanced away, sheepish. "I was the one who told Aram where he might find Silverlaine. He—I—led Malus right to them." He handed the letter back to Gazlowe.

"In an extremely roundabout way," Sprocket suggested. "Is that it? Is that the whole letter?"

"Nah, there's a bit more." Scanning lower, Gazlowe's eyes grew three sizes bigger. "Hang on, there's something about a legendary artifact in here. Something very valuable to them. Think it's worth anything?"

"Sounds like profit to me," Sprocket said, tapping at his nose through the jar again. "Our combined genius and expertise might come in handy for a joint business venture."

"And Aram is our *friend*," Charnas reminded them.

Gazlowe slid out of his lounger and stretched, fetching his shirt from where he had left it next to the chair. "Sure, sure, profit and friendship! The perfect match. What would they do without us, eh? Goblins and leper gnome to the rescue. Again."

CHAPTER TWENTY-ONE
THE RISING TIDE

Aramar Thorne was dreaming, dreaming of a thriving glade filled with flowers and trees. Pollen and bees danced on the air, the sweet scent of blossoms and dewy grass so thick he felt more alive with each breath, as if nature itself was breathing life into him, reviving him. He longed to hear the Voice of the Light, but it never came. He lay on his back, staring up at the stars, listening to the hum of the bees and the soft rush of wind through the flowers. He wanted to stay there forever, for all of it, from the colors to the softness to the perfume, reminded him keenly of Taryndrella, daughter of Cenarius.

The edges of the glade began to burn and burn quickly. The fire spread, speeding toward him, making red cinders of everything in its path. It reached him as he leapt to his feet and he felt the terrible heat lick at his toes, shocking him awake.

"Aram? Aram, by the Light, it really is you."

He knew that voice. But how? Was he still dreaming?

No matter how much or how hard he blinked, the vision didn't change. His father, Greydon Thorne, was there, kneeling at the bars of the cell next to his. Greydon Thorne. Alive.

"But you're—you're dead." Was he still dreaming? The trip through the portal had been disorienting, and either Malus had knocked him out flat or the journey had left him too exhausted to go on. And now he was looking at his father's weathered face, his kind, sad eyes, and his scarred hands, and Aram had no idea whether to be relieved or suspicious. He glanced outside the cell, though it was difficult to make out a single feature of their prison. The bars on his cell were twisted and strange, made of a blackened material that oozed and stank. Even the floor he sat on was hot, as if they were being slowly cooked.

"Malus merely took me captive," Greydon explained.

"I . . . don't trust this. Tell me something only you would know," Aram demanded.

"Each night on the *Wavestrider*, you would stay up late to sketch," he said. "You would hum the same song—one I remember your mother singing to you each and every night. How did it go? *When my love comes home, from the storm-tossed seas . . .*"

"You . . . saw me do that?" Aram gasped. "But—I was so sure you were gone. All this time you were here, and you were . . ." Trailing off, Aram covered his face with his hands, looking at his father through trembling fingers. "You were being tortured."

He hadn't even been looking for Greydon. All that time, his father was alive and in pain.

"Now you." Greydon's eyes hardened. For a moment he looked distant, even cold. His right hand shaking was the only indication that he might believe Aram, that he might give in to the relief. "Tell me something only you could know."

Aram swallowed hard, thinking. The perfect memory eased through the jumble of thoughts in his head. "Back home, back in Lakeshire, you scratched your name into the dock, the east dock, the shorter post. You got tired, though, I think, because the last few letters are hard to read."

His father's mouth turned up in a smile, tears gathering in his eyes. "Aram. My son."

"It's really you . . . I'm so— But how? How can this be true?"

"I know, Aramar, I know . . . It's good to see your face again, son. Wish it were under better circumstances, though." Greydon sighed, rubbing at his ribs. His father was not being well taken care of. There were burns and scars all over his visible skin, and his clothes were in tatters, burned away in places, revealing red, livid welts. "I can't tell you it will be easy here. They will try to torture you like they've tortured me. I'm sorry that I cannot . . . that I *did not* protect you from this."

Aram hugged himself, leaning against the confines of the cell. His skin had gone cold, even if the place they were being kept was boiling hot. He slid his hands into his father's coat pockets, finding the strange gift Drella had given him before he was pried away. In the shadows, he took it out, setting it on his lap, finding that it was a painfully bright blossom. By then it should have looked wilted and dead, but it remained alive, buttery pollen clinging to the insides of the vivid turquoise petals.

"Where are we?" Aramar asked, hoping that whatever the answer, holding that gift from Drella would make it easier to hear.

"Outland," Greydon said. "We dwell in the darkest pit of Highlord Xaraax, a demon of the Burning Legion, a nathrezim fiend I've been fighting since before I can remember."

"Outland?" If it was possible for Aramar's heart to sink lower, it did. "But where? Isn't Outland huge? An entire world . . . How will Makasa find us?"

Greydon shifted and Aram saw his skin grow pale. "Makasa? Aramar, your faith in her is admirable, but these are not forces she alone could face. Even if she could reach Outland itself . . ."

"I know," Aram muttered. "I get it. It's stupid to hope."

"Hope is never stupid, Aramar. I thought I taught you better." He vented a hollow laugh, then released a very long sigh. "We face a dire fate, son, but we will face it together. But the compass—"

"Malus has it, and the hilt of the Diamond Blade," Aram told him, shaking. "And it's my fault. But Makasa—"

"Aram. Are you not listening to me? You cannot expect that a girl of her age, alone, could storm the Dark Portal and—"

"I know," he whispered. His own words surprised him, shook him. "I . . . know."

Outland was another world altogether. He and his father couldn't be harder to find. Drella was gone, their bond severed in the cruelest possible way, and now he would face nothing but torture and despair. At least he had his father, at least he had . . .

Aram closed his hand around the flower Drella had left him. A flower. That was all. His wounded, battered father and a flower. What good was that? The Light had abandoned him, choosing Makasa instead. She was the better fighter. The stronger leader.

"We're together," Greydon said gently. "We do have that. To see you lifts my heart, and I had never thought to feel relief again."

Aram nodded, but he felt empty. Lost.

"I'm glad you're not alone anymore." It was the only thing he could think to say. Even Drella's gift brought him little comfort. "I'm glad." Aram said the words like a reflex, but stopped. He wasn't glad. Not about anything.

"Rest, son," he heard his father say.

Yes. Rest. Sitting. Sleeping. They were useless now, and Aram could do nothing but hope that Makasa served the Light better than he had.

CHAPTER TWENTY-TWO
LEAVING THE OVERLOOK

A broad ring of Sentinels aimed their bows to the sky, a less than warm welcome for the Horde zeppelin lowering through the clouds, its propellers blasting the trees that bended and swayed as the balloon landed at Thal'darah Overlook.

"I appreciate your understanding." Makasa watched the Sentinels carefully. Not a single shot was fired, but they remained vigilant, keeping their promise to her not to engage with the Horde vessel, even if it went against their direct order from Darnassus.

"We will understand," Master Thal'darah told her solemnly, "so long as they prove friendly."

"They will," Makasa assured him. She couldn't believe how swiftly they had come, and it was hard to contain her relief. Finally, some good luck. Aiyell's owl had returned, making the trip to the coast and back in less than a day. The reply from

Gazlowe lifted all their spirits, even Galena, who now gasped in wonder at the sight of the *Cloudkicker* idling in the glade.

"How does it work?" she breathed.

"I rode on the thing and I still have no idea," Makasa muttered. "But it flies, and that's all that matters. Gazlowe!"

The green-skinned, yellow-eyed goblin slid down the ladder that unrolled from the deck. He landed smoothly, with a flourish, casting a wary eye at the armed Sentinels before strolling over to Makasa. The wind from the *Cloudkicker* mussed her hair, and only she, Murky, and Hackle were brave enough to approach.

Above them, hanging over the embellished wooden railing, Sprocket and Charnas appeared, waving.

"Well, we're here!" Gazlowe stuck out his hand for Makasa to shake, and she did, warmly. "Sorry to hear about the kid. Kids. That's a real kick in the teeth. And I hear you lost some kind of legendary artifact?"

"Yes, the Diamond Blade," Galena interjected. Makasa elbowed her in the ribs.

"Diamonds?" The goblin's eyes lit up. "Man, that's gotta feel real bad. We're gonna get that back, though. And your friends."

Makasa nodded, but squared her shoulders, steeling herself. There would be time to tell the goblin the full story, but for now they had no time to waste. They needed to be on their way to Lakeshire, and fast. "Aram's compass was telling us to go to

Lakeshire; can you take us? We don't . . . we don't have any money."

"Nk! Flggrlm mur slrrrgl blem!" Murky hauled up one of his nets, fishing out a handful of scrubbed seashells and a bundle of bruiseweed. He thrust them toward Gazlowe expectantly, smiling.

"Keep that stuff away from me," Makasa muttered. "Bruiseweed gives me hives."

She heard a soft grunt from the pack on Galena's back. Valdread. He was probably already plotting ways to use the weed against her.

"Uh, thanks?" Gazlowe took the shells, spilling a few, which Murky immediately picked up and placed back in the goblin's arms. "Listen, kid, I know you're not exactly flush with gold at the moment. Think of this as a favor. This ride? It's on the house."

Makasa stared, mouth agape. "Are you sure?"

"Hey, hey, hey. What do you take me for? Of course I'm sure. Now just take the favor before I change my mind! I could be back on the beach sipping a Dos Ogris instead of playing taxi, but for you goofballs I'll be nice. Just this once. Besides, once we get that Diamond Blade back, you just remember who helped you out in your time of need, right?"

Murky pointed to the bounty of seashells Gazlowe cradled.

"No favor." Hackle bristled. "Murky pay you good price. Give you bargain."

"Right. Sure. I'm making out like a bandit." Gazlowe rolled his eyes and nodded his pointy head toward the zeppelin. "We going or what? Don't waste my time, kid. Sprocket and I had a real good thing going back on the coast. Drinks! Money! Sprocket crushed the competition again. You shoulda seen the DLVR-E fleet in action! Beautiful, just beautiful! Those things are fast as can be, fly anywhere, deliver anything! A real gem! Anyway, how much baggage you bringing?"

Makasa couldn't help but flush. Valdread. The Whisper-Man. She had forgotten to mention that bit in her letter to Gazlowe. She scratched at the back of her neck, a nervous habit she had picked up from Aram, and coughed. "It'll be me, Murky, and Hackle . . ."

The goblin chuckled. "Obviously."

"And one more—"

"*Two* more." Galena Stormspear closed the distance between them, Valdread's head and torso bouncing on her back, the Forsaken cursing her every clumsy step. "You're not going without me. I failed the Circle once; I won't do it again. If I can't prove myself by bringing Aramar Thorne back and protecting the Diamond Blade, then I have no business calling myself a druid."

"Yikes. That's a tall order. You wanna bring world peace and fix the Cataclysm while you're at it?" Gazlowe snorted, then turned and began walking back to the ladder, shoving the shells

Murky had paid him into his coat pockets. "Fine. Get your stuff. We can sort out your bunks when we're in the air. Hang on, what's that you got on your back?"

"How do you do?" Valdread drawled, clearly enjoying the way Gazlowe reeled back in shock.

"Ugh! Your mannequin is talking! And Noggenfogger's cogs, he *stinks*." Gazlowe hauled himself up the ladder as if he could somehow escape the stench.

"I am running precariously low on jasmine water," Valdread admitted. "And none of these strange fellows have offered to procure more."

Makasa silenced him with a glance and lowered her voice to the tauren. "You don't have to do this, Galena. None of us blame you for what happened to Aram and Drella. That was all Malus."

"A promise is a promise," Galena stated, meeting Makasa's eye with no shortage of pride. "Taryndrella would want me to come along, and besides, having a druid with you won't be so bad. I'll pull my weight." She gave a dry laugh. "And *his*."

"I resent that," Valdread muttered from over her shoulder.

"Then welcome aboard," Makasa told her, clapping the tauren on the arm. "Did you tell the order?"

"I told Master Thal'darah this morning and he approves. He's releasing me as his apprentice, and he wishes us all luck."

In fact, the old druid had come out to watch their departure, regarding them with hooded eyes from the safety of the inn's entrance. He had said little to Makasa since their return, and he kept muttering to himself, fiddling with the top of his walking staff. Occasionally she heard him mention Drella's name; he must be grieving over her loss just like Galena.

"You coming or what?" Gazlowe called from above, beckoning them aboard. "Next stop: Eastern Kingdoms!"

Makasa felt her heart skip a beat. It was what she wanted, to go and continue Aram's quest and find the rest of the shards, but she knew it would be difficult, maybe impossible, to face his family. What would the Glades think of this bizarre assortment of creatures showing up on their doorstep, dropping practically out of the air and into their lives?

She had rehearsed what she would say a hundred times, but none of it seemed quite right. She hefted her pack and Aram's, as well as the extra bundle of arms she carried—literal arms. Valdread's various parts had been divvied up among the troop, Hackle given the heaviest bundle with his legs. Each limb and hand and foot was tightly wrapped to dampen the smell, which would test even the most hardened gravedigger. The night elves who had saved them in the Charred Vale were there, watching silently, Iyneath, Llaran, and Aiyell all in a row, and Aiyell's trusty owl gave a piercing cry at their departure.

Then Makasa gave Master Thal'darah one final wave. He nodded in response, and the Sentinels saluted, their weapons no longer pointed at the *Cloudkicker* as Makasa boarded, turning at the railing to look her last. Her gaze traveled over the top of the inn's ornate roof, across the valley and the treacherous path filled with lurking spiders, and at last to the tops of the distant hills, where she fancied she could see the suggestion of a wild pink tree, growing strong, the breeze-rustled leaves waving *fair voyage, friends.*

Highlord Xaraax's dreaded imps had arrived for their daily tormenting of father and son. Aram never knew when to expect them, for the torture varied, and some days he thought they might not come at all. But he was always disappointed. The little laughing demons skipped into the prison, bouncing across the mottled stone floor with their burning torture implements held at the ready. Time had ceased to mean very much, as the cells remained dark constantly, and there was no way to tell if it was day or night.

Aram stood up, backing away from the imps, plastering himself against the back of the cell. But his father put up no resistance, resigned to the cruel punishment. The pair of imps split off, one giggling his way over to Aram's cell. The demon's glowing yellow eyes were unnerving, his skin crimson and split all over, cracked as if baked too long over a fire. He had skinny curved horns and a wide mouth fixed in a permanent smile.

"Don't you ever get tired of this?" Aram sighed, watching as the creature danced around to the opposite side of the cell, taking the hot poker he carried and jabbing it between the bars. But Aram was prepared, and he kicked the poker hard, knocking it out of the imp's hands. He had been planning this little attempt at rebellion all day, tired of being the amusement for Xaraax's minions.

Aram dropped down, sweeping up the poker before the imp had a chance to retrieve it.

"You'll only make them angrier," Greydon muttered. He hissed, cursing at the imp tormenting him as she drove the burning metal rod into his thigh. "'Tis better to be forgotten than draw your jailor's ire."

"I don't care!" Aram shouted, trying to jab back at the imp, who cackled and dodged away. "I'm sick of this, sick of doing nothing."

"Well. You had better get used to it, boy."

It was the first voice other than his father's and the giggling of the imps that Aram had heard in days. He squeezed up against the back of his cell again, still holding the poker, watching as Malus, his uncle, emerged from the shadowy arch to the left of their holding cells. Aram chided himself for even calling Malus his uncle. He didn't deserve the title. The rage that had transformed into sadness surged again, and he held the metal rod fast, hoping he could land just one good hit on Malus. Something was different about him. He had always had scars, but the right half of his face was reddened, mottled skin like a bad burn distorting his cheek and brow. Most of his ear on that side was missing. The whole wound was shiny with ointment.

Good, Aram thought. The man deserved much, much worse.

Aram remembered the smell of the mud and rain mixing, that cold, wormy scent that would forever remind him of their battle at Northwatch Expedition Base. In a flash, he was on the ground again, shivering and bereft, holding Drella while she smiled, her lifeblood seeping out around them. His clothes were still stained with it.

"Come to gloat, brother?" Greydon barely registered the next jab of the imp. He had withstood the torture so many times that he took it far better than Aram.

"That's enough, leave them be." Malus waved the imps away, though they only retreated to the shadows behind him, waiting, their yellow eyes glowing like little embers in the dark. The captain meandered closer, using a knife to deftly slice an apple and eat each slice slowly as he studied them. Aram's mouth watered. They had been given nothing but thin gruel and dirty water, only enough to scrape by and go on surviving.

"You don't look very well, Greydon," Malus observed with a smirk. "A bit of sunlight would do you a world of good. Or maybe a hot meal? It's a pity you'll never enjoy the simple pleasures of life again. Like an apple, for example . . ."

"Let me out of this cell, just once, you coward. I'd take your death over all the apples in Elwynn! What happened to your face? I didn't think it could get uglier." Aram rammed at the bars, then slammed the poker against them, causing as much noise as he could.

"My face is none of your concern. Goodness, did you raise him in a barn, Greydon? He's practically feral." Peeling off another slice of apple, Malus shook his head, clucking his tongue. "Oh, that's right. You were barely there to parent him, so perhaps it's that other man's fault, the one your wife ran to after you abandoned your family. You're good at that, aren't you? Betraying those you claim to love."

"You won't get a rise out of me, Silverlaine. Say whatever you need to say and be gone."

Greydon stilled, stoic as a statue, his eyes impassive as he stared out at his brother.

"No more pleas for my return to the side of the Light?" Malus taunted, drawing near enough to Aram's cage that he could almost be struck. It was only a way to taunt him, and Aram knew it, but it was still tempting to lash out. Aram kept his grasp on the poker, but he also slid one hand into his father's coat pocket, wrapping his fingers around Drella's gift. Just feeling it there soothed him, and he breathed deeply, forcing himself not to give Malus the satisfaction of his anger. His father was right. He should have just been quiet, then Malus would never have heard the commotion and come to see them. Anything was better than having Malus in the same room.

"You murdered my friend," Aram whispered.

Malus nodded, then sliced off a large piece of apple, flicking it expertly with his knife. It landed in Aram's cell, gleaming and tantalizingly fresh. But Aram didn't move. He wouldn't be bribed.

"You don't want it? Come now, boy, it's a small act of mercy. Maybe I'm not so irredeemable after all." Wonderfully pleased with himself, Malus tossed back his head and laughed. His beard had grown in fully, making him look even more like a darkly twisted version of Greydon, or an aging Aram.

"There is *nothing* you can do to fix what you've done," Aram ground out. He was taking the bait by even talking to Malus, but he couldn't help it. The anger festering inside him needed an outlet.

"Ahh, now that's the spirit. But before you place all that blame squarely on me, you might want to have a talk with your dear old dad. He's as much to blame for your present predicament as I am." Malus slowly turned, fixing his powerful gaze on Greydon, who bristled, moved at last. Then Aram's father snorted, rolling his eyes in a way Aram had seen Malus do many times.

"We're not the same, Silverlaine. We will never be the same. You're a monster. A *monster*. You turned your back on everything we worked so hard to achieve. You turned your back on the Light, and on that day, you turned your back on me forever. There is no penance that can repair the harm you have done," Greydon said, returning Malus's gaze with equal intensity.

The air crackled between them, and for a moment, Aram was certain Malus would draw his broadsword and end Greydon's life.

"How?" Aram heard himself say. He was curious, after all, about what had driven the brothers apart. Both men whirled to look at him, and Malus sneered.

"Your father's arrogance drives everyone away. He can do no wrong. Say no wrong. He's the chosen one, after all, the favored of the Order of the Seven Suns! Didn't you know that, Aramar? Don't you know the myth of the mighty Greydon Thorne?"

"That's enough."

They sounded so much alike that Aramar had no idea how he hadn't put them together as brothers before. Surely, Malus's voice was lower, twisted with a cold indifference, but it was not so different from Greydon's when he heard them speak, saw them side by side.

"I . . . made many mistakes," Greydon said slowly. "Had I listened to you in our youth, Silverlaine, had I given you your due, things may have turned out very differently indeed."

At that, Malus laughed, once, spitting at Greydon's feet.

He roared, loud enough to shake the bars on Aramar's cage. "Far too little, brother, far too late!"

"I cannot change the past, or undo it, or change the way I treated you," Greydon continued, flinching in the face of his brother's rage. He then looked sadly toward Aramar, his eyes wet with what looked like genuine tears. "The way I treated both of you. There was always a reason, but that doesn't make it right. Forsaking my family, ignoring how that hurt you . . . I suppose I'll have to work on that."

That only enraged Malus further. He stuck the knife in the remainder of the apple, stabbing it as hard as he might wish to stab Greydon in the heart. Then he took two steps back, placing it on the floor, just out of reach of either him or Aram.

"You'll never get the chance, Greydon. This place is your fate and your tomb, and I will enjoy every minute of your well-earned suffering."

With that, he was gone, stalking away, Xaraax's imps following in his wake. Greydon was trembling, but Aramar knew not what to say. He knelt and took up the piece of apple his uncle had flicked into the cell. His stomach growled, desperate for real sustenance. But he tossed the fruit away.

I won't take anything that monster gives me.

CHAPTER TWENTY-THREE
TO LAKESHIRE

Dawn broke across the red roofs of Lakeshire, Lake Everstill sparkling silver like a polished blade slicing through the emerald grass, dividing the banks. Only a handful of Alliance soldiers were awake, patrolling across the quaint stone bridge. An abundance of thick trees surrounded the village, cradling it in lush growth, the Redridge Mountains spearing through the forest to the north.

In the far distance, hazy through the clouds, the tall towers of Stormwind City could be seen, smaller towers and cottages dotting the landscape like sheep as the forest swept from the Alliance capital to the more provincial town of Lakeshire.

It was just as Aram described, just as he sketched and annotated in his sketchbook. She had shown the drawings to Galena, Murky, and Hackle, hoping it was all right to share, knowing that Aram would understand that she just wanted them prepared for what was to come. How ironic, how bitter, that they had at last arrived at their original destination, the place they had always meant to go, only they arrived without Aram.

"And there are no druids there?" Galena asked.

"I don't know," Makasa confessed. "But Aram never mentioned any."

"Brrl mrgle mer mrgy nerg."

Makasa nodded, frowning with concentration. She and Murky had been trying to find a way to communicate more efficiently. He had asked, and Makasa agreed to learn what she could of his language after their nightly reading lessons. Murky would never be able to speak her tongue, but there had to be some way they could understand each other better. Picking up where Aram left off, Makasa had gathered up Galena, Murky, and Hackle for a teaching hour. Aram certainly proved the more patient teacher, but Galena, more educated than all of them put together, helped out where she could, politely interrupting Makasa's lessons to expound on a word's etymology, and then explaining to them all what *etymology* meant.

"Where a word comes from," Galena had said, to Murky's wide-eyed appreciation, "how it came to be, and how it's changed over time. I would love to know where murlocs got their words."

"Gllgh lug!"

Murky had slapped his little knees, finding his answer hysterically funny.

"The sea," Hackle provided helpfully. "Hackle no see why funny."

Even less funny was the predicament presented by not only their mode of transportation, but their destination. As Lakeshire spread out beneath them, Gazlowe summoned Makasa to the deck, where he, Sprocket, and Charnas waited for her near the captain's wheel.

"You got a plan for this?" Gazlowe asked, taking a watch out of his pocket and consulting it before nodding toward the edge of the zeppelin. "Please tell me that you're aware of the political scorpid's nest you're dropping us into."

"Not . . . really."

Charnas intervened before Gazlowe could, calmly unfolding his hands, leading Makasa over to the railing and pointing to the shimmering lake below. "These folks aren't exactly fond of our kind. Or gnolls. Or murlocs, for that matter. And they're not going to welcome a tauren or an undead torso with open arms, either."

Makasa worried her lower lip. This was problematic. Nothing Aram had told her could prepare her for what life was like in Lakeshire. She knew it was tranquil, but she also didn't really know what that meant. All her life she had lived on the sea, in busy ports, or on the road, journeying from post to post, where trade was encouraged, and that meant folks from all over Azeroth were welcome or at least tolerated.

"We're a stone's throw from Stormwind City, kid, it's not Booty Bay down there," Gazlowe added.

"Got it. Maybe we should find a quiet spot to put down, then you can take the *Cloudkicker* and hide it somewhere in the mountains." That was as far as she got.

"We have some winter cloaks," Charnas said. "But they're small because of our size."

"That could work! We take the cloaks and hide Murky, Hackle, and Galena. Even if we just cover their heads, it will be better than nothing. Aram described his house for me a dozen times—he even sketched it. We head straight there and hope his family will let us in."

Gazlowe rubbed his narrow chin, sending the others a bleak stare. "It's . . . something. If you get yourselves killed out there, don't blame me."

"Stay with the *Cloudkicker* we can rendezvous in the forest each day," she said.

"I've got some flares in the storage crates. You send one up if anything goes sideways." Sprocket trotted away, his containment suit hissing as he disappeared down into the hold.

"You ready for this, kid?" Gazlowe took her by the elbow, giving a squeeze. "Like I said, this ain't Booty Bay."

Makasa snorted, leaning onto the railing, watching as they left the town behind and began their descent, traveling northeast to set down closer to the mountains. "It's a bunch of villagers and Aram's family; I'm sure I can handle it."

"Yeah, yeah, you think drunken cutthroats are testy? Wait until a bunch of sheltered humans get a whiff of outsiders in their midst. It'll make a brawl at the Salty Sailor look like a picnic."

When would it end? When would they be found? Aram didn't know if he could endure the torture for one more day, one more hour . . . A fever crept in. A wound from the beatings on his leg wasn't healing right. When the fever didn't burn him up, he was dreadfully cold. Shaking on the floor of his cell, he stared at the apple rotting outside the bars. If he could just reach the knife . . . If he could just do *something*.

When he wasn't consumed by hopelessness, he was consumed by rage at Malus, reliving the anguish of his last battle each night in his dreams. And yet, through all the pain, Drella's gift refused to wilt. When the imps left them alone, he held the flower and looked at it and remembered what it was to feel the wind in his hair and the rain on his face.

How much longer?

"Quiet now, wait for my signal."

Makasa led their strange little group, concealed under the goblins' winter hoods, around the back of the house and toward the brightly painted front door.

"This is ridiculous." She heard Valdread's muffled voice under Galena's cloak.

"I said *quiet*."

The sleepy village began to stir all around them. A pair of fishermen in rough-spun shirts and trousers brought their fishing poles to the docks, laughing as they went. The perfume of baking bread weaved through the village, cutting through the fishy smell of the nearby lake. Aram's house sat not far from the town center and the focal point of the inn, with a market nearby, the tradesmen chatting there, setting up their stalls for the day. She knew they had the correct house when she found the well-used forge built alongside the cottage. An empty doghouse sat a few feet from the forge, as well as a neat garden with rows of growing vegetables and a decorative patch of pretty white daisies.

"Let me do the talking," Makasa warned. "Stay here, I'll let you know when the coast is clear."

"Nk—"

"I'll be right back," she promised. "Now hush."

She had no idea if they could pull it off, but she had to try. Armed with Aram's sketchbook, she darted around the side of the house and up to the front door. Lights shone from inside, and through the wood she could hear the telltale sounds of a family beginning their day. Children laughed. A man's hearty voice boomed through the door. She took a deep breath and knocked, her pulse racing as footsteps hurried toward her.

A round-faced woman in a knit jumper greeted her with a smile. She dried a wooden bowl with a rag as she opened the door, keeping it open with her hip. At once, Makasa saw the resemblance to Aram, particularly in her full, gentle grin.

"Hello there," Ceya Glade said. "Can I do something for you?"

"I'm . . . It's . . ." So much for the speech she had practiced.

"Dear? Who's that at the door?"

"Just a young woman," Ceya called back. Her smile didn't waver. "Is something the matter?"

"A letter," Makasa blurted out. "I'm—I'm here to give you a letter. It's from your son, Aramar." *Who else would it be, idiot?* "I served with him on the *Wavestrider*, but it sank. It's . . . a long story, and I just wanted to—"

"Oh . . . Oh no. Not Aramar."

Ceya dropped the bowl, sinking to the floor. A moment later, a mountain of a man—it must have been Aram's stepfather, Robb—thundered up to the door, followed by about eighty pounds of drooling, sniffing fur. Aram's dog, Soot. Soot smashed through the barricade of humans, tackling Makasa to the ground and licking her face in exuberant greeting. Then he sniffed her some more, and nosed along her arm until he found Aram's sketchbook, barking and pouncing.

"Who are you?" Robb demanded, kneeling and comforting his wife.

"Just let me explain!" Makasa cried out. She pulled the

sketchbook away from Soot, holding it up for them both to see. "Aram's alive, but he's in a lot of trouble. I came to deliver his letter, and . . . and to let you know that he's been kidnapped."

"Kidnapped!" Robb's big brown eyes grew wider. "Who would kidnap our boy?"

"Where is he?" Ceya clutched her husband, staring in disbelief at Makasa and then the sketchbook.

"If you would just let me come inside, I could explain . . . everything. It's a long tale, and you deserve to hear all of it. I'm not alone; his friends are with me, too. We're going to get Aram back, I promise you that. We won't stop until he's safe, of that you have my word."

It didn't take a mystic to divine that the Glades were suspicious of their unexpected guests.

Makasa led her companions in slowly, removing each hood as they came and making introductions. They had quite the audience: the slobbering, utterly overjoyed Soot, black as his namesake and eager to sniff each newcomer; the inconsolable Ceya Glade attached permanently to her husband; and Aram's younger siblings, Robertson and Selya, miniatures of Robb and Ceya, respectively. Selya sat on the ground next to Soot, one hand tugging on her pigtails, the other clutching the dog's collar. Robertson planted himself at the front of the family, armed with his play wooden sword, prepared to cut them down, it seemed, though his little hands trembled with fear.

"First you tell me my son is kidnapped," Robb boomed, "and now you bring Horde scum, a gnoll, and a bloody murloc into my home?"

Murky cowered behind Makasa's leg, peering out at the Glades with huge, rapidly blinking eyes.

"Now just one minute—"

"I told you to let me do the talking," Makasa snarled at Valdread. She turned her attention back to the Glades. "He's . . . not a threat, I promise."

"He's not even ambulatory," Galena chimed in. "Able to walk," she added shyly. "That is. And I'm with the Cenarion Circle. Druids, you see, not the Horde."

"We're all in the sketchbook," Makasa promised the Glades, nodding toward the book, which Robb now held. At that, he flipped through the pages, glancing up whenever he stumbled upon one of the group as if to confirm the wild story.

Good magic, Makasa thought as she saw a hint of the earlier suspicion leave Ceya's face.

"We know all about you; Aram loves to tell stories about his home."

"Urum nalerga brk lrka," Murky chimed in, breaking Makasa's single rule. *No. Talking.* But he smiled, pointing at each of the children in turn. This delighted them to no end. "Rrrbrsun ekal nrga Srrla!"

"Rrrbrsun!" the young boy cried out. "That's me!"

"Right," Makasa said. "We know your names, and we're in Aram's letter, too. He explains quite a bit, but not everything.

And he definitely doesn't get to the part where Malus—Silverlaine—takes him prisoner."

"Greydon's brother?" Ceya had gone ghostly white. She crossed slowly toward Makasa, then took the letter held out to her. Her lips had gone bloodless as she unfolded the parchment and began to read. "I haven't thought of Silverlaine Thorne in years."

"He's been going by a different name, and captaining a ship, the ship that sank the *Wavestrider*," Makasa said. They all stood awkwardly at the front of the kitchen, the first room in the house, spacious but not with that many people and creatures crowded into it. Behind Robb there was a pantry, with stairs leading down into a cellar. The hearth blazed just near the stairs of the front room, and a large supper table with settings and chairs separated the Glades from their guests. A full breakfast of toast, eggs, dried fish, and potatoes was there, uneaten.

"You're Makasa," Ceya said slowly, stumbling over her name.

"Yes. Makasa Flintwill. Second mate on the *Wavestrider*. I knew Greydon well. He's . . . gone."

"D-Dead?" Ceya murmured.

"Not exactly!" Valdread, of course, had to poke his decaying nose into things. Makasa's urge to shut him up, however, quickly faded. Even Galena chirped with surprise, turning so that the Forsaken could speak more clearly, facing the family. Nobody particularly wanted to look at him, but Makasa wanted to hear what he had to say.

"Malus—Silverlaine, as you know him—has Greydon, too. He wouldn't have killed him. He's too cunning for that; he would never cut down an adversary that might be useful to him later. Greydon and Aramar Thorne handled the shards, the compass . . . They have information and insight Malus will want. I'm guessing he has them together somewhere, and I'm certain he's enjoying the irony of the reunion."

"Greydon is *alive*?" Makasa wanted to holler, but instead she remembered their surroundings. It was hard to believe, harder still because it was coming from Valdread. Would he lie about such a thing?

"Slipped my mind," Valdread said with a snort. "Probably from my untimely tumble."

Robb glowered at him, an intimidating man under the best circumstances, more so when he puffed up his broad chest and loomed over Makasa and Valdread. Bearded and brawny, freckled and brown from the sun, his blacksmith's forearms were the size of ham hocks. His voice shook the timbers of the house. "Do you find this funny?"

"I said Malus—Silverlaine—would enjoy the irony. Not me. No, I find this all rather depressing. My condolences, on the disappearance of your family members."

Makasa didn't interrupt him, and did not add that Valdread had been part of the Hidden, the vicious enemies that had abducted the Thornes in the first place. They would figure it out eventually, she thought, if they studied Aram's sketchbook with a careful eye. Valdread's apology seemed to quell them for the moment, and Makasa admitted that he sounded sincere. *Layers and layers*, she thought, shooting him a curious glance.

"I . . . don't know what to say," Ceya murmured, shaking her head. "I need time."

"Doggy!" Selya, meanwhile, had none of her mother's hesitation. The little girl shot up, noticing Hackle tucked away by the door, and toddled over to him, passing by Makasa before she could stop her, and hurling herself at the gnoll.

Hackle froze, putting his paws up as if in surrender.

"Human puppy," he barked out. "Why you touch leg?"

"Doggy!" Selya screamed, enchanted. "Talking doggy!"

"Selya! Get away from that mangy thing!" Robb thundered, knocking Makasa and Galena (and by extension, Valdread) out of the way.

But he had no need to fret. Hackle patted the girl's head gently, giving a quiet hyena cackle as she wrapped herself around his leather-clad leg and squeezed, holding on for dear life.

"Doggy talk! Doggy talk! Doggy talk!" she chanted.

And Hackle obliged.

"What me say, human puppy? Your den smell good. Smell

meat in home, and Hackle starving. Goblin ship have stinky food, not smell as good."

"Srrla drlll lerga tergrl brrlaagrlgl," Murky pointed out.

"Yes," Hackle agreed. "Human puppy very like barnacle on leg."

Soot joined in the inspection of the gnoll, padding over to sniff at the canine creature's fur.

"Goblin ship?" Robb repeated. He exchanged a look with his wife, who held Aram's letter to her chest, and she shrugged in apparent resignation. "There are goblins now, too?"

"And a gnome. Like I said"—Makasa tried to smile, helpless— "it's a long tale, and complicated. You might want to sit down."

By the time Makasa had taken the Glades from Aram's adventures aboard the *Wavestrider* to his exploits in Thousand Needles, the mood had shifted dramatically. Selya patently refused to dislodge herself from Hackle's leg, and the gnoll didn't force her away, only asking after a while if he could sit down because his poor leg was beginning to cramp. Not long after, little Robertson challenged Murky to a duel, for the honor and protection of Lakeshire, and to the murloc's credit, he faked a good fight, but ultimately let the little boy win.

"Mama? Papa? Can't they at least have breakfast?" the boy asked.

That softened Robb and Ceya right up. They relented, and the whole mess of them settled down to breakfast. Ceya put the kettle on, still keeping Aram's letter with her, and prepared more food, realizing that much of the spread had gone cold and they would need more plates and many more boiled potatoes.

Makasa watched her watching them. Some color had come back into Ceya's face, and she even managed a thin smile or two as the meal began. Robb, perhaps sensing that Hackle and Murky were harmless if they were willing to put up with his rambunctious children, turned his attention instead to Valdread, keeping a close eye on the dismembered Forsaken.

Galena wisely positioned herself and the undead at the far end of the table, nearest to an open window, allowing Valdread's troubling aroma to filter out into the open air. The morning stretched on and on, Makasa still weaving her complex story for Aram's family. Then afternoon came, Robb deciding not to open the forge that day, and Ceya preparing yet more food for the weary and hungry travelers.

"You're kind even to listen," Galena remarked at one pause in the story. "I haven't known Makasa and the others long, but they astounded me, too, when first we met."

They were just reaching that part of the journey, and Makasa left nothing out. Robertson and Selya, their eyes wide with wonder, leaned in close, forgetting their lunch altogether.

"Then, out of nowhere, this black drake swooped down and picked me up!" The children gasped and shivered. "Its claws went deep, and I couldn't get free. I thought I would be finished then and there, carried off to be a meal for some ravenous whelps!"

Another round of gasps.

Makasa pulled down the top shoulder of her travel-stained shirt, showing them the proof of the encounter, the still-healing wounds from the drake that had just begun to scab. "But then, a band of night elves from the Overlook appeared, and shot the drake right out of the sky. They were riding massive sabers, and one had an owl!"

It was harder to recount the story whenever Aram was in danger, and she stumbled when they reached Drella's death. Thalyss had been a hard person to lose, and Greydon, too, but thanks to Valdread, she now knew she could stop mourning his loss—though learning of his imprisonment still shocked her. That was a conversation for another time. There was no getting around it. She had to describe the battle on the hill, and she did, keeping the more violent aspects to herself, so as not to frighten the little ones too gravely.

When it was over, and the Glades fully informed, they stared at her in stunned silence. Robertson and Selya clapped, but their parents were not so eager to show their appreciation. Ceya's eyes filled with tears, but she somehow managed to keep them at bay, pressing the backs of her hands to her pale cheeks.

"It's hard to believe it all," Ceya murmured. "But Aram's

sketchbook . . . Those are his works, unmistakably, and you put your lives at risk to bring us his letter. If the Alliance soldiers saw some of you, they'd swing a sword and ask questions later. I—I don't know if I can say I like this, but if Aram trusts you, then I will do my best to help where I can."

Murky audibly gulped.

"I know . . . but it was the right thing to do. It's what Aram would do," Makasa explained. "And as I told you, Aram's compass was pointing here. We were bound for Lakeshire no matter what, but it was important for you to know Aram's story. And ours. And to know that we'll do whatever it takes to find him."

Robb narrowed his eyes, casting a cold glance around the table. "You mean whatever it takes to find those bloody shards."

Makasa's immediate instinct to go on the defensive made her hands clench, but she closed her eyes and begrudgingly recalled Valdread's advice. This was the hard, uncomfortable part of being the "leader." Even if she wanted to take a tone, and tell him how far they had come and how tired they were, she stowed it.

"The shards, reassembling the Diamond Blade, it's the only way we'll be able to take on Malus, to free Aramar," she said. "It's all connected, and I mean no disrespect, sir, but the faster we find those shards, the faster we find your boy—our friend."

"Robb," Ceya interrupted, putting a hand on his shoulder. It looked tiny on the blacksmith's muscled shoulder. "You heard the same tale as I, and you can see plain as I can that these folk were put down in his hand. He mentions most of them in the letter. Our boy's gone; now we must be brave for him and . . . do what we might not otherwise do." And here she glanced at Galena and Valdread, swallowing uneasily. "They must be guests in our home, and we should help them however we can." A tear escaped her eye, sliding down her cheek.

"And what do we do if someone so much as peeks in our window?" Robb demanded. His face had gone red. "We're at war. We would be harboring enemies and fugitives, Ceya; it puts our family at risk! I want to help Aram, too, but this is asking too much."

"Nothing is asking too much if it means saving Aram's life. It's the best we can do for him right now. It will have to suffice until he's brought home to us. Please, Robb. This is our *son*."

Robb stared at her for a tense, silent moment, then reached over and wiped the tear from her cheek. "We will have to be unbelievably careful. No risks. No mistakes."

Makasa nodded, stunned and humbled by Ceya's kindness. "Thank you. I know this isn't easy, letting us into your home. It's that kind of courage that will bring Aramar home."

It was a fine speech, but Ceya didn't smile.

"There's a spare room upstairs," was all she said, turning away, wiping at her face with her apron. "And a shed out the back. Perhaps the *strange* ones best stay inside, and not be spotted by the town guards."

Though the children giggled and played, deciding they would

take on the roles of Murky and Hackle and wrestle to see who was the better warrior, their parents demonstrated no such joy. Makasa allowed them their grief. It had gone better than she expected, for they were not imprisoned in the village jail, and nobody had been killed or kicked out. Yet. She glanced at Valdread, holding his gaze for a long time.

"Hackle go to shed, Hackle take stinky man," the gnoll muttered, unhooking the heavy pack from Galena's back, after which she groaned with relief and rubbed her tired shoulders.

"Hackle," Makasa warned him, following to the back door. "Wear your hood, and don't do anything stupid. I mean it. And Hackle? Don't beat him with your club."

The gnoll pretended not to hear her, pulling up his cloak and plunging out into daylight without another word.

"Hackle!"

A muffled complaint came from under the cloak, but then the gnoll disappeared into the little woodshed, Valdread bumping along on his back. Makasa was too drained to worry too much about it. It was, perhaps, a fruitless exercise to try and teach diplomacy to a gnoll. Meanwhile, Aram's mother waited at the bottom of the stairs, then led them up to a cozy second level. Thick, woven carpets were spread across the floor, and small brass lamps were fixed to the rough timber walls, a pleasant glow suffusing the hall.

"There's a bedroom just there," Ceya said softly. "And, well, I suppose one of you can take Aramar's room. It isn't— It . . ."

"Thank you," Makasa said again, and, impulsively, reached out to take the woman's hands. She didn't smack her away, and Makasa squeezed, watching as the urge to weep came and went from Ceya's face. "Thank you for accepting us."

She shook her head, and Makasa didn't know if that meant it was no trouble at all, or she hadn't accepted them. Then she fixed the girl with a tight-lipped look, her eyes wet and pleading. "Just find a way to bring him back. *Just find a way.*"

CHAPTER TWENTY-FIVE
DREAMS OF SHARDS

Makasa woke, finding herself in the dark, frogs and crickets singing at her from every direction, the moons bright and low in the sky. Alone. Cold. She shivered and rubbed at her arms. Wearing only her night shirt and a pair of trousers, she stood barefoot in the tall grass, a strange rock formation shining like diamonds in the grass under the stars.

Was she dreaming? How had she gotten there?

The stones. Look among the stones.

Makasa doubled over, wincing, the voice in her head painfully loud, blasting through her thoughts and blinding her for an instant. Clutching her temples, she stumbled forward, falling into the wet embrace of the overgrown weeds. The rocks were different sizes, forming a circle, some of them with designs scratched across the tops.

The compass led you here. The shards led you here. Look among the stones, Makasa. Look. Do not be afraid.

The Voice of the Light. She had dreaded its return, and now she could hear nothing but the crystallized words that seemed to sear her mind with fire. She picked up each rock, turning it over, then dug through the grass, wondering again how she had ended up outside. Glancing over her shoulder, she saw the Glade cottage not far away, the forge, and the doghouse, no lights burning inside. Had she been sleepwalking?

You have been led here. Search. Find Greydon's hope. Find the shard. The Diamond Blade must be whole; to save Azeroth, the blade must be whole. Look. Look . . .

"I bloody am," she grunted, shivering in the cold. A torch flickered down the way, a night patrol perhaps, and she clawed at the grass faster, faster, until her fingertips felt like ice. At the very center of the stone circle, covered by a deep layer of mud and pebbles, she at last felt the warm prickle of magic. The shard.

She closed her hand over it and gasped, a vision overtaking her, a blinding white veil dropping in front of her eyes, showing her the ghost of a man, Greydon, traveling to that same spot, kneeling in the grass, digging down to hide the shard and then marking it with the stones. He looked younger and less bearded; it must have been years ago. *He must have always intended to return to Lakeshire*, she thought, and not abandoned his family forever like most assumed.

"That's why the compass was pointing here," Makasa breathed. "There was a bloody shard buried in the backyard all this time."

Makasa cleaned off the shard and tucked it into her pocket, hurrying back toward the house. The back door was open, no doubt a result of her sleepwalking. She tiptoed back inside and retraced her steps to Aram's room, then used some remaining cinders in the hearth to light a candle and study the shard at his old desk. The desk, covered in scraps of drawings, soon held even more art, as Makasa retrieved his sketchbook from the bedside and opened it by candlelight. After confirming that they were, in fact, folk that Aram had drawn, the Glades had relinquished the sketchbook, and Makasa promised to take good care of it.

She wetted a finger and flipped through the book quickly, finding the picture Aram had drawn of the Diamond Blade hilt. With the shard she carried from his compass and now this newly recovered one, that meant they were still missing two shards. Makasa touched the pointed crystal chip on the desk, marveling at its smoothness, and the way it warmed to her fingers. While it was certainly a victory, how in the world could they find the remaining two pieces?

"We could really use your compass right now," she muttered, glancing around at the room, as if by virtue of it being Aram's she could somehow hear him. But she did feel closer to him there. His clothing was still draped over every chair and bedpost, though Ceya had done her best to tidy up. An aged globe sat in the windowsill, and he had left a fluffy rug out next to his bed, no doubt for Soot to sleep on. Given how much fur she found in the bedclothes, she didn't imagine the dog used that rug much.

Never in her life had she expected to miss him so much. He had been nothing but a lazy nuisance on the *Wavestrider*, taking to seafaring life like a fish to the sky. But now that she thought about it, there had always been a spark of something more there, a willingness to try, even if he failed. Makasa had to admire that. She hated failing, looking stupid, or not knowing what to do, which was why the mysterious shards bothered her.

Sighing with frustration, wishing she could just go back to bed and forget the whole business and wake up to find Aram downstairs at breakfast, smirking over his bacon, she snatched up the shard from his compass and squeezed it with her fist.

"Just tell me, you stupid rock, tell me what to do!"

At once, the shard warmed in her touch. She opened her hand and held the crystal flat in her palm, the shard spinning and spinning, then stopping, abruptly, glowing brightly, pulsing with light. She stood up, using her palm like the body of a compass, and moved throughout the room. Then she spun, slowly, watching as the pointed end of the shard, like a needle, pointed northeast. No matter where she went in Aram's room, the needle pointed the same direction.

"Great, so anywhere to the northeast," she muttered, then dropped back down into the chair at his desk. Slamming her head down onto her crossed arms, she squeezed the shard again. "You can't just . . . whisper it in my ear, can you?"

Close now. Less than a day's journey. Remake the blade.

Makasa nearly screamed, jumping up. That was certainly not a whisper, but a shout as clear as anything in her mind. The Voice of the Light. Maybe, she thought, if she just started walking northeast, she could divine where the next shard was hidden. But what could *close* mean? Did the strange thing in her head have any conception of human distances?

She was doing an awful lot of petulant sighing, but she blew out another breath anyway, watching it ruffle the pages of Aram's sketchbook. The parchment whispered softly as the pages rushed forward and back, then stopped, resettling. In grand stories, there would be some kind of map on that page, but there was no mystical, magical map, just a drawing of a cave.

Makasa stood up, knowing she would never sleep but determined to try anyway. Halfway to the bed, she froze, turning and racing back to the desk and Aramar's drawing of the cave. She kept her place with one finger, then flipped back through the book, finding that almost everything there was something Aramar had seen with his own eyes. Portraits. Locations. Scenes she knew he had witnessed in person. But this? When had Aram gone to a cave and happened across a dragon and a young man? She would definitely remember him telling her that, even if her mind had a tendency to wander during his longer stories.

Was it possible? Could Aram have somehow left them a clue in his sketchbook? It seemed absurd, but then again, she had just woken up outside in her bedclothes, guided in her sleep by a mysterious voice to a magical shard that was somehow a part of a sword that would save the world.

So all things considered, a fortune-telling picture was far less deranged than the rest of it.

"Northeast," she whispered, running her hand gently over the sketch. "A cave to the northeast. If you manage to get us to that shard, Aram, I swear, I'll never complain about you sketching me again."

CHAPTER TWENTY-SIX
DARKSTORM

"Here. Take mine, son; you need it more than I do."

Aram grunted.

"That leg of yours doesn't look good," Greydon added. "How is the fever today?"

"Not bad," Aram said, sparing him the truth. *Worse.*

The wooden bowl of gruel skittered across the floor toward him, sliding just under the lowest crossbar of the cell and bumping into his leg. Aram lifted himself up, his leg throbbing with pain. The beatings had continued, but lessened ever since the imps noticed his swollen, infected leg. The prodding and burning might have ceased, but not the fever, and Aram wiped at the sweat collecting on his brow, reaching for the extra portion of gruel with shaking hands.

"I'm sorry," Greydon said. He had told Aram that countless times as they wasted away in their twin cells. And like the last dozen times or so, Aram didn't respond. "I'm sorry I couldn't protect you from this. This is not how a Thorne should die."

At that, Aram finally showed some interest, and spooned a bit of the tasteless, gluey gruel into his mouth, gagging. "And how should a Thorne die?"

"With a sword in hand," Greydon replied, leaning back against his cell bars, his long legs stretched out before him. They were both so dirty and scratched, and his father was almost unrecognizable under his shaggy beard. "Or on the sea, fighting the storm. That's what we were doing, you know, your uncle and I. Fighting a storm. The Darkstorm."

It occurred to Aram that, even with the hope gifted to him by Drella's flower, it was likely they would die there together. This sudden confession from his father only deepened that sense. A strange kind of peace settled over him.

"The Darkstorm?" Aram prompted.

"Indeed. A force so terrible, so dark, it could unmake the world and destroy Azeroth entirely. Every living soul would be gone, the failure of our order. My failure."

"How could it be your fault?" Aramar asked. "If you were part of an order, that's not just one man."

Greydon shook his head, stroking his overgrown beard. "The Order of the Seven Suns was under my care," he recalled softly, as if even speaking too loudly of it might summon his cruel brother again to torment them. "Seven of us there were, Silverlaine and I among them. We were called to protect a naaru, a being of pure Light. It was foretold that this being could stop the Darkstorm, and Silverlaine and I vowed to protect it. Gladly. We dedicated our lives to the order, and I was chosen as its leader."

"But why summon the Darkstorm?" Aram asked, puzzled. "How would that even happen?"

"Xaraax." His father said the word like a curse. "A dreadlord of the Burning Legion. His only interest is in spreading the strength of the Legion, smearing it like a stain across every world. Azeroth is the only world to resist, a world the naaru has lent its grace to shield. We were to guard that shield against the malice of Xaraax. Silverlaine and I were to protect that shield, until he betrayed everything we fought for."

"So what happened? I thought Malus said you betrayed him, not the other way around."

"And so I did. I was the leader of the order, but he was the superior swordsman. The naaru granted me the Diamond Blade to bestow upon whomever I deemed most worthy. I kept it for myself. I saw it as a symbol of my leadership, but Silverlaine was furious. He, of course, deserved the gift of the blade, and I denied it to him because of pride." The weight of that choice returned to Greydon, and he sank down against the bars. "He *did* deserve the blade, but I dismissed him, thinking it was mere jealousy. Brothers can be like that."

"Sisters, too," Aram said dryly. His father raised a brow at that. "Makasa, I mean. We squabbled so much . . . I never thought we could really be friends, and now I think of her as my sister."

"Then you've been wiser than me," Greydon replied. "Silverlaine and I argued endlessly over the blade, and it tore our bond apart. I told him . . . he was not worthy. Then one day, he stole the blade from my quarters and simply left. I discovered later that he had gone to fight Xaraax and his minions alone, no doubt determined to prove that I had erred, and that he had the true right to the Diamond Blade."

"Brave, I guess. And stupid."

"Those things often go hand in hand," his father said. "Silverlaine was outnumbered. He survived the worst of the onslaught, but at the last, Xaraax tempted him to his side, promising Silverlaine great power and even greater revenge if he sided with the demons. Xaraax's worm tongue burrowed into Silverlaine's mind, persuading him that the naaru and I would discard him. He was weakened by his anger, I think, and accepted the demon's offer. We had no idea he had betrayed us until he returned and used the Diamond Blade to murder the naaru."

His voice hitched on the last word. Aram ate in silence, but he had lost his taste for the gruel and set it aside.

"The—the impact shattered the blade, and the shards of it were scattered across Azeroth, lost, I thought, for all time."

"But what about the Darkstorm? It must not have come,

because Azeroth is still here... *We're* still here. Why didn't Xaraax take what he'd won?"

"For a long time, I didn't know. The naaru was gone, the order as shattered as the Diamond Blade. No one remained to defend Azeroth, yet the world *wasn't* ending. And then everything changed."

"What changed?"

"The Voice of the Light. After years, I began hearing the naaru. How I had missed the sound of its voice! It called to me, telling me that the blade could be reforged, that it contained the naaru's essence. This was why the Darkstorm hadn't come: it *couldn't* come while the naaru still existed in some form. If I could find the shards, I could restore the naaru, and then it could stop Xaraax and the Darkstorm for good. This was my chance to mend my mistake, but doing so meant leaving you and your mother. The Diamond Blade is truly a double-edged sword: If I could reforge it in secret, I could save us all—I could save my family. But if I let the sword fall into Xaraax's hands, Azeroth would be doomed."

Another spell of silence. Aram didn't think it would hurt so much to hear the explanation, not when they were already imprisoned and in pain. But he pounded his fist into his palm, glaring across at his father. "Why didn't you just say something?"

"I didn't know if I would ever return," Greydon whispered, hoarse, his eyes shining in the darkness. "And I wanted to protect you. I see now that it was folly, and the naaru knew it, too. You are part of this, Aram; the Voice of the Light told me to find you, told me you had a great destiny. I struggled with it for a long, long time. The Darkstorm, the Diamond Blade, Silverlaine . . . So much loss, so many mistakes, how could I endanger you, too?"

"*That* was why you came back for me. The Voice of the Light . . ." That hurt more. Hot, angry tears spilled down his cheeks. "You never wanted to come find me. It wasn't even your decision!"

Greydon clambered to his knees, crawling toward Aramar, reaching for him through the bars. "No, Aramar, no. I only wanted to protect you from, well, this. Look what has happened. I listened to the naaru and now we are both doomed. You were much safer back in Lakeshire. I tried to tell you, Aram, I tried to tell you on the *Wavestrider* . . ."

Wincing, Aram did, in fact, remember. Just as his father finally sat him down to explain his actions, his abandonment, his absence, Malus had attacked, sinking the ship, leaving Aram to believe his father had been killed.

"For years I was desperate to return to Lakeshire and find you, but I was too afraid to get you wrapped up in this mess. I wanted to save you. That's what a father does."

"A father never leaves in the first place," Aram spat. But his father, weakened by the prolonged torture, looked only pitiful to him then. Withered. Alone for so much of his life . . . and there

Aram had been. Aram had always been surrounded by a loving family. First in Lakeshire, and then among his father's crew, and when the *Wavestrider* was gone and hope seemed lost, he gained yet another family, one he had cobbled together himself.

"The fate of the world was in the balance, Aram, and that world is yours, too."

The words hung heavily between them. Aram let out a single sob, wiped at his face, and found the anger had fled him. He was being just like Silverlaine, only seeing how things affected *him*. His father had been handed an impossible choice, and he had done the best he could, trying to save Azeroth and protect Aram at the same time.

"I suppose the whole world is more important than me," Aram murmured.

"Not by much, son. My regrets are legion, but being with you now, seeing you grow into this fine young man, that does not number among them. I have told my sad tale, Aram, but now I should very much like to hear yours. I have a feeling it is far more interesting than mine."

"It doesn't involve the end of the world," Aram said. *I don't think.* Or maybe it did. Aramar had been brought into the adventure by the Light, and it had spoken to him, so maybe he really was a part of his father's grand story after all. "Well, it begins with Makasa. I never would have gotten far without her by my side. Weird, I know, because at first? At first we couldn't stand each other. She was just so bossy and a know-it-all, and I never wanted to listen, but then we were stranded. After the *Wavestrider* sank, we didn't just give up. We made friends. We pressed on. I carried the compass and protected it through the wilds of Feralas, to Gadgetzan, and all the way across Kalimdor to the Stonetalon Mountains."

His father said nothing, but waited, clearly intrigued. It was Aram's turn to spin a tale.

"There's Murky, a murloc who saved me from a whale shark, and a brave gnoll warrior called Hackle, who faced yetis and ogres, and never wavered as my friend. And there was . . . There was . . ." He faltered, then drew in a shaky breath. "There's more, a lot more. Goblins and dryads and elves and druids, they all tried to help me, and I have faith in them. I know things are dire, but I have faith."

"Indeed," Greydon Thorne said, his voice hoarse. "Indeed, Aramar, I should think that they will try even harder now that you are gone. Faith is good; faith in our friends is even better."

Aramar nodded, satisfied for the moment. The desolation of the pits hung heavy on the air, screams erupting from random directions, piercing through the smoky darkness that surrounded them. Could they really be saved? Was there any hope at all for a father and son imprisoned in the depths, waiting in the unknown of Outland, with nothing to sustain them but a single bright flower?

Drella's lullaby returned to him, and he hummed it to himself softly.

> *There I walked in my grove*
> *With hope and pride.*
> *There I shall stay*
> *When I fear the rising tide.*

Had he dreamt of that very grove? Maybe their bond wasn't severed after all. Maybe Drella was with him, there in that cell, one beautiful blossom still thriving in the dark.

CHAPTER TWENTY-SEVEN
HUNTING A DRAGON

"**Y**ou cannot think to leave me behind like some sack of rubbish!"

Valdread was in a rage and Makasa didn't have time to indulge him. She had packed light for the day trip to the cave, only bringing water, a snack, Aram's sketchbook for guidance, and a rough map of the area Robb Glade had been kind enough to provide her. Hackle and Murky shored up their weapons, packed their own fish and meat for the walk, and waited in the protective shadows of the trees behind the cottage. Galena waited, too, but inside the woodshed, where the sweet smell of drying cedar gave them at least some relief from Valdread's persistent stench.

"Your words, not mine," Makasa told him. "We're not going far; can't you put on your big boy pants and just wait here?"

Galena smothered a laugh with her hand, and Valdread shot her a withering look.

"No, child, I cannot put on any sort of pants because you still *refuse* to grant me my legs. It isn't fair. I've been nothing but obedient. Practically a saint!"

"A saint?! You might have told me sooner that Greydon Thorne was still alive instead of springing it on me like that in front of Aram's parents. If I'm to lead us, you can't surprise me like that. I looked like a fool!"

"Fine. All right. One minor omission. It frankly slipped my mind until that moment."

It was Makasa's turn to glare.

"We are going to a strange cave that might have a dragon inside," Galena pointed out. "Bringing him along might not be such a bad idea. If nothing else, he's hard to kill."

"Galena, of course!" Makasa dug through the pile of Hackle's things next to the stacked wood, finding the body parts they had collected there. She found his legs and dragged them toward their natural place on Valdread's body.

"Change of plans. You *are* coming with us. You can be our walking meat shield."

"Meat . . . shield?" Valdread huffed with disgust, blowing a piece of dark hair out of his eyes. "Disgraceful. Ah well, I suppose it is better than staying here with all the creepy-crawlies nibbling on me at their leisure. I'm afraid at least one of you will need to assist."

"I'll try to help," Galena said slowly, not looking at all pleased by the task. "I memorized the CCAMP chapters on staunching wounds. Will that give me any insight?"

"I don't think anything will prepare you for reattaching my limbs, but it certainly couldn't hurt."

Makasa reminded them to use their cloaks, then left them to wait in the forest with the others. The sounds that came from the little woodshed would be burned into Makasa's mind forever. It was over quickly, thank the Light, and soon Galena and Valdread scurried across the open grass to them, their faces and bodies hidden in cloaks. Robb Glade had been kind enough to lend some of his wardrobe, reluctantly, but his garments were the only ones big enough to conceal Galena and her charge. Galena had, in turn, promised to wash the cloaks thoroughly.

"Keep to the trees," Makasa warned them. "We should be able to stay hidden if we follow the forest at the foot of the mountains."

As they set out on their search, Makasa cradled the compass shard in her palm, watching it for any variations as they moved quietly through the underbrush, sheltered by the thick, leafy trees that hugged the village. Valdread kept pace, and it was unsettling to have him stalking along beside her, armless and swift, his head tilting this way and that as he searched all around them.

"Let's pause here. We will be exposed on the road, but if we hike uphill through the woods we will soon be in gnoll country.

Hackle should go on ahead and give things a sniff," Valdread whispered, his eyes glowing in the shadows of the woods.

"How do you know that?" Makasa demanded.

"Use your eyes and ears, girl. Here's your first SI:7 lesson: Everything is important. Everything is intelligence. Lakeshire's outskirts are crawling with gnolls and murlocs, and where do gnolls like to live? In the hills. If they're clever, and most gnolls rather are despite common belief, then they will stack patrols in any mountainous areas."

"Stinky man right," Hackle grumbled, moving quickly to the north and the tree break, where the mountains reared up sharply, covered in reddish-brown dust. "Hackle look for gnoll. Good wind today for sniff."

He disappeared for a moment, crouched so low that Makasa lost track of him altogether.

"You have so much to learn," Valdread whispered to her.

"And I suppose *you're* going to teach me? Ha."

"Why not? I'm along on this ride for good or ill, you may as well benefit from my expertise. I'll make you a fine leader. King Varian Wrynn himself gave me my title. Baron. Years in SI:7 ought to be enough to convince you of my value. Yes, you'll learn much, but only if you listen." And here he chuckled, both of them watching Hackle return, his club resting over one shoulder.

"Clan move east, chasing boars. We go now!"

Hackle sprang forward, leading them through the underbrush, bringing them back into the brightness of the morning as they filed one by one up the shallowest part of the hill. Valdread struggled to keep his feet, but managed, and soon they found themselves in the midst of a sort of dish carved into the mountains, with steep rocks to the north and most of the south.

"No choice but to go east for a while," Makasa said. "Keep your eyes open for movement. Those gnolls could return anytime."

"Hackle sniff first. Gnoll no hide from Hackle."

It took them the better part of an hour to pick their way across the rocky path east. Either gnolls or wild animals had flattened down the meager grass, making the track easier to follow. The shard in Makasa's hand glowed brighter with each step. They traveled along a raised cliff, the view down to Lakeshire obstructed only by the occasional high, jutting stone.

"We're getting close," she told them. "It's getting brighter in my hand."

"Melllgl flerger, drgl nerp?"

"Hackle hope we see dragon, too, Murky."

"Remember the last time we encountered one of those?" Makasa called over her shoulder, a little sweaty and cross.

"Mrksa floooooooooog!"

She understood that one. "Yes, Murky. Mrksa fly."

"You know, that was my favorite bit of your story last night," Valdread teased. "A real crowd-pleaser with the young ones, too."

"If you ever want to see your arms again, I suggest you keep your mouth shut." Makasa pushed on, convinced they were close, knowing that more than anything, they needed a morale boost. Finding another shard, bringing them that much closer to Aram, would do the trick. After that, only one piece remained, and then they could decide their plan of attack.

"There!" Galena trotted ahead, pointing toward a dark spot in the mountainside. "It looks like a cave."

Her instincts proved right. It was a cave, a cave so dark and foreboding that Makasa found herself suddenly wishing for any excuse not to go inside.

"Here," Galena said, closing her eyes and moving her hands over each other in a circle. Gradually, a glowing white orb of lunar energy formed in her hands, shining brightly enough to illuminate the darkness. She beamed around at her companions. "CCAMP procedure, obviously; every Cenarion Circle member knows a simple lighting spell."

"Perfect! You can go first, then. Do watch for any sudden drops or snakes!" Valdread said.

Galena gulped. "I—I will. It's . . . not so s-scary."

"Why don't you go right along with her, Baron? You are the meat shield, after all."

After a brief bit of grousing, Valdread joined the druid, for once walking beside her and not bouncing along on her back. They pushed deeper into the cave, which was blessedly free of snakes, but full of twists and turns. Makasa consulted the shard at every forking path, and hoped she was divining its directions correctly. The air grew thinner and colder, the floor wet beneath their feet.

Galena summoned large thorny roots along the way to keep track of their path. And when they rounded a corner only to stumble upon one of those markers, Hackle growled in frustration.

"We go in circle! Nothing in stupid cave."

"No, Hackle, it's here," Makasa murmured.

"Let's go back. Maybe we missed a turn." Galena led them through the tunnels, keeping the lunar orb in her hands burning bright.

"Stop."

It was Valdread. He had noticed something at a fork in the passage, one of the deepest twists in the cave system.

"Everyone be silent."

Nobody moved, and Valdread leaned forward, resting his armless body against the smooth surface of the cave wall, pressing his ear to the stones. "Water. There must be another passage somewhere."

He hurled himself back, beckoning Galena forward with a nod of his head, then searched the cave floor, walls, and ceiling closely. A bit of leafy vine hung down from the ceiling, brushing the top of Valdread's head. "Of course. Easy. Druid, pull that vine just there."

Galena's hands were full, so Makasa did it herself, then readied her harpoon in her free hand. The cave immediately began to rumble; then slowly a break in the wall appeared, a slab of stone moving to the side and revealing a wide-open cavern beyond. The sound of water rushed out to meet them. An underground spring. Strange blue lights floated along the air, throwing shadows up the curved cave walls.

The shard in Makasa's palm began to steadily vibrate.

"It's close now," she whispered. "Everyone be on your guard."

No sooner had she uttered those words than an ominous rumbling echoed throughout the cavern. It grew sharper, then deafening, a screech as bloodcurdling as the cries of the drakes that had attacked them in the Charred Vale. She shivered, squinting into the low azure light of the cavern, watching with her mouth open wide as the glassy pool below them rippled and then broke, a shimmering blue dragon rising from its watery depths.

CHAPTER TWENTY-EIGHT
TELAGOS

Galena Stormspear felt her breath catch in her throat. Not since meeting Taryndrella had she felt such wonder, as if the combined years and effort of her training and study were colliding, the excitement so strong she could hardly keep from jumping in the air.

The excitement soon gave way to fear, however, as she realized this drake was not going to be as friendly as Drella. It was the size of two stags, perhaps, with smooth blue wings and a slender head, two horns curling back from its prominent brow. White vapor streamed from its nostrils, the rhythmic beating of its wings echoing in the cavern, magnifying the sound.

Its sharp white eyes found them at once, and just as quickly, it dove toward them, unleashing a high and piercing cry. Galena had seen the drakes circling over the Charred Vale, and asked Master Thal'darah about them, and he had explained that the ones she could see from the Overlook were far older and more grown than the smaller whelps that foraged along the ground. This, she reasoned, must be closer to a whelp, then, but its youth did not make it any less intimidating as it soared toward them, mouth dropping wide as if preparing to swallow Murky whole.

Galena dropped her lunar orb in a fright. Valdread called out for them to duck. Hackle raised his club, and Murky dove off the ledge, spearing into the water.

And Makasa, whom Galena had never seen shaken or hesitant in the heat of battle, did not raise her harpoon. It seemed to be the time for that, in Galena's admittedly unexperienced opinion, but the weapon remained fixed to the human's side. Instead, Makasa held up Aram's journal, wielding it like some kind of magic shield.

"Wait!" she cried. "I know you. You guard a shard of the Diamond Blade. The Light sent me here to retrieve it, and my brother foresaw us coming. *Look.*"

It was a gutsy strategy, and the dragon did not seem interested, flattening Makasa's short hair back with another scream. Galena clutched her ears, falling to her knees.

"Look! This is you! You're—you're not just a dragon," she shouted. "You have another form. *This* form." Makasa pointed desperately at the page.

The dragon drew up short, baring its razor-sharp teeth, its glowing white eyes now just a handbreadth from the book. And amazingly, miraculously, it fell quiet, hovering there, beating its great wings and staring at Aramar Thorne's drawing.

Makasa whispered carefully, "We didn't come here to harm you; we came here because my brother knew we were destined to find you."

Galena peered up from where she had crumpled on the ledge, finding that the drake really did have a scar curving over one cheek.

The drake flashed its teeth again, perhaps unmoved, but then it circled, performing an incredible flip, before blowing a cone of frosty breath across the pool at the bottom of the cavern. The water froze instantly, sealing Murky beneath it. Then it landed and flapped its wings, conjuring a silvery veil around its entire body before the mist evaporated, leaving in its wake a young man.

"By the Earth Mother!" Galena gasped. "Aramar's drawing—"

"It looks just like him," Makasa agreed.

The young man—tall and thin, with ash-blond hair and pale, wintry eyes—cocked his head to the side, then strode across the ice to the ledge of the cavern, climbing until he stood face-to-face with Makasa. She continued holding out the sketchbook, and the young man leaned over to examine it.

"What sort of magic is this?" he asked. He had a soft, scholarly voice, one that Galena thought belonged in a library or mage's college. In his human form, he wore a suit of trim blue scale mail, cinched at the waist with a belt. Six or so scrolls were tied neatly to his belt. "The likeness is sublime. Faultless. The expression is mine exactly. But I don't recall meeting any of you, much less sitting for a drawing in this form."

Aramar had captured the young man's quizzical look, the way his right eyebrow remained permanently lifted with curiosity, and of course, the scar on his cheek.

Good magic, she thought.

"A blue dragon!" Galena kept her distance but was desperate for a closer look. "Your kind are so rare! How did you come to be in a cave in Lakeshire?"

Galena was full of questions—she also wanted to know how he had transformed so seamlessly from dragon to human. There were legends, of course, of dragons that could take many forms, not a magic they learned like druids, but an innate ability. The young man did not meet her gaze, and instead took the sketchbook from Makasa, studying it from every angle.

"'Tis a protracted and tedious tale, one I may yet tell, but not before you explain this book to me. What manner of magic is it? That you could know me and not know me."

Protracted and tedious? Galena could see he was grating on Makasa already.

"My brother drew all the pictures in that book, and he must have had some kind of vision of you. We've been trying to locate crystal shards; they belong to a sword, like this shard." Makasa held up her palm with the glowing, needlelike splinter of the blade. "Aram's sketch led us here."

"And which of you is Aram?" the dragon asked.

"He's not actually with us . . . He's been kidnapped. We need to gather the missing sword shards before we can get him back." Pointing to each of them in turn, she made quick introductions. "My name is Makasa Flintwill, and these are my companions, Galena and Hackle. The armless undead man is Reigol Valdread. The arms thing is also a protracted and tedious tale. And that's . . ."

She had been so distracted that she had forgotten about Murky in the pool. Muted thumping came from under the ice, and the faint sounds of panicked burblings.

"That's Murky under the ice!"

"You may call me Telagos, and I will retrieve your amphibious friend."

The dragon—Telagos—gracefully dropped down from the ledge, then placed his hands on the ice. A perfectly round hole melted away, revealing Murky's huge eyes. He flopped out of the water and onto the ice, then looked to Makasa as he shivered and shivered.

"Mrksa? Blggr lerg?"

"Telagos, he's the one from Aram's drawing. I think trapping you under the ice was a mistake," she said with a shrug.

"Absolutely. And I apologize for the error, young Murky." Telagos swept the murloc a deep bow, the scrolls on his belt rustling softly.

"Frund?" Murky asked, peering at the curious young man.

"I'm . . . not sure," Makasa said.

Galena closed her hands around Makasa's wrist and squeezed, the druid clearly casting her vote for *friend*. "We don't want any trouble, Telagos. We just want the shard."

"I wouldn't trust him," Valdread whispered, leaning in. "Look in the shadows. Those are skeletons. They're picked clean."

"And nobody asked you," Makasa replied. She regarded the dragon. "So? What will it be? Friend or foe?"

Telagos placed an open hand on his chest, fluttering his silvery lashes. "I'm offended. Were we foes, this conversation would not be taking place. I am intrigued by your brother's vision, and by your knowledge of the shards. The shard here was entrusted to me by a friend, a man, a Thorne, who sought to protect Azeroth. The shard has remained here with me for some years . . ."

"Did I just hear you say a Thorne?" Makasa reeled back for a moment. "As in Greydon Thorne? This sketchbook belongs to his son, Aramar Thorne."

The young man's pale eyes widened and he smiled, then his expression shifted to one of deep concern. "That is the very man. He said the shards would need to be protected, but he did not say they would be reunited."

"I've been hearing a voice—the Voice of the Light," Makasa hurried to tell him. "And so has my brother. That can't be a coincidence, can it? It has to mean something, it just has to.

We've come so far, and you've seen the sketchbook! You knew—*know*—Greydon. Trust me, when we get him and his son back, he can tell you everything."

Galena was beginning to wonder more and more about Aramar's father—he had known *dragons*?

Telagos watched Makasa with keen, bright eyes. "Greydon Thorne is similarly kidnapped?"

"Yes," Makasa said. "And part of our mission is to get him back, but for that we're going to need the shard."

"Indeed . . ." It was not the dragon agreeing, and for a long time he said nothing.

"Then you'll give us the shard?" Valdread asked. It sounded pushy to Galena, but sooner or later they would need to ask.

"It is yours"—Telagos bowed again—"but I go with it. Greydon Thorne asked me to watch over it, and watch over it I shall. If you are truly a friend to him, then you will accept my presence."

Now Makasa paused. "Are you sure?"

Galena squeezed Makasa's arm harder, and she suddenly felt like her human companion was about to push her into the icy water hole. "This will get messy and dangerous, and I'm going to stop at nothing to find my brother, wherever that leads."

"Well, 'tis fortunate, then, that I can fly." Telagos grinned, coolly, and Galena realized that, true to the lore she'd studied, there was a cunning beneath his smile, a cunning that her group would be foolish to underestimate. Maybe Valdread was right.

The skeletons in the shadowy recesses of the cavern were spotless. A dragon had to eat, after all. But they needed the shard, and she knew Makasa wasn't about to tangle with a dragon who could freeze them all with a single breath. Besides, Telagos knew Aramar's father, and if Greydon trusted him, then she imagined Makasa did, too.

"I suppose you can come," Makasa said, though there was an unspoken *but I don't like it* to her tone.

"Of course I can," Telagos stated. "Do not look so fretful— you have asked a great deal of me, and now, in turn, I ask a great deal of you."

He had a point.

"Shard, then," Makasa said. "I guess that means you're coming with us."

Galena gave a not so subtle, "Yes!" under her breath.

"Hackle no club?"

Makasa smirked, watching as Telagos lifted his right hand, then reached into his left sleeve and, with a flourish, produced a gleaming sliver of the blade.

The shard.

Two found, one more to go, and a dragon ally to boot? Now they were getting somewhere. Makasa's grin deepened. "Hackle no club."

CHAPTER TWENTY-NINE
HARD TRUTHS

Tucked against the large, gnarled roots of an oak, Makasa had been studying Aram's sketchbook for clues. Galena had found them a secluded grove in an area of the forest not far from the Glades' cottage. With Ceya's help, Galena brought them into the safest part of the forest, using her abilities to scout a spot away from the prying eyes of the villagers.

Makasa glanced up from the book, finding Valdread looming over her. He did so *love* to loom. He also loved to get a rise out of her. In an unusually good mood (two shards already, and they had only been there for less than three days!), she decided not to take back the arm they had granted him after returning from the cave.

Valdread had, after all, been on his best behavior. And Makasa was not a fool—there was a dragon in their midst now, and even with just one arm, Valdread could hold his own in case Telagos turned traitor.

Valdread grinned. "Going soft, are we?"

"A pretty wise dryad once told me that it was good to be soft. Not all the time, but I think she was on to something."

Valdread nodded.

Behind him, Hackle practiced club moves with Murky, showing the murloc how to give a good swing. Murky was using one of Robertson's toy weapons as a stand-in for the real thing. The two slid back and forth across the grass, Hackle solemnly giving instruction while Murky, face screwed up in concentration, did his best to impress his "frund." Cross-legged in the grass not far from that, Galena and Telagos sat in deep conversation, heads together while Galena showed him her CCAMP manual. Every once in a while a little sparkle of magic came from their direction as they showed off to each other.

"I do believe someone has a crush." Valdread chuckled. "Not a match I'd ever expected to see. A tauren and a dragon."

"He's easy on the eyes," Makasa said with a snort. "But not exactly my type."

"Too verbose?"

"Too proud," she said. If that was what "verbose" meant, anyway. "I think they might just be bookish."

"Dragons tend to be like that. My old SI:7 colleagues would tell me stories of those they had met. More and more had been migrating to Winterspring, and the Alliance needed to be ready to tangle with them, if need be." Valdread turned his attention back to Makasa. "Any luck with the book?"

"Not yet." She sighed. "There are plenty of drawings, but some of them are just . . . nonsensical. Look, this one is just some rock. Thanks a lot, Aram."

The Forsaken gave a hearty laugh, and Makasa had to admit it felt good to impress him. She didn't exactly crave his approval or anything, but he *was* unmistakably dangerous and capable, and every once in a while, he could bring a smile to her face, too.

"I'm beginning to think Greydon must have scattered these pieces all over Lakeshire. If I were him, I wouldn't hide them too far from one another, making it easier to check on them quickly if need be. And if he was the only one aware of the locations, there would be no real danger to his family here." Makasa flipped through the sketches again, finding the same nondescript locations Aram had depicted. "I just keep thinking if I look at these long enough, Aram will, I don't know, speak to me or something. He's been my only family for months; you would think I could read this stuff like tea leaves."

Valdread cleared his throat, moving almost imperceptibly nearer. "You're going to go blind to the information," he said. "Look at anything long enough and it just becomes a blur. Sometimes you need to take a step back." His tone was light, but he seemed oddly intent. "What you need, I think, is a distraction. Like a game. I know, perhaps a game of questions."

"Is this your idea of a joke, old man?" Makasa chuckled. "How are questions a game?"

Sighing, he scratched at his bony chin. "I thought you were smarter than this. Think of how much you can learn, with the right tool applied in the right way."

Makasa studied him. He was a spy. This wasn't just a way to clear her head; he had ulterior motives. He *always* had them. Still, she relished the thought of getting inside his mind, maybe learning a few deep spy secrets. The temptation won out over the quiet voice warning that he was up to something.

"Huh. All right. Who goes first?" she asked, putting down the sketchbook.

"I do," Valdread said, a little smug. "Tell me, how do you take your coffee?"

"Black," she said, but Valdread answered the same in unison.

"I thought I was supposed to ask you something," she said, narrowing her eyes. Valdread shrugged, glancing away.

"My mistake. All right, you ask something," he prompted.

It wasn't hard to come up with her first question for him. "Why are you really helping us?"

He grinned, and it looked something like admiration. "Good question. I always pick the winning side."

Flattery, probably, but Makasa didn't press him on it. Instead, she tried to think like he would. What would flattery get him? What was this game really about? She had to laugh. It was ridiculous, playing a child's game with a lifelong spy and one-time enemy.

"Do you really not know where my brother is?" she asked, not caring if it was her turn or not.

"I may have an idea," Valdread replied. He was skillful in the art of manipulation. All spies were, but to her he seemed genuine. Or at least, like he wasn't trying too hard to lie. "It's my job to understand my enemies and my friends. Ssarbik wouldn't like to know how far I dug into his past. The same goes for Malus. In the end, I've drawn conclusions on how they would proceed."

He cleared his throat, glancing over at Murky and Hackle before asking, "Any strong feelings on bruiseweed?"

"I . . . break out into little bumps." But he already knew that . . . Why bring up bruiseweed again? Oh. She sat up, quickly, spinning to see if she had accidentally plopped down in a bush of it.

"Interesting," he commented, ignoring her panic, no longer scratching his rotting chin but stroking it. "Very interesting. And how do you feel about venison?"

"Can't stand it."

"Seasickness?"

"Not a problem."

"Webbed toes?"

Makasa was going to vomit. This was getting creepy. "How did you know that? Nobody knows that. I've never even shown Aram my weird toes."

Valdread grinned, tilting his head to the side, one piece of dark hair falling roguishly in front of his eyes. "It's your turn," he told her, "to ask a question. That's the game."

Her stomach churned, but she knew what question had to come next. "When we dueled . . . you mentioned the captain of the *Makemba*. How did you know my mother?"

His shrug was all too casual. "I happened to meet her . . . about eighteen years ago."

Eighteen. *Eighteen.* Before she could say another word, Valdread took his turn.

"Tell me," he said softly. "Did you know your father?"

Makasa covered her face with both hands, struggling to breathe. Eighteen years. Her mother. A father. Her father. Reigol Valdread, the Whisper-Man, her father. It wasn't possible, and yet . . . She knew in her souring gut that everything he said made sense. But just because something made sense didn't mean it was fun or exciting. The truth could be comforting, but it could also burn.

No . . . No. She wasn't ready to accept that.

"How?" she asked, peeling her hands away and glaring up at him. "You're— You're—"

"The curse of Lordaeron befell me after I happened to meet

your mother," he said, no longer so glib. An eerie, haunted light came into his eyes at the mention of his undead nature. "It was part of my job, as an SI:7 operative, to investigate rumors of a plague. It was my sworn duty that bound me to this body. For a time, I was a mindless servant of the Lich King, until my mind was restored to me by Lady Sylvanas. None of this"—he gestured at nothing in particular—"was planned. I was not so monstrous. Once."

She found that hard to imagine. And yet, if he was really her father, she wanted to believe that was true. "And Malus? You claim you were not always monstrous, but how did he come to feature so prominently in your life?"

Sighing, he turned away, then paced back toward her. "What life was I to have in this form? I took my leave of Sylvanas, and Stormwind wanted nothing to do with me. I had no choice but to take work where I could find it, to become a mercenary. My only connection to Malus is through coin, and now, through my desire to see him brought low."

Makasa leapt to her feet, dizzy, and stumbled away from Valdread and the tree. Everything he was saying, everything she now knew, was crashing over her like a wave. The truth ought to be illuminating, but she felt plunged into darkness.

"I—I need to be alone."

"Makasa! Wait!"

But he couldn't follow her out of the grove and risk being seen by the village guards. She ran, clutching Aram's book, her feet carrying her a long, long way, until it was dark and she couldn't run anymore, as if somehow, someway, she could outrun the knowledge that an undead mercenary and all-around villain was her father.

Makasa dangled her legs over the edge of the quarry, picking up pebbles and tossing them into the water that filled the abandoned pit. On the *Wavestrider*, Aram had told her about swimming there with Soot, and she could just imagine the two of them, scruffy and ridiculous, paddling around, splashing in the summertime pond until sundown. It was dark, and she couldn't much see the rocks plopping into the surface of the pool, but the sound was satisfying. The rhythm soothed her, the simplicity of it.

Throw. Splash. Plop. Predictable. She did it over and over again, until the nervous churning in her stomach ebbed and she no longer felt the urge to cry. Those days on the *Wavestrider* with Aram and Greydon felt a thousand years away, and almost surreal, as if she had imagined it all—the wind on her face and the salt-sea air filling her lungs. It was hard work, living on a ship, but just like the rocks going into the water, there was a system to it, the same chores day in and day out, the same calluses from the rigging, the same food, and the same shanties.

This was why she hated surprises. She didn't need to know

Valdread was her father. What did it change? Nothing. Greydon Thorne was the father she chose, and that was what mattered. But to know, finally, that Valdread was her kin? She laughed, then spit into the waters of the quarry. "He worked for Malus," she whispered, closing her eyes. "He could have killed us. He *would* have killed us."

Then again, he hadn't. When Drella was threatened, he tried to save her. He seemed truly disgusted at Malus's actions, and had been helpful, if stubborn, since joining their side. She had never allowed herself to really trust him. Could she?

No. He was the enemy. It didn't matter that he had become briefly useful; he had willingly worked for Malus, and that was a black mark that might never be removed. Then again, he had seemingly tried to guide her, mold her, even, into more of a leader. It made sense now, she thought, that he took such an interest in her decisions. He must have known for some time. *Stupid.* That was the word. She felt stupid. There she was, thinking herself so tough, so smart, and all along Reigol Valdread had been untangling the truth, piecing the facts together, and waiting to see if she might make the connections herself.

She hadn't, and now . . . now it was nothing but confusion and emptiness.

Greydon was the father she chose. What did that make Valdread?

It made him a distraction, and coming at the worst possible time.

They were still desperate to find the last shard—upon which the very fate of Azeroth relied, apparently—and Aram and Greydon were still missing. The victory of finding the cave, Telagos, and his precious guarded shard began to vanish. *That boost of excitement didn't last long,* she thought with a sigh, hurling another pebble into the quarry.

She had brought Aram's sketchbook with her when she ran, but it would be impossible to see his sketches in the dark. She realized suddenly that it wasn't the sketches she wished for company, but Aram himself. Her brother, who had similarly been abandoned by one father only to find comfort and guidance in another man, one whose influence had shaped him in more important ways than blood. Was this how Aram felt about Greydon when he first came aboard the *Wavestrider?* Suddenly, his anger, his petulant behavior in those early days, felt somewhat reasonable, at least while she picked through her own feelings about Valdread.

It was growing darker. Soon the lights of the town twinkled in the distance. The wooden houses with their red roofs and glowing windows seemed so cozy and inviting, but she craved solitude. They were wasting time. *She* was wasting time. This trip to Lakeshire was about so much more than just delivering a letter or finding the shards; it was a bridge, a bridge connecting her back to Aram, wherever he was. They had started the journey of the Diamond Blade together, and they would end it that way, too. She promised herself, and him, that.

Aramar's strange drawings filled her head. The rock, the cavern, the dragon, the patch of grass with footprints under the tree, the mine shaft. The rock, the cavern, the dragon, the patch of grass with footprints under the tree, the mine shaft—

The mine shaft.

Makasa stared down into the water; the stars and slivers of moons reflected back, and nothing else. It was like black glass, unbroken now that her pebbles no longer rippled it. She was sitting on the edge of a quarry. The mine shaft . . . It had to be right. She was certain that Aram's sketches were so much more than just mindless doodles. No, they were magic accidents, seemingly random visions that were so much more.

Listen, Makasa. The Voice of the Light split her thoughts, and she winced, grabbing her head. *Listen to me, Makasa, and listen to yourself.*

That she could do. But how? The quarry was flooded, and any mine shafts that might hold the shard would be impossible to reach. She climbed to her feet, staring down into the dark glass of the water, listening, listening to the nighttime noise of the crickets, to the bugs skimming the pool, to the far-off music seeping out from the Lakeshire Inn, to the voice inside herself that told her to trust. Told her to believe.

Aram's letter had led them here, and then his sketches had opened a window into Greydon's mind. Telagos, insufferable or not, was right. Their fates were entwined—with one another, and with this place.

Listen to yourself.

A new star appeared in the water, though this one was gold, not silver. It grew in brightness as she watched. Makasa bent down and picked up a stone, then tossed it into the water where the star had appeared. The ripple passed along the other stars, but not the golden one. A shard. It was there, glowing up at her from deep inside the quarry.

"Your friends are beginning to worry."

She nearly toppled into the water, but spun instead, heart racing, to find Telagos watching her. His hair shone like the silvery stars above them as he swaggered toward her, then leaned over and looked into the water.

"Now *that* is fortuitous," he murmured, seeing what she had.

"No," Makasa said. "It's fate. It's the Voice—it brought me here to find the last shard. It's probably stuck in a shaft at the bottom of the quarry, like in Aram's drawing, but how do we get it?" She glanced over at him. "You didn't happen to bring Murky in that belt of yours, did you?"

"He is rather too slimy. However." Telagos raised his hands, closing his eyes, his face going slack as the air around them grew charged with magic.

Makasa watched as the shard at the bottom of the quarry blurred, something obscuring it. Then, as she stared, a tunnel grew up toward them through the water, a tunnel of ice, and the shard along with it, rushed through the frozen pipe until it flew up out of the pool. With a laugh, Makasa caught it, feeling its warmth as the icy water dripped away. The other shards, hidden in a pouch on her belt, began to vibrate, then grow warm. One by one, the shards flew out of the satchel, racing to meet their long-lost kin. The final piece. She and Telagos watched, silent, awed, as the scattered shards locked together, drawn by some unseen, blinding force, flashing all in unison before melding into one unbroken, beautiful blade.

It landed in the grass at Makasa's side with a soft *tink*.

"I can't believe it," she breathed. "We did it."

"Quite beautiful, a satisfying outcome," Telagos remarked.

"Thank you. I'm glad they sent you to find me."

The dragon boy shook his head, pursing his lips. "Oh no, I came of my own volition. I grew weary of listening to the decomposing one fret. He worries about you. He attempts to conceal as much, but the concern is evident."

Makasa frowned and picked up the reforged blade. The blade in her hands was so warm it was almost too hot to hold comfortably. "He's . . ."

Could she say it? Could she admit it to herself, and more than that, state it aloud?

Fate. The Voice of the Light. If it connected them all together, her, Greydon, Aram, Murky, Hackle, Galena, Drella, Telagos, and . . . Valdread, then her relationship with him was more than just a cruel surprise. It was something more, this knowledge, something meant to be.

"He's my father," she said, and strangely, it only hurt a little.

"Then we should hurry you back to the village," Telagos said, taking her gently by the arm. That he didn't react with disgust to Valdread being her father was . . . surprising, but also oddly comforting. Maybe Telagos wasn't so insufferable after all. Was she going soft? If so, it was Aram's fault—that boy had rubbed off on her in all sorts of incredible, if sometimes insufferable, ways. "Ceya Glade is preparing an elaborate configuration of meat and noodles, and I do wish to study her technique. Human culinary ingenuity is endlessly fascinating."

Makasa snorted, and they started back toward the Glade house together in the dark. "It's a stew, Telagos."

"And? Is that not extraordinary?"

"Sure," she said, looking forward to the warmth of the hearth and of Aram's family, and her friends. "Sure, that is extraordinary. It really is."

CHAPTER THIRTY
VALDREAD'S SECRET

The mood was celebratory in the Glade house that evening, at least for the travelers. It took a moment for the Glades to understand the importance of what had happened, and what it might mean. The children couldn't take it after a spell; impatient for dinner, they scrambled over to the adventurers, lingering just behind Murky and Hackle until they were noticed.

"Dlrga brrlaagrlgl," Murky said, pointing with his thumb over his shoulder.

"Yes." Hackle grunted. "Barnacle back." He swiveled to face the children. "What you want Hackle say?"

"Puppy man!" Selya squealed.

Robb hurried over, wiping his hands on a towel that looked hilariously small in his hands. He had been chopping meat for the stew. "Selya, don't bother them. Come back over to the fire with us."

"Is good, she safe," said Hackle.

"They can be . . . rambunctious." Robb smirked, gazing down at Hackle expectantly.

"Less wild than gnoll pups. Hackle like. Hackle have some of his own some day."

Robb seemed taken aback at that. "You . . . want children?"

Hackle shrugged. "Why no? Hackle brave. Only brave ones have pups."

The children would not be dislodged regardless, and they shrieked with laughter while Murky and Hackle entertained them. Valdread couldn't be sure, but Robb and Ceya seemingly regarded them with less suspicion. The longer the children giggled, the more they laughed, too, even wandering over to listen while Hackle told them all the tale of facing the yetis with Aram.

Their true gesture of goodwill came when Ceya cooked a mouthwatering stew, though Valdread could eat none of it. He dined only on the overjoyed reactions of the humans, dragon, and tauren who ate it. The young boy, Robertson, had been kind enough to fish up a bounty of small lake fish for Hackle and Murky, for they could not do so themselves, the water too exposed and risky for the odd travelers.

Selya regaled them with a song she made up on the spot, the words comprising mainly of praise for Talking Doggy and Frog Friend. Beyond all understanding, the murloc and gnoll had charmed the Glade children, answering a veritable barrage of questions with the utmost patience.

Valdread sat apart, near the window, painfully aware of his own stench and the chilling effect he had on the company. It had ceased to bother him long ago; it was merely a fact of his prolonged, cursed existence. Perhaps it began to irk him, for it had been difficult to watch his daughter avoid him, her nose wrinkling at his approach. He had no idea if he would ever grow to love the girl, or truly be her father in any regular capacity, but he did wish to *know* her. To have a real connection with life, other than beginning it.

When she returned to the cottage, dragon and final shard in tow, she gave Valdread a thin smile. The time alone seemed to have done her some good, and she sat closest to him of anybody, eating a third helping of stew and laughing along to Selya's silly songs.

When the food was cleared and the little girl was done giving her concert, Robb Glade produced a mandolin and played a few skilled tunes while Galena and Hackle helped tidy up. Hackle mostly just licked the plates clean. Robertson and Selya pored over their brother's drawings, trying to pick which they liked best.

"Dead man!" Robertson suddenly screamed.

Ceya spun around, then realized Robertson had found a drawing in Aram's sketchbook. "What was he thinking, drawing . . ."

Her voice trailed off as she reached her son and saw what Aram had drawn. Valdread. It was a clean, precise portrait, capturing the mercenary's roguish smile. Unfortunately, he was seated among Silverlaine and the Hidden. All of their enemies were there, and Valdread unmistakably among them. He winced.

"Oh," she said, fretting. She paced nervously back toward the basin. "You were siding with Silverlaine? Is this—is what Aram drew—"

"I'm sorry I didn't tell you," Makasa protested. "It's— He's— complicated. He was betrayed by Malus and left for dead, and if we hadn't helped, he likely would be. Trust me, he's no friend to those people, not anymore."

Ceya stared down at her washrag. "That sounds . . . very complicated indeed."

"It could be. It doesn't have to be, I think," Makasa said, working it out as she went. "We all have things in our pasts we aren't proud of. Me. Valdread." She closed her eyes. "Greydon. But what we do, how we fix things, that's what matters."

Aram's mother glanced up at her, eyes unreadable.

"I spent many years in service to King Varian Wrynn, before this curse befell me and I fell in with Malus." He looked Ceya in the eye. "I will use the information I know, the skills I have, to find your son." Valdread said it quietly, and for a moment he was sure she would still turn him out of the house.

"Well, I suppose I owe you just as much as the others for helping to bring my boy home." She sighed. "What's past is past."

From her spot near the washing basin, Ceya remarked that it was amazing how many people Aramar had met, and how they had all come to embrace him. Not many boys of twelve could boast so many varied and strange friends. Telagos studied the mandolin, awed by its apparently complex design. Everything, it seemed, was fascinating to the dragon.

The dragon. Valdread did not trust him, but he could not deny the usefulness of such a creature. Nothing struck fear into the hearts of enemies like a dragon—even one as young as Telagos—taking to the field, and his frost breath would prove helpful in controlling the battle. Valdread indulged in a brief moment of whimsy, imagining himself charging blade first at Ssarbik, Telagos soaring above, laying down icy justice while Valdread prepared to make the killing blow—

A blow he could not make without first committing further honesty. What an exhausting day. First, confronting Makasa with their strange connection, and now it was time to come clean, and tell her where Aram and Greydon were being held. It was the final piece, the final card he had to play. Maybe, just maybe, it would win him back his other arm.

All throughout dinner, Makasa could talk of nothing else. They had the shards; it was time to prepare for the final assault and bring Aram and Greydon home. But how? Her eyes had traveled deliberately toward Valdread over the course of this discussion, and the reason was plainly evident: Valdread was one of the Hidden, and surely, cunning as he was, he would have eavesdropped enough to absorb the details of Malus's plans.

Just like her father, she was a quick study. And she was right.

Valdread stood and stretched his one arm over his head, then moved toward the back door. "I believe I shall take some air."

"Not so fast." Makasa, as he knew she would, jumped up to follow. "You're still technically our prisoner. Wouldn't want you wandering off."

"Oh goodness, I had no idea you cared."

She rolled her eyes and followed him out the back. They were safely concealed by the darkness, and the coldness of night drove most villagers inside. Valdread wandered toward the woodshed, taking his time.

"What's this really about?" Makasa asked.

Valdread turned west, imagining he could see the tops of Stormwind's towers, the familiar, comforting sight of them soaring above the trees. When he closed his eyes, he could still smell the sulfur of the forges outside SI:7 headquarters, and the oily tang of sword polish, and the leather of so many well-worn boots. The canals of the city sometimes stank, but that didn't make it any less of a home. That was long ago, and the nostalgia only filled him with anger, anger for what he had lost in service to King Varian Wrynn. What he had lost . . . Valdread sighed out of dead lungs. It was time to let go of what had been taken from him, and turn his attention toward what he still had to gain.

The respect of a daughter. The revenge of a wronged man. The dignity of a soldier.

"Before I tell you what I know, I need you to promise me something," Valdread said, turning his back on Stormwind and facing her.

"And what's that?"

"The hour of battle approaches, Makasa, and you must be ready. Knowing now how we're connected . . ." By the Lady, that was bizarre to say. "I feel a duty to you, a responsibility to make certain that you are prepared in every way. This will not be like the Thunderdrome, or the scuffle at the Northwatch base. This will be the bloodiest battle yet, and many of your friends are likely to die."

"Where are you going with this? We have the shards, we have a *dragon*. It's time to take the fight to Malus."

Just like her mother. He had not known Marjani long, but she had left quite an impression. Impulsive, strong, with a sharp tongue that could slice the flesh off a man's bones if need be . . . and impatient.

"It is *time* to form a plan. And . . . if you're interested, there are some things I might teach you," he said. "But only if you promise to be patient. To strike when the time is right, not when the time is convenient."

She took a step toward him, furious, her hands curling into fists at her sides. "We have no time. I never asked this of you, and what could you teach me anyway?"

"Don't be flippant. You know my skill set. You know my past.

Hate me if you will, but do not discard my advice. You're smarter than that."

"You keep saying that," Makasa muttered. "It's annoying. Maybe I'm not smarter than that, hmm? Maybe I *will* discard your advice."

"You won't. You're smart."

She fell silent, staring at him through the thick darkness. He could see the temptation to scream written all over her face. Her brows were pulled down, her mouth puckered, and those fists of hers were practically banging against her legs in frustration. But Valdread waited. He had meant what he said: She was smart.

"Fine. Fine! I promise to be . . . patient. Whatever that means. Now what did you want to tell me?"

Now came the difficult bit. Valdread coughed into his one hand and glanced at the sky, but nothing was going to give him more courage, and a stiff drink certainly wasn't an option. He had only just somewhat won Makasa to his side; she didn't need to watch wine pour out of every hole in his throat.

The truth, then. It was time.

"I haven't been completely transparent about certain things," he began. "The Thornes, for example. I know where Malus is holding them. They're in Outland, likely near the southern border of Hellfire Peninsula. Malus is too reliant on arakkoa support to go anywhere devoid of their strongholds."

Even in the dark, he saw the hurt flare in her eyes.

"*What?* How could you keep this from me?" Makasa demanded. She looked ready to hit him. "You're . . . you're . . . *my father.*"

"Yes, and like I was in my youth, you're stubborn, impulsive. I knew you would rush out the door without a plan and get yourself killed." Valdread threw up his hand, aggravated.

Makasa's lip quivered, but she somehow managed not to shout. "So what are we up against?"

"Malus isn't who you should be worried about. He's human, and I understand his weaknesses. No, you should be concerned about his master. Xaraax. He's a dreadlord of the demonic Burning Legion, powerful beyond your comprehension, and by comparison Malus is a dimwitted ogre sixteen pints deep."

Her anger quickly turned to unease. "A dreadlord?"

"Of the Burning Legion, yes." He sighed and pushed on. "He's determined to annihilate Azeroth with some kind of magical catastrophe. He called it the Darkstorm, a way to spread the corruption of the Legion across all of Azeroth, wipe out life as we know it here completely."

"Then he has to die."

"You're rushing ahead already! Did you forget your promise to be patient?"

That stopped her dead in her tracks. Makasa turned slowly to peer at him, her face strangely absent of a scowl. She looked only shocked. Or perhaps unnerved.

"What?" he asked. Unseen gears turned in her head and then, unexpectedly, she nodded.

"All right. I'm listening. I'll . . . try to listen. To you. I'll try. But you can't blame me for wanting to hurry. If this is true, our advantages in the battle, like Telagos, mean little."

Valdread nodded, wishing he could put his hand on her shoulder, but he knew neither of them were anywhere near ready for that. He needed to take his own advice. Patience. "Indeed. There *is* so much to do, and the preparations start now. They start with you. We need to reforge that Diamond Blade; without it Xaraax will never be defeated."

"Xaraax. Diamond Blade. Outland, all right. We need a way to get there. And we'll need support, lots of it. Any ideas?"

At that, Valdread's thin lips widened into a smile. "Plenty. Which is why, daughter, we need a plan."

CHAPTER THIRTY-ONE
DEELIVERRGGEEE

Makasa had planned the attack before Valdread even met her in the clearing. He had taught her to study her foes closely, and so she did, noting that he was always on time to their meetings. And so she climbed the tree a quarter of an hour before he arrived, waiting in tense silence, finding a strong but well-concealed branch as her perch. When the time was right, she would slip gracefully out of the tree and finally—finally—get the drop on Valdread.

Just as she expected, he sauntered into the clearing at the appointed hour, a heavy cloak drawn up around his head to hide his rotting face. She could smell the jasmine water on him from her hiding spot, and she nearly coughed. Instead, Makasa held her breath and carefully slid onto a lower branch, trying to get the perfect foothold before she dropped. The leaves around her rustled, but only a little, no more noise than a squirrel might make.

"If you want your opponents to know you're about to strike them this badly, why not just announce it?"

Startled, Makasa lost her footing, tumbling out of the tree and landing on her rump with a yelp. Furious, she leapt back up, finding her balance, knowing she couldn't show another weakness. "You're infuriating!" she yelled, charging him. "I was being eaten alive by bugs up there, and for what?"

He was ready for her onslaught. "Your swing is perfect, but your footwork is sloppy. What's the matter with you today?"

Valdread, even with only one arm, was a formidable dueling partner. Sweaty, out of breath, Makasa called for a time-out, dropping her harpoon and putting both hands on her head, trying to catch her breath.

"How much longer?" she asked him, no, implored him. "I'm ready. I *feel* ready."

"You're ready when I say you are. That tree move was smart, but you botched it at the crucial moment. Still, I like where your head is at."

Blast, but Valdread knew how to get under her skin, and that did it. "Please, remind me again why we're playing games here in Lakeshire while Aram and Greydon rot in Outland?"

As with every day, their sneak-attack duels had an audience. Galena and Telagos, while talking about whatever higher subjects they liked to talk about, looked up, both of them putting down their books. Hackle and Murky stopped their own duel, though Murky got in one last sly swing, hitting Hackle on the knee with his toy club.

"I've been cogitating . . ." Telagos piped up. "Galena informs me that you arrived here in an airship. First, I would very much like to inspect this contraption, and second, it may prove sufficient to fly us to the Blasted Lands."

"What's in the Blasted Lands?" Makasa asked, rolling up her sleeves to vent heat.

"The Dark Portal," Galena replied. "It is deep in the ruinous valley, surrounded by demons of all sort."

"And this portal can take us to Outland?" Makasa prompted.

Telagos grinned, adjusting the collar of his doublet beneath his scaly armor. "Ah! Indeed! It is certainly the most expedient route to Outland, unless we were to somehow acquire passage to Northrend, then to Dalaran, and then convince an archmage—"

Makasa held up her hand. "So the Dark Portal is our best bet. And you know the way?"

"I do," Telagos replied serenely.

She could feel Valdread's eerie glowing eyes boring into the back of her head. It really wasn't necessary; she had taken her promise to heart. She was listening, learning, and trying to be patient. She could see in the light of day that they'd have one shot at defeating Malus and his master, and they needed to be clever.

"That still leaves us short an army," Valdread mumbled.

Not many boys of twelve could boast so many varied and strange friends. Ceya's words came back to Makasa in a rush. She turned to Murky, who suddenly seemed to have the same idea.

"Murky mirga mmmurloks flegl, amagloo blrrrrrr!" It was Hackle's turn to get in a quick smack while Murky weighed in on their predicament. The murloc rubbed his injury, pouting at his gnoll friend.

Makasa understood a few choice words in that sentence. *Murloc*, for example, and *army*.

"But how?" Makasa asked.

Murky gave one of his short, bubbly laughs and pointed due east. "Mrggl mirga, Evrgil mmmurloks, perlooga legleg. Murky gerla flllrrrla glooga brbrrrg Mrrrla!"

She looked to Hackle on that one; she was still not quite as advanced when it came to Murky's language. Hackle nodded along, then clawed at his furred chin in thought. "Murky say Everstill murlocs not far to east. He go visit, ask for help. His cousin Merla lost once, end up here, have tadpole that live there."

"Maybe the familial connection will move them to assist us," Valdread said, sounding just as thoughtful and intrigued as Hackle.

"Indeed, Mistress Glade rightfully noted the number of unlikely allies your Aramar Thorne made on his journey," Telagos noted. "The human may have stumbled upon the answer."

Hackle raised his club, jabbing it excitedly skyward. "Hackle know Woodpaw loyal. Woodpaw brave. Woodpaw gnolls help club Malus to save Aram! Aram help Woodpaw gnolls and yetis be friends, fight Gordunni ogres. Woodpaw gnolls and yetis now help Aram!"

"But how would we reach them?" Galena asked, standing and wandering into the middle of the clearing to stand near Makasa. The tauren had changed out of her heavy Cenarion robes, dressed in a simple, pretty linen frock.

"Deeeeliverrrrggeeeeee!" Murky hopped up and down, miming something like a bird with his free hand.

"What is he trying to say?" Makasa asked, but Hackle was helpless.

"Sprockle deeeeliverrrgeee! Deelivergee!"

Makasa was growing impatient, which she was working on, and knelt, beckoning the little murloc closer. "Are you saying delivery? Yes, Murky, that's what we need to do, deliver messages to the gnolls, the yetis, everyone who helped us along the way."

"Hackle know!" The gnoll pointed to the north, toward the mountains. "Metal gnome man, he make machine, win big prize. Goblin man no shut up about it at Overlook."

It struck her like lightning. Makasa gasped, whirling to face Valdread, all of her impatience gone, replaced with hope. "Gazlowe and Sprocket won the MEGA event with some kind of delivery contraption. DLVR-E. Hackle's right; he was babbling on about it when he picked us up. They have a whole fleet of them. They might be fast enough to deliver the messages in time."

Valdread smirked, nodding once. She hated to admit it, but the look of pride he gave her felt pretty nice. "It could just work, especially if it means we get an army of angry yetis."

"Then it's settled." Makasa stood, pointing to each of her companions in turn. "Murky, you sneak off east, ask the Everstill murlocs for help. Hackle? You prepare a message for your clan. Galena? I need you to fetch Gazlowe and tell him our plan. Telagos will guide us to the Dark Portal, and with any luck our friends will be there to fight with us." Then she glanced over her shoulder at Valdread. "And then—"

"And then we're ready," he said solemnly. "Let the final preparations begin."

CHAPTER THIRTY-TWO
A DRYAD'S GIFT

The fever didn't abate. The pain was spreading. Aramar Thorne clutched his leg, gritting his teeth. He was going to die in that cell, taken by infection. His eyes closed on their own, and he was too weak even to call out to his father, who slept fitfully in the neighboring cell.

This was not how he wanted to die. What was it his father had said? *A Thorne should die with a sword in hand . . .* How could the Voice of the Light have been wrong? How could it lead him here?

The pain was blinding. Incredible. He rolled onto his back, desperate, hot beads of perspiration rolling down his cheeks. Then he was freezing cold. Then hot again. He tried to go somewhere else, anywhere else, to escape the pain.

How? he thought. *How can it end this way?*

It does not end this way.

Ha. He really was dying, he thought. He was even hallucinating! Drella's voice echoed around the chamber, as clear as a bell.

Everything is dark. I'm sorry, Drella, I'm sorry. I failed you, just like I failed everyone else.

There in the darkness, gripped with fever, Aram could swear he felt Drella's hand take his and squeeze. Then her voice flashed through him again, just as powerful as when the Voice of the Light called.

Use your gift, Aramar. Use our bond.

Aramar shivered, wishing he could understand . . . the gift. The gift! With the last of his strength, he reached into his pocket, drawing out the flower. It glowed warm at his touch, soothing. Without thinking, he pressed it hard against the tear in his trousers near the knee, smashing it against the cut that had gotten so swollen and infected. For a moment nothing happened, but then, gradually, he felt a cool sensation spread across his skin. The fever lifted, the weakness in his limbs easing. As he held the flower there, he felt the swelling go down, the wound no longer sweltering to the touch.

Then, like magic, it was healed.

Aramar smiled in the darkness, taking the gift and clutching it to his heart. Drella was with him there in his cell; she was with him so long as he cherished her last gift.

"You really think this will work?"

Sprocket turned with a whirring of gears and mechanical clicks toward Gazlowe. They stood in the hazy, glow-bug-filled gloom of twilight, the DLVR-E systems calibrated and ready to fly.

"This is an award-winning invention—"

Sighing, Gazlowe shoved his hands into his pockets. "Not that, the . . . this! This harebrained plan. You think it's got a shot of working? Because I'm not feeling any closer to my diamonds."

Sprocket considered his question for a long time. Serious questions deserved measured thought. This was how he approached his inventions. One careful decision, one methodical experiment at a time.

"The odds are difficult to calculate," Sprocket replied.

"Yeah? Not for me. What did Flintwill say again? A dreadlord of the Burning Legion? I wouldn't want to go up against whatever that is." Gazlowe had brought a bottle of his favorite port from the *Cloudkicker*, and it rested on the storage crates for the DLVR-E systems. He pulled the cork with his teeth and took a swig. "Kinda . . . kinda feels like these kids are doomed."

Sprocket lowered his mechanical legs a touch, bringing himself face-to-face with one DLVR-E that didn't seem to be quite level. The machines needed to be in perfect condition before leaving, or risk never reaching their destinations. "And you will have taken a risk with no reward. I see your hesitation."

"Right? I'm right, right?" Gazlowe snorted. "Don't tell Charnas about this. He's too sentimental."

"He is fond of Thorne; it's true." The DLVR-E leaned back to the right, perfectly flat as it hovered, waiting to be dispatched. Sprocket glanced over at Gazlowe. He could see the goblin working on more reasons to drop out of the plan. "And if I understood Makasa correctly, they can't really get the Diamond Blade unless they confront this Xaraax."

At that, Gazlowe groaned. "Sure. Of course. There's always a catch. I'm starting to think this diamond thing isn't even real."

Sprocket turned away, smirking. "But you know, there are benefits to sending out the fleet. *Lucrative* benefits."

Gazlowe's ears perked up at that. "Say again?"

"Well, usually when you help, you know, *save the world*, people give you some kind of reward. Can you imagine the kinds of treasure we might get for helping with their little quest?"

It was partially true, of course, what he had just told Gazlowe. Sprocket didn't really care much about the Diamond Blade. He had easily inferred, with his superior and scientific mind, that the Diamond Blade was likely a magical relic, and not simply a sword made from precious stones. But dispatching these systems was a challenge—one that might bring fame to his inventions—and Sprocket loved a challenge. Plus, these were good kids, and they were trying to do the right thing. Yet if Gazlowe decided not to lend assistance, then Sprocket would have no reason to send the machines at all.

A minor deception, Sprocket reasoned, for the greater good.

Or maybe just *his* good. He looked toward the village, thinking of the strange children that were so determined to risk everything for their mission. Yes, the greater good.

"Gazlowe."

"Yeah?" He joined Sprocket at the machines, gazing up at them.

"I have made a calculation. Your odds of coming into a fortune—diamond or otherwise—increase by sixty-seven percent if we assist Makasa and her companions."

Gazlowe rubbed his chin, his eyes suddenly glittering, filled with the dream of diamonds. "Sixty-seven percent, eh? Huh. I'm liking those odds better. All right, fine, Sprocket, send your little machines out."

Grinning inside his suit, Sprocket felt a twinge of glee, sending the first of the DLVR-E machines soaring into the air. "I'm going to be famous," he murmured.

At his side, Gazlowe gave a hoot. "And I'm going to be rich!"

The candles burned low, the shadows on the kitchen table growing longer and longer until at last, it was night. Makasa stared at the parchment laid out before her—their approach, their strategy, who would rush who and what weapons they would use, the best-case scenarios and the far bleaker contingencies. All of it had been carefully planned.

Makasa at last understood why Valdread wanted her to be

patient, because now they had two meticulous plans. If their allies arrived in time for the battle, then they would proceed one way; if not? Well . . .

Makasa glanced at her crew. At Hackle, curled up near the hearth, sharing a rug with Soot, whom he had grudgingly come to tolerate, even if he couldn't understand why the dog took orders from the family. Galena and Telagos dozed in the corner, books open and propped on their legs. Murky was still gone, and Makasa could only hope he returned soon and in one piece. The undead man sat across from her, who'd offered many valuable and unexpected insights as she plotted out each step.

All the pieces were on the board; now it was time to put them in motion.

"Makasa . . ."

She nodded, hanging her head.

"It's not great," she said, motioning to their contingency plan. "But it's something. We can't expect anyone to help us, and I just don't think we can wait any longer."

The messages had been sent. Sprocket was more than happy to put his DLVR-E fleet to the ultimate test, plugging in locations remotely so the speedy little disks could fly to the delivery points across the sea. Six, nearly seven days had passed. So much time. Would Aram still be alive by the time they reached Outland? Of course he would be. Makasa had decided long ago that if her brother died, she would sense it. Their connection through the shards, the Voice, and as family would tell her. She couldn't explain it, but she knew he was still out there.

Waiting.

"Do you think Malus will expect us to come after him?" she asked.

Valdread considered this with his chin propped in his one hand. "No, I don't think he will. He's arrogant. It doesn't matter that you've nearly stopped him so many times. He left you alive at the Northwatch encampment, and that tells us much. He doesn't consider you all a threat. More than that, even if he knew I was alive, he doesn't have the imagination to consider we would ever make an alliance."

"It *is* pretty unlikely," Makasa teased.

"All the better for us. Unpredictability may win us the day." Valdread's voice dropped, growing hoarser. "May."

They both knew victory lived in the slim margin between extreme luck and almost assured catastrophe.

"You don't have to help us," she reminded him. "We . . . The odds aren't in our favor. You could just leave."

"Now, why would I do that?" Valdread chuckled and nudged her shoulder, a nudge she should have minded more. "Ssarbik needs to be taught a lesson. Malus had me flung off a cliff and left me for dead. And I'm not so keen on letting Azeroth be destroyed anymore; I rather like some of the people here. Besides, I'm already dead, Makasa; what could be worse?"

"Torture? Prolonged, eternal torture at the hands of a demon army?"

Valdread raised both shabby brows. "Our resemblance becomes more unmistakable by the day."

Makasa rolled up their battle plan, tucking it under one arm. A chair screeched behind them, and she turned to find Ceya Glade watching them from the kitchen. Her eyes fell on Makasa and Valdread as they pushed away from the table, nodding toward the back door.

"I'll just be outside; someone should keep watch for the murloc," Valdread said.

He dodged around Ceya, then vanished silently into the night. Aram's mother slid up to the table, a dishrag flopped over one shoulder. For a moment, she just drank in the sight of the strange children she had temporarily adopted. Every meal, she cooked. She helped them with laundry. She let her children play fight with Hackle and Murky. Her home was open to them, and Makasa still marveled at her generosity. Her strength.

Drella was right. Strength could be soft. It could be a warm slice of bread with honey in the morning. It could be lovingly made stew at night. It could be the offer of shelter and the kindness of a hearth.

"We'll be out of your hair soon," Makasa said quietly. "Thank you, Ceya, for everything you've done."

Ceya nodded, biting down on her lip. "Just tell me how many meals I should pack."

"You don't have to—"

"But I do. You've all been working so hard. You don't think I see it, but I do. My son is out there somewhere. Greydon is out there. The day you showed up on our doorstep, you promised to bring Aramar home."

Makasa risked putting a hand over Ceya's on the table. "And I will keep that promise."

"The way you bring him home is with your feet, with your hands, with that harpoon you carry everywhere. My way of bringing him home is with this." She took her free hand and flipped it palm up. "Food. Shelter. Hope. If I can give you all those things, then I will."

"We have a good plan," Makasa assured her. "It will work."

"I saw you dashing off all those messages," Ceya said with a smile. "Who are they for?"

"It was your idea."

Ceya blinked. "Mine?"

"Yes. You were telling us at supper one night how Aramar made all these unusual friends, and he put them in his sketch-book to remember forever. Well, we're hoping they remember him, too. We sent a fleet of flying machines to his allies, and we asked them for help. For Aramar."

Ceya's eyes filled with tears, and she pressed her knuckles to her lips. "Do . . . do you think they'll come?"

"If they can, then they will. That's why we haven't left yet," she explained. "We're giving them time to meet us in the Blasted Lands."

"That doesn't sound very cheery."

Makasa smirked. "They'll do it," she said. "For your son."

It was hard to say good-bye, but the zeppelin was waiting, and Murky's gamble had paid off: Every available Everstill murloc in fighting form agreed to help, mustering in the hills near the *Cloudkicker*. (Apparently, the murlocs were less impressed with Murky's familial connection than they were with his heroic exploits as "Murky the Unstung." They wanted to seek glory, too, and they couldn't get that by harassing the humans of Lakeshire.) Even if no one else came, at least they would have a small army of murlocs helping them fight. Gazlowe needed to return to Gadgetzan, and he agreed to drop them off at the Dark Portal, but that was it. After all, he was a lover, not a fighter, and he had already performed too many favors.

"I have a reputation to protect!" he told Makasa. "But I'll do this one last thing for ya. Let's bring that kid home."

The Glade family joined them at the clearing where Gazlowe, Sprocket, and Charnas had been hiding the *Cloudkicker*. It was yet another astonishing sight for the Glades, particularly

Robertson and Selya, the little boy proclaiming that he would make one of those someday, but bigger and covered in swords.

The airship hovered just off the ground, the massive spinning turbines flattening the sparse grass in the rocky clearing. Gazlowe, Charnas, and Sprocket helped the Everstill murlocs board. A line of yellow and green murlocs, decked out in their finest armor, spears, and nets, steadily filed up the ladder and onto the ship. Murky watched over their progress proudly, his little chest puffed out as he helped them up onto the ladder.

Makasa waved him over, and the murloc joined their group, the Glades on one side, the odd assortment of travelers facing them.

Ceya darted forward to hug Makasa, holding her for a long time. "I think I shall miss having you all here."

"The larder certainly won't miss them," Robb teased, clapping Hackle on the back.

"Just think of it! What other woman in Lakeshire can boast of hosting a tauren, a dragon, a pirate, a gnoll, a murloc, and a—" She glanced precariously at Valdread.

"A baron," he supplied with a polite half bow.

"Yes," Ceya said. "A baron."

"Thanks again for everything; we couldn't have done this without you." Makasa hugged the woman back, seeing in her such warmth. Aram really was lucky. Murky burst into tears, throwing his slender, slimy arms around Selya and Robertson, who also were inconsolable at their parting.

"The next time we see you," Makasa said, pulling away and hefting her harpoon, "it will be with Aram and Greydon."

"Please be careful, and thank you. I know Greydon and Aram would be touched to know you were risking so much for their sakes," Ceya said, waving as the group gave their last hugs and good-byes, Robb eventually peeling his children away from Murky and Hackle.

A palpable bittersweetness hung in the air. Makasa boarded the ship last, hesitating, not only because she hated flying but because she would genuinely miss the Glades. They were nothing like her family. Less exciting, maybe, but steady, more reliable. If she could have Ceya's stew for dinner every single night, she would.

And beyond missing them, she knew what boarding the *Cloudkicker* meant for her personally, and for Aram's chances. Even if she promised Ceya over and over again that her son would be okay, Makasa knew there was a good chance none of them would ever see Lakeshire again. Valdread was right—a bloody and terrible battle loomed, and it would take equal parts luck and skill to get out of it alive.

With tears stinging her eyes, Makasa left the safety of the ground, watching from the deck of the *Cloudkicker* as the Glades grew smaller and smaller, the ship roaring into the air, Robertson and Selya waving, she knew, until long after they could see the zeppelin.

With so many new companions, the *Cloudkicker* felt a mite

cramped, but they managed, dividing into cabins as best they could, Murky deciding to stay with his brethren and get to know them better.

"You have to hand it to the little guy," Valdread said as a dozen or so murlocs crammed into one small cabin and began chattering away. "He came through."

"Murky once saved Aram from a whale shark in the Shimmering Deep," she said. "He's small, but he *always* comes through."

"What do you think we'll find at the Dark Portal?" he asked, leaning onto the railing as the *Cloudkicker* looped over the town and headed south. They had a long way to go, and Makasa was just thankful they didn't have to make the journey on foot.

"Hope for the best; plan for the worst," she said. The verdant forests of Lakeshire gave way to the darker green smudges of a swamp. Makasa closed her eyes, feeling the cool air rush fast against her face, rustling her hair and the gold hoop earrings she wore every day. "But I just—I just . . ."

"Yes?"

"I've been to exotic places, met fascinating people, seen wondrous things in my travels. Each new experience I thought of as isolated: a pretty bead in a jeweler's drawer—separate, never strung together to mean something bigger. But since the *Wavestrider* sank, since the Voice of the Light began guiding me and Aram, I've started to think about it more."

Valdread nodded, silent.

"Flipping through Aram's sketchbook has made me string the beads of our adventures together and look at the whole of it. I don't know if I believe in fate or anything like that, but I have to think this is all happening because something or someone is making it happen. That we're *meant* to stand against Malus and reforge the Diamond Blade, that we've done what we've done and met who we've met so that we'll have allies in our fight."

"Your optimism is impressive," Valdread said with a short laugh. "But better to expect the worst, like you said. Even if those flying contraptions delivered every single message—"

"I know," she murmured. "I know. They would have to cross an entire sea, and I'm not sure how good gnolls are with seafaring. Or yetis, come to think of it. Perhaps Magistrix Elmarine can portal them, if she gets the message in time."

"If we can free Aramar and Greydon, then we can add two more to our number," he pointed out. "That's why it's in our battle plan, Makasa: It could be enough to tip the balance. And I'm confident Throgg is winnable to our side; Malus disrespected the ogres' traditions when he declared himself king of Dire Maul, and then he used the ogres for his own ends. His friend Karrga is less certain; she's inexplicably loyal to Malus. How anyone can still follow him after they saw him just cast me aside . . ."

"What you did was hard," Makasa said. "Standing up for

Drella, trying to save her life—I never properly thanked you for that. You should give yourself more credit."

Valdread stared. "Was that a compliment?"

"I'm going belowdecks. This might be our last chance to rest up."

Her words proved prophetic. A storm thundered over the Swamp of Sorrows, rocking the ship so badly Makasa feared it might fall out of the sky. Makasa clung to her cot, listening to the army of murlocs on board burble and shout with fear. Side to side, side to side, the ship tossed, then dipped up and down. The wind whistled hard, tearing at them from the north.

"It's our lucky day, boys! We ride this squall all the way past Nethergarde!"

Gazlowe whooped and hollered on the deck, and she heard him prancing around in the storm, doing a little jig. She had no idea what Nethergarde was or how the goblin could be so cheerful about the storm until she felt the whole ship accelerate, pushed along at speed by the wind gusting from the north. They were going to reach the Dark Portal in a day if they kept up that pace.

But eventually the storm ceased, leaving them all in sudden and eerie silence. Makasa crawled, woozy, out of her cot and peered out the porthole. The last sludgy pocket of water from the swamp oozed against a rising set of hills, the soil turning from dark, loamy brown to red. The whole landscape to the south looked as if it had been dyed with blood, nothing but the hardest scrub bushes daring to grow. Night fell slowly around the ship, and Makasa returned to her cot, forcing herself to close her eyes and sleep. By the time dawn came, they would have reached the portal, and she had every intention of meeting the enemy rested and strong. Trained. Prepared. She was a better fighter now, honed by Valdread, and she was ready to show Malus all the deadly tricks she had learned.

Closing her eyes, she concentrated on the gentle hum under her head. She had placed the reforged blade of the Diamond Blade under her pillow for safekeeping. The blade seemed to warm under her as she pulled the blanket up around her neck and tried to sleep. Maybe it sensed it was almost time to become whole, to end Xaraax and the threat to Azeroth.

"I'm coming, Aram," she whispered to the darkness. "Just hold on. I'm coming."

CHAPTER THIRTY-THREE
DESPERATE ALLIANCES

The dry red stones of the Blasted Lands seemed even more bleached and desolate under a cloudless sky. The sun beat down on them mercilessly, baking all the passengers aboard the *Cloudkicker* as it eased southwest, passing over sharp hills, red boars, and pockets of Alliance patrols traveling the roads. They looked tiny from the sky, those soldiers, like toys. Valdread closed one eye and placed his thumb out in front of him, pretending to rub out the patrol. The view from the *Cloudkicker* made one feel godlike, and everything below inconsequential.

Valdread was getting a taste for air travel, but sadly it was soon to be over.

The Dark Portal bled into view: a tall, strange window set against the mountainside. From that distance, it simply looked like a massive door, but the unsettling, swirling mass inside it hinted at its dangers and its mysteries.

He had heard plenty of tales of Outland, some from those that had been there and seen it with their own eyes, but he had never thought to go there himself. The portal itself was far larger than he expected, flanked by two solemn statues, hooded figures with hidden faces and glowing eyes. A massive snake was carved along its top, coiled as if ready to strike.

Soon they would know the odds. Soon, at least, the wondering would be at an end.

"Here."

Valdread turned to find Makasa Flintwill standing behind him, holding a familiar hand out to him. Familiar because it was his own. Smiling, he accepted the gift, then with a mighty twist, reattached the arm at the shoulder socket. Flexing his hand and then stretching, he felt, at last, whole.

"You earned it," she said. "You're part of the crew now. Don't make me regret it."

Nodding, he turned back around, and she slid up to the railing next to him. He noticed more things about her every day. She had her mother's hair and dark, even skin, but she had his narrow, elegant nose and proud chin.

"Look at that thing," she breathed, catching sight of the portal. "I didn't think it would be so, so—"

"Intimidating?"

"Yeah." She gulped. "I can't believe we have to walk through that."

"Close your eyes when we do," he suggested. "Traveling

through portals is disorienting. You can get turned around, twisted. You'll feel less nauseous on the other side if you just keep your eyes closed."

"I don't think I'd want to look anyway."

He watched her squint into the distance and knew at once what she was searching for. She cupped a hand over her eyes, worrying her bottom lip.

"You didn't really think they would come, did you?" he asked softly.

"I guess I did. Stupid, huh?"

Valdread shook his head. "A good leader tries for every advantage. You did the right thing, trying to acquire their aid."

"I just hope they tried to get here, you know? Even if they couldn't quite make it in time, I hope they tried."

"Tell yourself they did, if that makes it easier to face the fight ahead."

She was tough for a kid. Tougher than he had been at seventeen. She would have trounced him easily in a fight, were they of the same age. Makasa had inherited her mother's build, excellent for one-on-one combat, a brawler's stature. Somehow that didn't make her any less quick with a blade, or harpoon, and he admired that.

"Ready the others," he said. "This is your command, not mine."

Makasa gave a weak smile. "An army of murlocs at my beck and call. Think they'll name me queen?"

"That depends. How are your net-mending skills?"

She chuckled and turned away, going to muster the full might they had brought aboard the *Cloudkicker*. It wasn't much, Valdread thought, but if they were smart, fast, and coordinated, they might just surprise Malus before he could mount a proper defense. There was always a chance that Malus had sent some of his agents away. It would make sense, in fact, for him to send out seeking fingers, looking, looking, spying to try and divine just where Makasa had gone with the missing shard from Aram's compass.

That must have put him in quite the rage, Valdread thought, *arriving back in Outland only to discover that the compass didn't have any of its magic left*. He only hoped he got to rub it in the captain's face, and let him know it was stuck to Valdread's boot all along.

The ship began its descent, the portal growing in size and doom as they drew up closer to it. A few scattered and abandoned command tents littered the field in front of the portal. Loud, throbbing energy hummed from the depths, its strange, black surface tinged with pale green along the edges, where portal met stone. He shivered, dreading it, wishing there had been another way to their destination. It would be a story for the ages, though, provided he survived long enough to make use of the tale.

"Hey, where's the welcome wagon?" the goblin Gazlowe shouted from the helm. He, like Valdread, had noticed the emptiness of the valley below. No gnolls. No yetis. Help had not come.

"Where is everyone?" the artist, Charnas, added, hoisting himself up to the railing to look over the edge. "Aram took the time to draw them all, to help them, that must mean something!"

"Try telling that to a yeti," Valdread drawled, strolling up to peer over the tops of their green heads. "Perhaps young Aramar should have given them a few bear carcasses instead of the gift of his talent."

Charnas muttered, "So ungrateful."

"It *was* a long shot," Valdread reminded them. "Powerful as your invention may be, Sprocket, Kalimdor is halfway across the world. We will simply have to rely on ourselves, and thankfully, you all have me. I'm practically a one-man army."

"Sure. Good thing you got all your parts back or you'd be a one-*armed* army," Gazlowe muttered, holding his nose while Sprocket and Charnas chortled.

"Would you four get serious? This isn't funny."

Makasa had a point. She had organized their small force, the murlocs in uneven ranks behind Murky, spears at the ready, Galena, Telagos, and Hackle waiting in a line by the ladder. The druid fidgeted nervously, tugging on her dark braids, while Hackle smacked the butt of his club, ready for battle.

"Taking us down. Hold on to your butts," Gazlowe called.

The *Cloudkicker* jerked to the side, then lowered more elegantly, at last hovering several feet off the ground, red dust rising in a hazy circle around them.

"This is as far as I go," Gazlowe said, leaving the helm to say good-bye to Makasa and the others. He extended his hand, but Makasa swooped down, pulling him into a hug. "Unless you're hiding diamonds somewhere. That's my price, you know? I don't do things for free."

"You've done more than enough," she said. "We wouldn't have made it here without you. I promise you'll get . . . We'll pay you back somehow."

"Have courage!" Charnas called, watching as the murlocs began scampering down the ladder. Galena and Telagos followed, then Hackle and Murky, who had been delayed saying good-bye to their friends.

Valdread went last, weapons strapped to his back, the dry red dust obscuring the way down, making it look as if they were climbing into a sandstorm. Well, they were dropping into a storm, certainly, for nothing but chaos and uncertainty awaited them on the other side of the Dark Portal. From below, where the ladder disappeared into the gritty haze, he heard Makasa cry out. Had she fallen?

He dropped down nimbly, waiting for the dust to clear as the *Cloudkicker* rose again, hovering above them. Slowly, Valdread saw the veil of red dust lift, revealing the command tents he had seen from the sky. He had seen the tents, certainly, but not what was inside.

Makasa had not fallen and hurt herself, no. She had called out in joy, finding squads of volunteers waiting for them. The messages had not been sent in vain. The gnolls had come, and so had the yetis, and the four bat-winged wyverns, one larger and three younger beasts, waiting under the tents, making camp, no doubt seeking reprieve from the harsh sun.

"Who are all these people?" Valdread asked, noticing a mismatched pair that had marked their arrival—a gloriously bearded tauren and a rather glamorously beautiful high elf. A stout, dangerous-looking quilboar stepped out from behind the elf, bristling.

"Friends," Makasa whispered. "That's . . . The tauren is Wuul Breezerider, and the elf is Magistrix Elmarine. The spiky one is Shagtusk. You might remember her from the Bone Pile."

Valdread noticed that the tauren was missing one leg. *Where have I seen him before?* When Wuul caught the undead's lingering gaze, the tauren beat his hand against his chest and shouted, "I survived the gladiator arena of Dire Maul. Keep looking at me like that, dead man, and I'll split your skull for you!"

Valdread smiled. "Impressive."

The group rushed ahead, but Valdread took his time, aware that his presence might only arouse suspicion.

"Sivet!" Hackle hurled himself into the yipping and cackling gnoll army. "Jaggal! You come!"

"Yes, we come; we not miss battle!" Sivet called. She had a more feminine voice than Hackle, and wore a charming necklace of severed fingers and ears of various origin. She wielded a club, too, as well as the larger gnoll, whom Hackle had called Jaggal. They all embraced warmly, though none quite shed a tear. That would have been a sight to see.

The yetis emerged from their larger, taller tent, roaring with eagerness. They were led by the largest creature Valdread had laid eyes on—larger than Throgg or Karrga, brown-furred and heavily scarred, with giant, sweeping horns rising from his head, the color of a cloudy sky.

Makasa appeared at his side. She had explained their connection to these assorted creatures while they made their battle plan, but now she pointed out faces and names for him. "Those are the Woodpaw gnolls, Hackle's clan, and that's Feral Scar; he leads the yetis in Feralas."

"Suggul! Kureeun!" Murky exploded out of the band of murlocs, leaping into the arms of another large gnoll.

It was quite the reunion, and even Makasa clapped hands with the leaders of the gnoll pack, their meeting more civil and less emotional.

"How did you get here so fast?" Makasa asked Sivet.

The petite gnoll smiled up at her, flashing razor-sharp white teeth. "Feral Scar make deal with pirate. Feral Scar pound pirate into dust if not help. They give ship."

"That's . . . not making a deal." Makasa snorted.

Sivet didn't seem to care. "Jaggal get sick on water, so, so funny! All get good laugh!"

She did an impression of the gnoll vomiting and moaning in pain. "Good laugh!"

"Not sick, not weak," Jaggal insisted with a huff.

Wuul, Elmarine, and Shagtusk joined them, the tall, graceful elf sweeping a bow as she came. "I offered to portal them after I received your message, but they were rather more fixated on forceful persuasion."

"Whatever happened, we're glad you're here," Makasa said. She reentered one of the command tents, and introduced the Woodpaw gnolls, Feral Scar and his yetis, the wyverns, Wuul, Shagtusk, and Elmarine to the Everstill murlocs, and then to the new additions to their troop. (Telagos and Galena both seemed quite taken with the high elf.) It took quite a long time, for the scorpion-tailed wyverns, Old One-Eye and her cubs, had to be explained, and then the volunteers had to be introduced to the plan.

"Telagos is a blue dragon," Makasa explained. An "oooh" of appreciation chased around the assembled armies. "And this is Galena Stormspear, a tauren druid with the Cenarion Circle. And this is Baron Reigol Valdread. He . . . takes some getting used to."

Thank you for the glowing recommendation.

"At your service," Valdread said gallantly, bowing, hoping to salvage the mediocre introduction. Dozens of angry animal eyes stared back at him. A gnoll in the back growled. "I don't work for Captain Malus anymore," he said. "And I know my appearance takes some . . . getting used to, but I assure you, I'm more than ready to risk everything for the cause."

Nobody seemed charmed.

Hackle bristled, raising his club. "At first! Hackle no like Stinky Man. Is true, he stink, he ugly, he missing many part. Once, Hackle try to club on head, but now Hackle know, and Hackle trust. Gnolls and yetis and wyvern, quilboar, and tauren trust, too, or Hackle club *you*."

"I appreciate that, friend," Valdread murmured.

That seemed to be good enough for the assorted creatures, who no longer stared at him with such open hostility. Makasa barreled along, kneeling, clearing a flat space in the dirt and revealing their battle map.

"Valdread thinks Malus and Xaraax will have the bulk of their armies here, between Falcon Watch and this bramble arak-koa stronghold to the south," she said, pointing, and the soldiers crowded around her, straining to see over one another. "Don't worry, we have a long march to get there; you will all get a chance to see the map. Telagos, the wyverns, and a few of the fastest gnolls will scout ahead, clearing out anything that might get in our way. We want to move fast and reach Falcon Watch before Malus can get organized. Be ready for a swift journey. Get rest now; we leave through the portal in two hours."

Hackle fell in with the Woodpaw, barking directions. They reignited their campfires, assembling spit roasts they had been using while they waited for the *Cloudkicker* to arrive. Water and food were passed around, and the battle map, Murky proudly displaying it to his cohorts and explaining to them what to expect.

The rest of their crew grouped up under their own tent, silent, heads bowed as they sat on half-demolished benches. Magistrix Elmarine joined them. Nobody seemed interested in eating the food Ceya Glade had packed for them. Rummaging in his bag, which had been returned to him shortly after his final arm, Valdread withdrew a small flask, bit off the cork, and downed the last of what was inside. It had been years since his living taste buds could savor the drink, but the comfort of the action eased his restless mind.

"I can't believe we're so close to Outland," Galena breathed, covering her face in fear or excitement, perhaps both. "What will we see? What will it be like? I've heard so many stories—strange creatures and plants, so many new things to catalog and study. I only wish we had more time."

"Survive this assault and you can return to catalog bugs and weeds until you're old and gray," Valdread teased.

Galena frowned at him. "You shouldn't say such things. We are going to win . . . aren't we?"

She looked to Makasa for reassurance. But the ex-raider simply pressed her lips together and stared at the ground. "I don't know, Galena, I can't possibly know that. All we can do is try."

"Come now," Valdread said, shocked that they were the glum ones for once. He wasn't exactly hopeful, but the most crucial element of any battle was controlling morale. "You have struck against Malus countless times, but only on your own. There are more of you now, many more, and he has no idea that you've practically assembled a working army. Besides, nobody remembers battles where the odds were fixed. This will be a subject of legends, of songs and tales for years to come. Imagine it: an unlikely alliance, assembled at the last moment, a ragged band of mismatched travelers facing off against a demon army and its vicious leader."

The others stared up at him in wonder, and Makasa suddenly stood, stomping her foot.

"He's right. We've already done the impossible. We lost Greydon and Aram, we lost Thalyss and Drella, and we never gave up. We only grew stronger. More determined. This is our legend now; we make it end how we want."

"Hear, hear!" Telagos leapt up, too, and then Galena.

"Well stated," Elmarine agreed, her eyes flashing.

"This might be a messy crew," Makasa said, flashing Valdread a grin. "But it's *our* messy crew."

"For Taryndrella!" Galena said, clapping her hands together.

"For Aramar," Makasa added, putting her arm around the druid. "And for *us*."

CHAPTER THIRTY-FOUR
MARCH ON OUTLAND

Throgg had never moved so fast in his life, galumphing down the tall, arched corridor, his lungs stinging as he gasped for air.

Malus was going to kill Throgg. There was a famous saying about messengers and killing them, but Throgg wasn't known for his memory. Or his speed. But Throgg did his best, batting aside arakkoa and imps as he finally reached the rise of steps that would bring him to Malus. The human captain had carved out a spot for himself in Xaraax's big castle; it wasn't grand, very sparse for a man like Malus. It only occurred to Throgg then that maybe it was supposed to look sad and empty. *A cunning russsssse*, as Ssarbik would say.

Throgg skidded to a stop, leaning against the wall for support, his size and weight making the shoddy timbers creak. A sprinkling of dust fell from the ceiling.

"Malus!" Throgg gasped for air. "Malus . . ."

The captain emerged from the shadows of his chamber. He was dressed in his shirtsleeves and clean trousers, with high, gleaming boots rising to his thighs. The hilt of the Diamond Blade was in his right hand, and he inspected it from every angle, hardly sparing Throgg a glance. The nasty wound on his face still hadn't healed.

Behind him, a strange circular doorway glowed, a portal of some kind. A few of Xaraax's minions tended to it, guarded by a dozen or so Gordunni ogres. They made the small room feel even more cramped.

"What is it?" he demanded, sharp.

"Ogres, what they doing here?" Throgg asked. He had almost forgotten why he came.

Malus spared them a quick glance. "Bodyguards. Mine. They serve their Gordok."

That was wrong. All wrong. Throgg bristled.

"You promised. You said! You said no more Gordok after you have compass. Now you have compass, so no more Gordok." Throgg squared his shoulders, but Malus only smiled.

"Would you like to fight them all?" Malus asked. "One word from me and they will attack you. I have the compass, but not the shard. A technicality, you may say, but I've decided to keep the title of Gordok." He nodded toward his "bodyguards." "It's proving useful."

Throgg glared at them. It felt bad, like being stung a whole bunch of times by wasps or stepping in a wyvern's nest. Throgg's anger wouldn't go. Malus had broken his promise.

"Why are you here?" Malus hissed.

"Scout . . . scout return. They have yeti size of two Throggs!" Throgg remembered his reason for coming, but couldn't shake the feeling like he had been stung, badly.

"Who does, you imbecile?" Malus shouted. He finally glanced up from the sword hilt. Something on Throgg's face must have concerned him, for he went a little pale and lowered his voice. "Explain."

Throgg tried, but the details were hazy at best. The portal behind Malus thrummed, growing in power.

"Bird scout go into valley. Yeti and gnoll and all type of thing there. Not belong . . . Not right! Getting close to den, Malus, an *army*."

Throgg watched the captain's eyes slide back and forth rapidly. Throgg didn't know what any of it meant. He only knew that gnolls and yetis never came to Outland, and they certainly didn't come in organized forces, working together. Throgg remembered the carnage of Feralas, of the brutish gnolls that fought with clubs and axes, and the yetis that could smash an ogre's head if they had a mind to.

Finally, Malus laughed, cruelly, smacking the hilt of the blade against his thigh in amusement. "Is it possible? Are they really that stupid? I can't believe it . . ."

"Who?" Throgg asked. "Who stupid?"

Malus turned back toward his portal, disappearing behind it

for a moment while he collected his flashy captain's jacket and pulled it on. He was striding down toward Throgg, passing him, moving swiftly down the corridor. The screeches of the demons and arakkoa filling the fortress could be heard all around them, but Throgg didn't notice them anymore. Throgg followed Malus, careful not to tread on him, but wishing he could.

"It's those fool children. They seek to free their friend. How unbelievably arrogant."

"We crush!" Throgg smashed his stump arm like a fist into his open palm. Battle. Throgg was ready. Throgg was always ready for battle. Karrga noticed him most when he fought, and sometimes Throgg even wanted to blush when he caught her admiring him after a particularly vicious kill. His warrior lady! There would be more opportunities to impress her, then. "Rematch!"

"Indeed." Malus chuckled again, sliding the hilt of the Diamond Blade into his belt next to his broadsword. They emerged from the tall hall and into the massive, open-air fortress, the ceiling made up entirely of tightly knit brambles and branches. Arakkoa and demon nests dotted the palace, the armies of Xaraax practicing their torture methods in the rotunda below. The occasional scream of a tormented prisoner punctuated the chaos. The whole place smelled, in Throgg's opinion, too strongly of bird droppings and sulfur. Horrible stenches wafted up from the demonic pits below, pits that Throgg avoided at all times.

"Find me that scout," Malus said, standing watch for a moment at the top of the high walkway that overlooked the vastness of the fortress. "I want details. I want to know everything. And then, Throgg, we end this. Those children will be dead by sundown."

From the ridge, Makasa watched an army pour out of the fortress. The lower half of the citadel was difficult to see at all, hidden as it was by hills and brambles. The upper half, their destination, looked, if one was not observant, like merely a series of caves dotting a gradual slope, arakkoa nests and more immense brambles tumbling over those caves in an effort to conceal them.

"I'll bet that's Xaraax's army," Makasa whispered. They made their way along the ridge to the north of the valley below, where the yetis and gnolls waited for the onslaught. Their friends were hopelessly outnumbered, but the yetis stood firm, absorbing the first wave of demons as they came pelting toward them with axes and swords raised. Xaraax's numbers wore blackened armor with green tabards, glowing fel runes hammered into their helmets. Creatures with many arms swarmed the field, their hideous cries forcing a yelp of shock from Galena.

"So many," the tauren murmured, covering her eyes. "How are there so many?"

"You no see demons on march. Woodpaw kill all in path," Hackle said, proudly sticking out his armored chest. "This real fight now."

"No," Valdread reminded him. "The real fight is with Malus and Xaraax. Come."

Makasa followed him, skirting carefully along the steep ridge with Galena, Hackle, and Murky. Telagos waited to play his part elsewhere, but soon he would take to the field. Down below, the ridge flattened out into the dish where the battle commenced, Malus's bramble fortress behind the demons, and the distant sin'dorei towers of Falcon Watch behind their friends.

The murlocs, wyverns, and other volunteers waited in reserve, Valdread's idea, as the murlocs were swift, light, and good ambushers, the wyverns could wreak havoc from the sky, Elmarine could do crowd control with her arcane magic, Shagtusk could mop up weakened enemies, and Wuul could split the demons' skulls for them. The murlocs had gone ahead of Makasa and the others, running along the ridge on sure, flappy feet, rounding the bend and waiting in the brambles for their signal. It was impossible not to look at the chaos below as they picked their way along the hillside, nearing the upper entrances to the Hidden citadel.

"I've never seen anything like it," Galena whispered, shaken.

"Battle is never pretty," Valdread muttered, crouched low, gracefully stealing along the path, quiet as a whisper. "Tales make it sound glorious, but the truth of it is ugly, bloody, and loud."

"Have courage," Makasa reminded the druid. The tauren had

not assisted them much during the fight at the Northwatch base, and they couldn't afford to have her fall to pieces like that again. "Do it for Taryndrella. She would want you to be brave."

"Yes, yes," Galena said, looking away from the battle. "I'll be brave for her. I must be brave."

As they crept above the fray, the demon army broke against the immovable phalanx of the yetis. It was like they had run headlong into a wall of fur and claws. The yetis tore at them, bigger and stronger, but slow, flinging demons into the air, batting them hard across the field, leaving giant swaths of fallen fel soldiers that the faster gnolls could leap upon and finish. They worked well in concert, the yetis smashing, more like siege engines than soldiers, using their long, log-thick arms to cut a path through the sheer numbers of Xaraax's army.

The gnolls leapt in where they could, retreating behind the yetis when they were in danger of being overwhelmed. Even so, Makasa saw many gnolls lost to the crush of the demons. The fel creatures were numerous and feral, imps and felhounds (as Valdread called them) that shrieked loud enough to mimic a storm, and they simply kept coming; there was no end in sight to the seething mass of them unleashed by the fortress.

They soon made their way into the fortress, the ridge curving hard to the north, their way forward narrower and narrower, Galena navigating clumsily, her hooves too wide for the treacherous ledge. Makasa helped her balance, Hackle behind her, ready to steady her.

They stilled, catching their breath, and Makasa looked back down at the battle in the valley. The first yeti had fallen, but that only seemed to enrage the others, who fought harder, roaring with fury, swinging from side to side, flattening dozens of demons with each swipe. A few enterprising gnolls had leapt onto the shoulders of the yetis, throwing spears and firing crossbows from that vantage, keeping the demons from swarming too quickly and dragging the yetis down.

"You would think they'd fought together for ages," Makasa said. "Look!"

She pointed to the wide arch of brambles where the demons had come from, the army trickling to a thin stream of lone stragglers. That was the moment they had been waiting for.

"Murky!" she called. "Give the signal!"

"Mrgle, mrgle!"

The murloc pulled a white shell from his belt and took a deep breath, his little white belly going round as a bubble. Then he blew into the conch, a high, reedy horn sounding across the valley. The murlocs hiding in the brambles above the fray descended, falling one by one onto the heads of the demon stragglers. They pelted them with rocks and stuck them hard in the sides with their spears, then moved on to the larger force, flanking them.

They were joined by the rest of the volunteers, the wyverns harrying the demons with their claws and stingers while Magistrix Elmarine bombarded the enemy with a barrage of arcane missiles.

"It's working," Galena said, wide-eyed. "It's working!"

"And now for the final touch," Valdread said with a grin.

The conch and the reinforcements had been the signal for Telagos. High above, he emerged from behind a bank of clouds. He dove down, down, swift as a heron spearing a fish, and let out a great, frosty breath, a cone of frost that hardened, sealing off the demons from retreat, and making it difficult for more enemies to leave the citadel.

"He's just amazing," Galena trilled. "So graceful!"

"All right, we're here," Makasa said, redirecting their attention. "It's our turn. There's no telling what we may find inside, so we need to be prepared."

Telagos circled the battle, diving now and then to freeze a demon into place for the gnolls to hack. Then he rose up again, gliding toward them, his blue scales shimmering in the unforgiving heat. He slowed and landed with a soft thump in front of them.

"Onward?" he asked, his gentle voice rumbling out from a dragon's belly.

"Onward," Makasa replied, loosening the chain around her chest and readying her harpoon. The blade of the Diamond Blade was strapped to her back, hidden under her jerkin. "I'm ready. Let's give Malus his big surprise and find Aram."

CHAPTER THIRTY-FIVE
RELIEF AND BETRAYAL

Seven will become One. Listen . . . Listen.

Aram lifted his head weakly, his leg no longer hurt after using Drella's blossom on it, but he was shaking with hunger and thirst. The imp standing guard over them seemed to hear something, or perhaps his master had somehow summoned him, and the little red creature bounced away, muttering to himself. Drella's voice was still echoing in his head when he heard Greydon stumble to his feet.

"What is it?" Aram whispered, his lips parched and cracked.

"Something's happened," Greydon replied, calling for silence with a finger.

Aram did as commanded and listened. Far away, high above them, he heard the shrieks and cries of the arakkoa and the thundering voice of the demon overlords ordering about the imps. That in itself wasn't new, but now they sounded *panicked*.

More voices. More chaos. The entire prison shook, as if a ground quake had started, threatening to tear the place apart.

"It's a battle," Greydon told him, his eyes shining brightly. "I would know that sound anywhere."

"Father!"

The imp had returned, and he hadn't returned alone. A floating demon with glowing green eyes and a trail of emerald fire in its wake drifted into the chamber. Huge, hunched, and hideous, the sagging skin of its chin had been braided into itself, hanging down to its waist, where it wore an iron girdle imbedded with gleaming fel stones. Its black horns were wet with blood, and so were its immense hands.

The jailer demon looked at each of them in turn, then fixed its gaze on Greydon and floated up next to his cell. Greydon stumbled backward, defenseless, pressing his back to the bars while the jailer appraised him and laughed, the sound as deep and ominous as thunder. Then dark, shimmering chains wrapped themselves around his father's wrists, created by the demon's will. Greydon froze, his eyes rolled back, his mouth dropping open in agony as he screamed, strange purple ripples emanating from his skin.

"Stop! Stop it, you're killing him!" Aram pounded on the bars, but it was no use. His father was beginning to go limp. The imp giggled and clapped with delight, dancing in front of his father.

"Father! Don't go, don't go!"

"Silence!" The demon turned its attention toward Aram, eyes aflame. "His essence is needed. He is of the Order of the Seven Suns. The Darkstorm feeds upon his life."

"You will never have him!" Aram shouted. "You will never summon the Darkstorm!"

He couldn't lose him, couldn't suffer the torment of the prison alone. But then he realized—the sounds of battle. Something major had happened, and now the demons were moving faster, anxious to raise the Darkstorm. The jailer didn't just mean to end Greydon; he'd use him to bring about the annihilation of Azeroth.

But how? Had Xaraax reassembled the Diamond Blade?

Thunk.

The demon attacking his father went still, the green light going out of its eyes. The strange purple chains wrapped around Greydon suddenly vanished, leaving behind dark welts. Greydon gasped and wheezed, clutching his throat.

Then the imp screamed, launching himself into the darkness. The jailer slumped over, a spear lodged in its skull. Aram's heart all but stopped. It wasn't possible . . . It couldn't be over; it was too good to be true . . .

But there they were: Murky, Hackle, Galena, and a pale young man Aram didn't quite recognize. He sank to his knees with relief, watching as, right before his very eyes, Galena's dark fur shimmered, turning yellow and then orange before growing longer, fluffing out into feathers. Her horns shot out and up, growing quickly until they resembled large antlers. She gave a shout as her snout curved sharply into a beak. Great talons sprang from her hands, and her hooves and fingers became avian and toughened. A feathered moonkin! She gave a strange, birdlike roar, and conjured a beam of pure moonlight, striking down the imp before he could escape.

"Urum!"

Murky hopped across the floor, retrieving his spear before using it to bash the bars of Aram's cage.

"Not like that!" Hackle sighed and dropped down next to the jailer demon, then popped up again holding a set of massive keys.

"Where did you come from? How did you find us?" Aram asked, tears of happiness and relief streaming down his face. Greydon, for his part, was struck silent until he gave a barrel-chested laugh, as shocked and disbelieving as his son.

"'Tis a protracted and tedious tale," the young man said. "Best told when we are free of this place."

"Wait, I—I know you," Aram cried. "You're the boy from my drawings. The one with the dragon!"

"He *is* dragon," Hackle said, fumbling with the keys and then

finally jamming them into the lock on Aram's cage. "Blue dragon! Ice breath. Wings. You see soon!"

"We have to get you out of there and help Makasa!" Galena said. She had shifted almost instantaneously out of her moonkin form, feathers springing back into fur as she shivered and ran toward them, a few feathers floating down from her shoulders. "She went to confront Malus!"

"On her own?" Greydon demanded, thunderous. "Is she mad?"

"Valdread is with her," Galena replied.

"What?!" father and son shouted in unison.

"We found the rest of the shards, Aramar," she said as Aram tumbled free of his cage. "We'll take the hilt from Malus and reforge the Diamond Blade. It's time to end this."

"No, no, this can't be—" Greydon tore at his hair, and didn't emerge from his opened cell until Aram guided him out of it. "That's too dangerous. Not with Xaraax so near!"

The others said nothing, stunned, but Aram knew exactly what his father meant. They couldn't know all the details of the naaru and the blade, and more importantly, of the Darkstorm. "We have to get to Makasa," he said, running to find the door, ignoring the pain in his joints, his hunger, his thirst . . . "We can't let Xaraax get his hands on the Diamond Blade. Without it, we can't restore the naaru! The naaru is the key, the key to ending the Darkstorm once and for all!"

*　　*　　*

"The rest of the blade is near. I can sense it," Highlord Xaraax said.

Malus couldn't believe his luck. He wasn't a man who believed in fate or destiny, but a man who believed in planning, in doing whatever it took to achieve his goals, no matter the cost.

He stared at Highlord Xaraax's back. The demon lord watched the battle in the valley below from his vaunted sanctuary, a twisted rock chamber as tall as a cathedral, gold and green lights casting eerie shadows along the thin windows. A balcony of brambles and spikes jutted out from behind his throne and altar, and it was from that balcony that the highlord watched. And waited.

Xaraax, tall and broad, with leathery wings and sharpened horns, could fill any fortress, any room, any space with the potency of his malice. A fog of terror lingered around him like a shroud, his eyes strangely unblinking, as if he could see you always, no matter the distance or angle. Or perhaps he never blinked because both eyes bore scars, and now he would never be caught unawares again. The blackened armor and jeweled belt he wore were spotless, polished to a high shine.

"I told you it would all come together," Malus said, kneeling at the altar, paying his respects. It was the stone base for a purple mass of liquid shadows, ever moving, ever whispering of unspeakable secrets found only in the Twisting Nether. This was a crucial moment, the moment when all their plans paid off. It had been a long road, paved in loss and death and sacrifice, but now, with the moment of triumph so near, Malus felt giddy with the thought of it. The Diamond Blade. It could be reassembled, the power of the Darkstorm granted to them, all of Azeroth at their mercy.

"Patience," Malus added. "Patience was all that was needed."

"This stroke of ridiculous luck has nothing to do with *patience*, Malus." The highlord's voice came as if from the lowest pits of Outland's core. It was brimstone and terror, a voice that demanded respect and obedience. The voice that whispered to him so long ago, the voice that lured him to carry out the will of demons. And now it mocked him, and Malus seethed.

"Your blunders will not be forgotten. My legions are being wasted upon the lowliest creatures of your world because of your incompetence. Your *laziness*. You have disappointed me again, and perhaps I shall wound far more than your face and hand."

"Highlord, that isn't true," Malus said, looking up. The sunlight framed Xaraax's tall horns as he beheld the plight of his armies. "They do not have the hilt of the blade, and we have the essence of the Order, one who served, and one who is of his blood. They cannot stop us without the Diamond Blade. I might have easily found them, but without the hilt their cause is lost." He stood, irritated. The loss of Xaraax's minions was minor; they were about to obtain their real goal: the final destruction of the naaru and of Azeroth. "Now is the hour of our victory."

"And your demise, Malus."

The nathrezim whirled, torn cloak billowing as his wings beat once, carrying him in a single leap to land at the altar, his shadow plunging Malus into darkness.

"My lord, I don't understand—"

Xaraax laughed once, staring down at him not with anger, but with indifference. "No, you do *not* understand. Like any tool, you eventually wear out your utility. Your willingness, your desperation to serve, was commendable once. Charming. I fear, however, that your usefulness is at an end." The highlord closed his eyes, a hideous smile splitting his face. He breathed hard, as if swept into a moment of passion. "Soon the Diamond Blade will be handed to me, and the annihilation of Azeroth will begin. Nothing will stand in my way. Without the blade, the naaru is truly dead. All will burn, and *you* will burn with it."

His eyes snapped open, and he lashed out, kicking Malus in the ribs, sending him sprawling, tumbling down the steps of the altar. How could this be? Malus had done everything Xaraax asked, everything, bending over backward to please the highlord. Murdering the naaru. Betraying his own brother!

Shuddering in pain, Malus covered his chest with his arms, anticipating another blow. It came, and swiftly, Xaraax descending on him, pressing his searing hooflike foot onto Malus's chest, pushing and pushing until Malus felt certain he would die.

"Your service is noted," Xaraax murmured, bending down to

snatch the hilt of the Diamond Blade from his belt. "And now, like all pitiful things, it will be forgotten."

He inhaled rapidly in that strange way again, eyelashes fluttering. "It is time to summon the others. The Hidden must witness my triumph. The blade approaches. Come to me now . . . Come to me. I can feel it, so close, so close. Soon the naaru will be destroyed and with it, this world's final protection. Azeroth shall *burn*."

CHAPTER THIRTY-SIX
WIELDING THE LIGHT

Finding where Malus and Xaraax lurked was no trouble at all. The Hidden's fortress, laid out in concentric rings of brambles and stone, rose higher and higher, ending in a foreboding black gate that guarded the entrance to the highest ring. Valdread drew his blades, whirling into action, dispensing two tall, helmed demons carrying pikes. They hadn't expected anyone to break through the fighting outside the fortress, and they didn't make a sound before the baron had dispatched them.

Makasa retrieved a silvery key from the belt of one of the dead guardians, opened the gate, and raced higher into the fortress. The training Valdread had given her paid off, and they had managed to win most battles before they even began—using stealth to strike deadly, silent blows. Her training had been incredibly useful, but now they came face-to-face with two massive ogres, their bodies blocking the archway and the sanctuary beyond.

Throgg and Karrga. They were not so easily surprised, and

Throgg hefted his mace at once, a massive piece of studded and banded wood lashed to his stump arm.

"What this?" Throgg arched a heavy brow.

"Why you fight with puny girl, dead man?" Karrga demanded. "You fight with us."

Valdread put out his hand, keeping Makasa from darting forward and engaging. "I did fight with you, yes, but that was before your charmer of a boss threw me off a mountain." There. He saw it, a quiver in Throgg's slimy lip. Insecurity. "You didn't like that, did you? I know honor is important to you, Throgg, which is why I'm surprised you're still here."

"Throgg loyal!" the ogre thundered, and both Valdread and Makasa winced from the force of it.

"Karrga loyal, too!"

"Loyal to whom, exactly?" Valdread pressed. An ogre wasn't something he liked to fight head-on, let alone two. Wits would serve them better. "Malus subjugated your people. Are you loyal to him or them? He's just a human; you've left behind the entire legacy of the ogres. And for what? A man who would turn on his own. Kill his own. It's a miracle I survived that fall, and our so-called enemies were the ones to piece me back together."

Throgg lowered his shield, just a little. Progress.

"What you doing?" Karrga demanded. "He lie."

"No," Throgg said. "Throgg see Malus with more Gordunni ogres. He still call himself Gordok. *Malus* lie."

"Exactly!" Valdread said, smirking. "Malus isn't the friend or the commander you think he is, and he will toss you aside if it serves his purposes, too."

"No! No listen to Whisper-Man!" Karrga forced the issue then, stomping toward them with her weapon raised high. Blast. And he had been so close to breaking through to Throgg, too.

Throgg's shield lashed out even before Makasa could skid to a stop, knocking her flat on her back. Valdread dodged, but Throgg spun again, this time with his mace, narrowly catching Valdread in the middle. He winced, knocked onto his side momentarily, but it was enough. Makasa tried to stand up through the pain, but Throgg knocked her with his shield again, then grabbed her by the chain wrapped around her chest, dragging her into the cavernous chamber beyond. She watched through dazed eyes as Valdread fell to yet another blow, this time from Karrga, who capitalized on Throgg's first hit. The blue ogre slammed him in the chest and then the throat with the pommel of her broadsword.

Valdread still had fight left in him, but Karrga sheathed her sword and scooped up the Forsaken, crushing him to her chest with both arms. Squirming, shouting, he could do nothing as he, too, was carried into the chamber.

"Ah. Our guests arrive, and with them, the blade that will seal Azeroth's fate."

* * *

The voice made Makasa tremble. It was like nothing she had ever heard before . . . Evil. Pure evil. The sound made her blood run cold, not loud but threaded with unnatural depth, as if the strange gray sky preempting a thunderstorm could speak. Not even a nightmare could conjure something like that. She twisted to find the source, finding a demon, taller than even the ogres, presiding over his court. The Hidden. They were all there, Ssarbik and Ssavra, heads bent together as they smiled eerily in the corner, Zathra with her scorpid chattering away on her shoulder, and Malus, kneeling in the center of the black sanctuary. The demon lord had his hand on Malus's shoulder, forcing him to the ground. She didn't expect to see him like that, his face stretched with misery, burned on the right side, bruises darkening on his neck.

And the hilt. The demon wielded the Diamond Blade's hilt, the shards among it glowing hot and bright, sensing the nearness of their brethren.

Makasa drew in a long, shaking breath. What had they done? She glanced toward Valdread, who continued struggling, though he grew still at the sight of the demon. The blade strapped to Makasa's back started to heat up until it burned, the heat searing her through her shirt, and she gritted her teeth against the agony.

"Ssssearch her," Ssarbik hissed. Zathra jumped at the chance, grinning lopsidedly, loping over with her head held high. Makasa cursed and spat, and Zathra ignored it, shoving her hands into Makasa's vest pockets and then, of course, her trouser pockets were searched. Finally, the troll reached a hand under Makasa's jerkin, grasping the blade and pulling it free.

"Ach! It be burning!" Zathra juggled the blade hand to hand, its core burning so brightly it was hard to look at it directly.

"Bring it to me."

"I can't! I can't!" she screamed as it clattered to the floor.

"Incompetent troll," the demon thundered, eyes blazing with fury.

Ssavra slid across the room quickly, chattering to herself, running toward the blade, but as soon as she drew near, it flew out of her reach, then lifted into the air. Nobody spoke, a hush falling over the room as the hilt in the demon's hands exploded with Light, then soared across the chamber, reuniting itself with the missing blade.

"The Diamond Blade," Makasa breathed, watching as the weapon reforged itself, whole and brilliant and bright. Somehow it seemed to hear her, hear its name, and flew toward her.

"What it doing?! What it doing?!" Throgg flailed, blinded by the Light. He dropped her, and Makasa saw her chance. She jumped up, determined not to fail, not when they were so close to defeating the Hidden. Her heart pounded, and she reached, reached, opening her hand . . .

"NO!"

Yes.

The Diamond Blade felt good in her hands. Right. She swung

in every direction, warning off Throgg and Zathra. Ssarbik aimed a bolt of shadow magic at her, but it dissolved as soon as it approached the blade. Then the weapon glowed and glowed, expanding and contracting, the hilt lengthening, the sharp end curving until it resembled a honed and deadly harpoon.

Wield the Light. Defend Azeroth.

The Voice boomed in her head, and she followed its command, unleashing a mighty shout as she sprinted across the chamber, aiming directly for the heart of the tall and terrible demon. The true master of the Hidden. She could end it, she thought, she could end it all then. They were so close, so close—

But Xaraax wielded a blade of his own, a fel sword, twisted and ugly, veins of glowing green fire wrapped around the hilt. Pale emerald flames leapt from its sharp edges, and Xaraax stepped over Malus's kneeling form, meeting Makasa's thrust with a powerful swing. Too powerful. All of her planning, all of her work, all of the days Valdread trained her and taught her, and for what? Xaraax was too strong. The bones in her hands felt as if they might shatter, the Diamond Blade knocked out of her grasp. It clattered to the floor, taking on its former shape, a sword of Light once more.

Without it, she was defenseless, and before she could try to reclaim the blade, Ssarbik and his blasted magic recaptured her— black, shadowy tendrils racing across the floor to bind her up.

And that was enough. She had failed. Xaraax dropped his fel

blade, no longer in need of it, and took up the Diamond Blade, claiming it as his own. Makasa watched in mute horror as liquid black ropes climbed from Xaraax's hands onto the hilt, ensnaring it, the hilt corrupted to a dark purpose before their very eyes.

"Yes. YES. The Diamond Blade is reforged, and I, Highlord Xaraax, dreadlord of the Burning Legion, ruler of the Hidden, am now, at last, architect of Azeroth's doom! The Diamond Blade is mine, the naaru at my mercy, and with its destruction, the Darkstorm cannot be stopped." Xaraax, eyes burning with excitement, thrust the hilt upward, the Diamond Blade igniting, more and more fel, black corruption staining it, climbing up the hilt toward the blade . . .

"NO!" It might have come from her or Valdread, but no, it was Malus who screamed. He cried out in pain, in anguish, and he stood, shaking, grabbing the demon's abandoned fel sword. With the flames still shooting off its end, he thrust the fel sword into Xaraax's back, through his chest, spearing him completely.

Xaraax stared, frozen, a strangled gasp seeping from his throat. The Diamond Blade slipped from his fingers and fell to the floor.

He slowly crumbled, impaled, his mouth going slack as Malus turned him around, one hand on his back, the other still on the fel blade, and pushed him toward the strange altar at the back of the chamber. Makasa watched as the purple shapes there, twisting and pulsing, swallowed Xaraax whole, and Malus was forced to pull back the blade, his former master disappearing into the vortex.

"To the Twisting Nether with you, Xaraax. May you forever suffer."

Ssarbik hissed, clawing his talons at Malus. "What have you done? You have ssslain the Masster!"

The captain glared, brandishing Xaraax's sword. He flashed it in the arakkoa's direction, and for one moment, Makasa let herself hope that Malus had at last had a change of heart. Maybe Xaraax had pushed him too far. Maybe he knew that his citadel would be overrun, the Hidden disbanded and his head on the chopping block.

"Don't question me. Unless you wish to meet the same fate as Xaraax. Summon as many imps and as many ogres as it takes to fuel the Darkstorm. It will be starving, but they shall sate it until we give it the true meal of Greydon Thorne." Throgg shouted in protest, but Malus ignored him, swinging the sword experimentally, its fel energy glowing brighter, seething, the same black, corrupted stain climbing up his arm, faster and faster, overtaking him, until his eyes blazed as hot and green as the fel fire he wielded.

Ssarbik disappeared for only a few moments, returning with a slew of confused, chained ogres, shuffled along by a demonic jailer. All of the ogres had been bound in shadowy chains. Fiery red imps hopped along beside them, but they soon shrieked in surprise as Ssarbik led the procession toward Malus and his grim, determined smile.

Behind him, a shadow grew and grew, until its slithering mass became a portal. Whispers emanated from within, louder and more sinister, the language too frenzied to make out.

"No!" Throgg thundered, but the demonic chains holding the ogres were too strong. The jailer gathered them near the portal, and soon they were nothing but glittering dust, the ogres and a dozen imps sucked into the expanding and swirling vortex. The portal twisted, becoming a black funnel that began to rise higher, the Darkstorm gathering. Seething. Ready for the sacrifice, hungry and whispering for the essence of the Order.

So much for his change of heart.

"Malus . . . Malus, what you doing?" It was Karrga who asked, dumbfounded.

It must have been too much for her, too strange, for Valdread suddenly broke free of her grasp, sliding out from under her arms and dodging across the floor. Zathra got off a shot with her crossbows, but missed, and Ssarbik also failed to snare Valdread. The Forsaken reached the Diamond Blade, but instead of taking it for himself, he kicked it across the floor. It spun, sending shards of golden light in every direction, before it at last reached Makasa, its energy dispersing the shadows that held her.

She grabbed it at once, and she needed it, for Malus soon charged her, his fel sword aimed for her head. Gasping, she blocked at the last moment with the harpoon of Light, the reforged weapon humming with readiness in her grasp. The portal, the beginnings of the Darkstorm, screamed with a thousand voices.

"Demons! My armies! To me!" he thundered. His voice had altered, deepening, twisting, sounding more and more like Xaraax's with every word. Gone was the Malus they had fought so many times, replaced with a shadowy demon, an even darker reflection of who he had once been.

CHAPTER THIRTY-SEVEN
GALENA'S REVENGE

The Light had stayed dormant for too long, separated, broken, undone. Now it sang with life once more, wielded by a young woman strong and noble and pure of heart. Its joy surged, and with it, its power. Life. Life must be protected. Life, like the blade, reborn. Protective Light shone out from it, blazing, stirred to action by the horrid fel weapon seeking to destroy. The fel blade crashed upon it again and again. No. The Light would fight back this time. The blade would not be broken again.

Seven will become One. The Light would endure. *Azeroth* would endure.

Aram reached the apex of the Hidden citadel just as the roof exploded.

"Look out!"

Hackle grabbed him by the collar, yanking him back. A giant block of bramble-covered stone slammed into the ground at their feet, very nearly flattening Aram. He stumbled against Hackle, wiping at his face.

"Thanks."

"You stay back," Hackle said, shoving a paw to Aram's chest, making him step behind the gnoll. "Too weak. Too hurt. Hackle protect."

"Mrgalrgalrglrllglgl!" Aram might be hanging back, but the same could not be said for Murky, who ran directly into the tall chamber, dodging debris as it fell. The blazing, blinding Light inside died down, and at the center of it, he saw Makasa. She wielded the Diamond Blade! But somehow it was different in her hands . . . a harpoon. Aram had dreamt of wielding the weapon himself, but looking at Makasa, strong and sure, he felt nothing but pride. They had all worked to bring about this moment. They had all sacrificed. That Makasa fought for them now, the way she had always fought for them, felt *right*.

The explosion of Light from the blade had sent Malus reeling. The swirling black vortex looming over the chamber shuddered, growing quiet for a moment. The Diamond Blade had reacted to something, blasting everyone but Makasa back, and cracking a gaping hole in the ceiling.

Murky leapt over fallen chunks of the citadel, landing at Makasa's side. Reigol Valdread, of all people, stood with them, his blades dancing nimbly in his hands as he fended off Zathra, sending her retreating across the floor.

"Malus! Malus!" Throgg and Karrga galumphed over to Malus, helping him stand.

"Fight, you idiots, fight!" he screamed.

Aram could hardly believe what he was seeing. The chamber in ruins, no sign of Highlord Xaraax, winged demons mustering in the skies, preparing to dive, and Malus, climbing to his feet, wielding a dark, ugly sword that seemed to have grown *into* *him*, corrupting him with its shadowy tendrils.

Throgg hefted the mace lashed to his arm, but not before Murky took his shot, aiming his sharp little spear for Malus and throwing. It was a perfect toss, the spear whistling fast across the room, passing some kind of strange altar, heading right for Malus's throat. But the captain saw it coming and reached for Throgg's leg, pulling until the ogre tumbled down right in front of Malus, the spear lodging harmlessly in the ogre's breastplate.

"What you doing?" Throgg glowered, grabbing the spear and chucking it away. "Throgg no like this new Malus. He betray Gordunni. He have no honor. Not fit to be called Gordok. Throgg his own master now!"

"Get out of my way!" Malus discarded them, running back into the fray, setting his sights on Makasa. But she was well defended, and she fought with the fury of a storm, whirling, parrying, deflecting every magical bolt Ssarbik and Ssavra sent her way.

"We have to do something," Aram said, but Hackle wasn't

listening. Greydon hobbled up behind them, slower because of his wounds, leaning heavily against Galena in her moonkin form as they reached the top of the fortress.

A hundred horrible screams split the sky, the hairy, winged demons gathering above the chamber following Malus's commands. They dove down, the sounds of their leathery wings as unsettling as their cries. One nearly carried Murky off, but Valdread intervened at the last moment, batting the demon away with a kick. Aram couldn't believe Valdread was fighting for their side, or maybe he could. He had tried to keep Malus from killing Drella, after all, and it seemed he had come around to the right side.

Hackle darted into the commotion, raising his club to attack Throgg, only to watch the big, horned ogre smash a flying demon with his own mace.

"Throgg good now?" Hackle scratched his head with one claw.

"Throgg is Throgg!" he roared, swinging wildly, knocking demon after demon out of the sky.

"Karrga good, too?" Hackle asked, turning to face the seven-foot-tall ogre, whose tattoos were now indistinguishable, covered in demon blood.

"Malus betray Throgg. Malus good for nothing!" she cried out as she blocked scrabbling, sharp, demonic claws with the flat of her broadsword.

That didn't mean Ssarbik, Ssavra, or Zathra had switched sides. They clustered around Malus, protecting him, occasionally making an attempt to reclaim the Diamond Blade from Makasa, but she held her ground.

The skyward demons had begun to notice Aram, Greydon, and Galena lingering in the doorway. They were more sheltered there, less of the roof having collapsed, but now three of the demons broke off from the main mass, raising their claws and soaring toward Aram.

"Stand back!" Galena shoved herself in front of him. She summoned bolt after bolt of moonfire from the sky to strike down the demons, but they were too swift, too nimble, dodging the gleaming silver rays of light.

"That's for Taryndrella!" she said. "That's for taking Aramar! That's for taking his father!" She tossed another bolt at them. "And that's for *me*!"

She quickly transformed back into her larger, stronger moonkin form and threw up her winged arms, trying to protect her face as the demons dove past her onslaught. They were too quick, too determined. Aram smelled them before they even got close, a sulfurous stink clinging to their strange, batlike bodies. Their claws were coming, their teeth bared and sharp.

But the slash of their claws never came. It was suddenly very cold, an icy wind rising seemingly from nowhere. Then Aram saw the dragon from his vision, brilliant blue, with startling white eyes and powerful wings. Its breath froze the demons as they came in for the kill, and they dropped like stones to the floor, shattering.

"Isn't he perfect?" Galena sighed, shimmering back into her tauren form and watching the dragon loop back around, returning to the skies.

"Sure," Aram said, a little confused. "Come on, I need a weapon, and so does my father."

Galena protected them with quick flashes of moonfire as they picked their way across the battlefield. Malus's remaining loyal minions had rallied in a protective half-moon around him as they pressed toward Makasa in the center of the room.

"Malus," Greydon growled. "The coward. Never fighting his own battles . . ."

"Here." Aram knelt, finding Makasa's beloved chain and harpoon on the floor among the dead demon bodies and stones. He wondered how she had lost them, but clearly she had found a more potent weapon. "Take these, I'll find something else to use."

"I'm weak, Aram."

"No, you can do this. *We* can do this. We can't give up now, not when we're so close to victory!" Aram dove to his father's side, pressing the chain and harpoon into his scarred, trembling hands. "This is why you left us all those years ago. To protect Azeroth, to protect *me*. And if we die—"

Slowly, Greydon nodded, looking into his son's eyes with a small, sad smile under his overgrown beard. "We die with a sword in hand."

CHAPTER THIRTY-EIGHT
BROTHERS

Greydon Thorne knew what had to be done. He had always known, of course, but the truth filled him with the strength to go on. His hands ached. His back felt as if it had been crushed by a boulder. The burns and gashes in his side throbbed with every step. But he saw his brother ahead, hiding behind his minions like an utter coward. Silverlaine—Malus—seethed with power, but it seemed his newfound abilities didn't matter to him. Better that others die than Malus take a single blow.

This was not the brother he loved. This was no longer a man, but a creature, twisted and lost. Maybe this had begun the moment Silverlaine took the Diamond Blade in his hands and decided on murder. Or perhaps it had begun when he actually struck the blow. It didn't matter. The corruption made manifest now had started when Silverlaine turned his back on the Order of the Seven Suns, when he hastened the Darkstorm, when he chose a dark master and abandoned his name.

Malus.

Greydon fought for every step he took, his body screaming in agony. One more battle. Just one more. His son was right: This was *his* fight, his burden to bear. If he had been a better brother, a better leader—but no, there was no time to think that way. His brother was mad, trying to kill *children*. Trying to kill the *world*.

An orange-skinned troll broke away from Malus's group, hurtling herself across the room. She gave a loud, terrible cackle, a scorpid on her shoulder, lashing out with its barbed tail. Greydon began to swing the chain, knowing it had been too long since he fought with such a weapon. The battle was chaos. He was all on his own . . .

"Hey, stinky troll!" The strange, gruff bark came from his right. His son's gnoll friend leapt onto a piece of tumbled stone, then blew his tongue out at the troll.

"Furry pest, it be way past time you die!" The troll aimed one of her small crossbows at him and let fly. The gnoll ducked, giving a hyena's cackle. That only made the troll angrier; she sent her scorpid screaming toward him.

"Bring him down, Skitter! Tackle him, my love! I be reloadin'!"

But Greydon saw what she did not—the gnoll was not their only aid. From above, a blue dragon dipped down, saving him once more, its frosty breath encasing the troll in a block of gleaming ice.

That was his chance. There was still some fight left in the old man. He lurched forward, swinging the harpoon. In his prime, he was formidable, strong, and some of that old vigor returned when he needed it. The blow landed against the ice so forcefully that it broke clean in half. The troll tumbled free, stunned, but clinging to life. The gnoll nimbly jumped into the air, tucking and rolling, just in time to smack her once with his club. But the scorpid had not given up, correcting course, living up to its name and skittering quickly over fallen stones.

"Gnoll!" Greydon yelled.

The creature dodged, just at the right time, the scorpid's tail not hitting the gnoll, but burying its barbed, poisonous spike into its master's heart.

"S-Skitter. Y-You missed him. You missed . . ."

The troll rolled onto her side and moved no more. The scorpid seemed to lose its appetite for battle then, crawling over its master, protecting her body even as it no longer twitched at all.

There was no time to thank his gnoll rescuer; instead, Greydon marched on, emboldened by the victory. And there was his brother. Malus. His protectors scattered, their attention drawn by other targets. Perhaps they were lured. It did not matter. Greydon fixed his eye on Malus and crossed to him, gaining speed and determination. The battlefield narrowed to the two of them, the sounds of the demons and of the chaos suddenly distant, as if only he and Malus existed.

"Brother!" he called, not willing to surprise him with a blow to the back.

Malus spun to confront him, his face, neck, every visible inch of skin pulsating with ropey black veins, green fel fire glowing faintly beneath. His eyes blazed with hatred and corruption, and he grinned, showing nothing but blackened teeth.

"Greydon, you old relic, I hardly noticed you. You're half the man I knew," Malus said with a sneer, raising his immense, demonic blade.

"At least I remain a man; the same cannot be said for you." Their blades clashed. "Give up, brother, and put down that weapon. I will give you a clean death and rid you of this foul corruption. You cannot wish to live this way, and you cannot hope to win. The Diamond Blade is ours."

Malus blinked, then laughed, swinging once, missing Greydon's chest by a hair.

"I don't need the Diamond Blade to defeat you, Greydon. My power is that of the Burning Legion itself, terrible and eternal. The fel flames, they whisper to me; they whisper of my victory. If only you could hear the whispers; they sound so sweet. It was the same whisper that convinced me of your worthlessness, that showed me the beauty in destruction. And destruction there will be. Your deaths first, and then? The world's."

"No!" Greydon lifted the harpoon, absorbing the full might of Malus's strength.

Greydon fell back at once, reeling. The power . . . He had never felt someone swing a sword like that before. It was over so quickly. Just like that? But how? It could not be possible. The Voice of the Light had spoken to him, urged him; he had made it so far, he could not die to this twisted shadow of his brother. But when Greydon tried to stand, his legs gave out. Malus raised the sword high over his head, preparing to strike.

"Good-bye, brother."

CHAPTER THIRTY-NINE
SEVEN BECOME ONE

"Father!"

Aram felt time distort the way it had when Drella fell to Malus's cruel stroke. Too slow. The battlefield was littered with weapons, but none he knew how to wield. A broken crossbow bolt or a shield wouldn't help much, and it left him feeling utterly useless. Still, he searched, hoping to find some way to come to his father's aid. He watched his father on his knees, too far for Aram to help, the others engrossed in their own battles, and the killing blow falling, falling . . .

Aram's hand shot out and with it, a blast of golden light, as bright and brilliant as the sun itself, a solar flare that sparkled with heat.

"What in the—"

Aram watched in disbelief. The spell—for he knew it could only be magic—streamed across the carnage and the chaos, colliding with the blade of Malus's sword just before it cut into his father.

The flower in his pocket, Drella's gift, began pulsing light, then it flew out of his pocket of its own volition, hovering in front of him. He could swear he heard Drella's sweet voice in his mind as the ever-blooming flower burst into a shower of sparks, bathing him in its pink-and-green radiance.

We are bonded. That bond will never die. Go. Protect the Light. Protect our friends.

Aram released the spell, the beam of solar light vanishing. It left behind a slight glare in his eyes. There was no time to question it. The shock of the spell had staggered Malus, but he was rallying.

"Together!"

He heard Makasa through the din, the clash of claws on swords, the magical shadow bolts ricocheting throughout the room. At last, he would fight by his sister's side once more. Aram ran toward her, dodging stones and swords and fists, ignoring the pain of his imprisonment, the scars and burns it had left on his body. All that mattered was reaching his family.

They were so close now, so close—

"Impossible." Malus snarled, kicking Aram's father hard in the chest, knocking him to the ground with a groan. He didn't go for Greydon again, however; instead he set his sights on Makasa and the Diamond Blade.

"Murky, Hackle!" Aram shouted, then pointed to where Ssarbik and Ssavra cackled and attempted to ensnare Makasa with their shadow magics. Galena and Telagos worked together to fend off the threat from the sky, Telagos freezing the demons in place for Galena to snipe with a carefully timed bolt of moonfire. Aram wondered if he could use that same power Drella had gifted him again, and he aimed for one of the frozen demons, evaporating it with a shock of solar energy. Each time the beam left his hand, he felt a jolt of power run through his entire body.

Throgg and Karrga were busy playing their own game, trying to bat as many demons out of the sky as they could, laughing and joking together, oblivious to everything else around them.

"That six! Me got six! Throgg big loser!" Karrga shrieked and slammed her sword into another demon. Aram ignored them, trying to reach Makasa, but Malus had already engaged her, slamming his sword down again and again on the blade of her glowing harpoon. He pinned Makasa back against a piece of fallen stone, and she tripped over it, but regained her balance quickly.

"Not so invincible, are you?" Malus taunted. "All alone. All afraid."

A dagger materialized from out of nowhere, or so Aramar thought. It hit Malus in the chest, burying itself just shy of his heart. But it was enough to distract him, and he glanced up from his prey, Reigol Valdread already flicking another throwing knife into his hands as he stood atop a tumbled stone. "Get away from my daughter, you filth!"

"Errack?" Ssarbik froze, giving another one of his hideous laughs, his noise of confusion earning him Valdread's quick attention. He swiveled at the waist, releasing the throwing knife with a simple flick of the wrist, elegant and precise. It landed true, better than true, doing to Ssarbik what it had failed to do to Malus. It sank deep, directly into the arakkoa's heart.

"And that's enough out of you," Valdread spat. "By the Lady, that felt good."

Aram would have time to figure out what Valdread meant, and why in the world he seemed convinced he was Makasa's father. Ah well, stranger things had certainly happened. And there was no time to waste. A trio of winged demons dove toward Valdread, and Aram let his power fly again, concentrating hard, thinking of Drella, opening his palms while a blinding solar beam seared through the sky, knocking the demons off course and into the ground.

Malus plucked the dagger out of his chest and tossed it away. But he was well and truly outnumbered then, with only a pitiful number of demons circling above, and no loyal minions left but Ssavra, who soon realized that, too, and fled. Galena froze her in place at the door, roots growing through the floor, tangling Ssavra up as surely as Ssarbik's magic had entangled them so many times.

"It's over," Makasa said, standing, bringing the Diamond Blade to bear.

Malus was trapped, backing up rapidly, swinging his sword out in front of him in desperation.

Aram felt a presence with him then. Drella. He heard her giggling somewhere in the distance, and that warmth he had felt from her, and from her gift, filled him again. It was the same warmth he felt when he wielded her powers, the glow that flew from his hands and felt, strangely, natural.

Murky soared by, riding a demon he had managed to snare in his net. He crashed the demon into the altar, then rolled away, a little dazed. Wobbly, he found his spear and jabbed it at Malus, flanking him.

The crew assembled, a smile tugged at Makasa's lips. Demon blood, dirt, and scratches covered her face, but she was glowing. With that, she looked up slowly, taking a single step toward Malus. "It's over, Malus. Surrender. You don't have to live like this—this thing."

"Never. *Never!*" He tumbled back again, eyes wide and panicked. Over and over, he jabbed at them, but he was surrounded and roundly defeated. Broken. "I will never surrender. You're fools if you think anything can defeat the might of the Burning Legion! I will never, never—"

His eyes burned, furious, and for a moment he seemed almost calm. Almost like he might change his mind and truly surrender. But then he drew in a long breath and his eyes settled on Makasa. He seemed to summon one last burst of strength, hurling his sword at her, the blade flying true. But Aram was swift, ready, and a bright beam of sunlight flashed from his hand, sending the sword end over end until it clattered, useless, to the floor.

Makasa did not wait, did not even hesitate. She saw her opening and took it, leaping forward toward Malus, the Diamond Harpoon glinting in her hand, her stroke sure and steady as she brought the sharp end down, cutting through Malus's scream before it could even begin.

The demons in the sky, sensing their master's destruction, dispersed, vanishing in every direction, nothing remaining but the distant sound of their beating wings. The starved and thwarted Darkstorm—for surely that was what the roiling black vortex was—raged for an instant longer, its energies churning, shrieking, before it dissipated, its strange voices quieting until it was nothing more than a hushed whisper. Its darkness ebbed, no trace of it or the sad souls it had consumed remaining.

The battle was over. Throgg and Karrga groaned, all of their fun at an end.

"You good at whack-a-bat," Karrga said, slinging one meaty arm over Throgg's shoulder. "Maybe you good at other thing, too. Like kiss. Like hug."

They lumbered away together, arm in arm, not even staying long enough to appreciate Malus's demise.

"We get them?" Hackle asked, nodding to the two ogres.

On the way out, Throgg whacked Ssavra a good one, and she shrieked, clawing at the thorny roots holding her fast.

"No . . . they're all right," Makasa said with a smirk.

Galena walked up next to Aramar's side, no longer in her moonkin form, but back to the bashful, braided tauren he remembered. He smiled at her, at all of his friends, most of them still standing there in stunned silence.

It was over. It was *over.*

Malus was defeated, the Diamond Blade safe and reforged. The naaru's power preserved. There would be no Darkstorm that day.

"Good riddance to bad rubbish, I always say." Valdread dusted off his hands, cocking his hip to the side as he collected one of his fallen throwing knives and slid it back into the holster across his chest. "Fitting, really. Now he and his beloved Xaraax have shared the same fate. I hope they end up together somehow and drive each other absolutely mad."

"That's a given," Aram said with a snort.

"How did you do that?" Makasa had turned to him, nodding toward his hands and the golden solar magic that still encased them. "Since when are you a mage?"

"Not a mage," he whispered sadly. He wished Drella could be there to share in their win, but maybe, he thought, squeezing his fingers, she was. "A druid. It's Drella's magic. She passed it to me through our bond before she died."

"I felt her here," Galena said. "That bond . . . I think it flows through all of us."

"Seven must become One," Aram murmured. "And so we did." He gazed around at each of them in turn, amazed that they had come so far and stuck together. To be one of the seven was an honor, but it required Makasa, of course, who was steady and stubborn in all things. And it needed Valdread, the most unlikely addition. Telagos, too, only slightly less unlikely. Hackle, Murky, and Galena had done their part, too, valiant in battle, and stalwart in their friendship. It was truly miraculous, that so many strange companions could put aside their differences and beat back such a terrible threat.

"Yes. We did, but Hackle do best job. Many clubbings, more than Sivet and Jaggal combine!" The gnoll sidled up to them, cleaning off his war club on the leathery straps of his trousers.

"Murky mggla drrdaagar!" Murky insisted.

"You count wrong! No way you fight more than Hackle!" Hackle fired back.

Greydon Thorne stood, with help, of course, from Aram. He didn't seem amused by the bickering, only aloof. And sad. He stared at Malus's crumpled form for a long time, his eyes hooded, his lower lip trembling.

"I'm sorry we couldn't save him," Aram said softly, touching his father's shoulder.

"Me too, Aramar, me too." Greydon took one last lingering

look at his fallen brother, then drank in the sight of his son, and his daughter, and all of the strange and wonderful travelers that they had befriended along the way. Down in the valley, triumphant horns sounded. The rest of their allies were celebrating. The day was won.

"Some men cannot be swayed back to the Light," Greydon concluded, brushing off his tunic and straightening his shoulders. "Silverlaine Thorne chose his path, just as you did, Aramar, and this is what you chose: these friends. This family."

"Best choice I've ever made," Aram said, accepting a tight hug from Makasa, who nearly bowled him over. He was glad to see her again, too.

"I couldn't agree more," Greydon Thorne said, his eyes softening as he embraced both his son and his adopted daughter, Makasa.

"You've come so far," he said, leaning back. He took a moment to just look at her. "To make it here, to build an army, to wield the Diamond Blade . . . I knew you were something special on the *Wavestrider*. I should have known you could do whatever you put your mind to."

"Couldn't let you two rot out here," she said with a shrug.

"I told you," Aram added. "I told you she would come for us."

Greydon nodded, giving a warm, relieved chuckle. "I was a fool to doubt." It was then that he noticed Telagos off to the side, his shining scale mail spattered with demon bits. "Incredible. I had not thought to see Telagos again, but here he is, aiding the Order of the Seven Suns once more."

Hearing him, Telagos merely gave a short, elegant bow.

"Well," Greydon said with a sigh, gazing around at the motley assortment of allies that had come to defeat the Darkstorm. "It appears there are many introductions to be made. Friends and allies to meet . . ." With that, Greydon turned his eyes to the door, and to the path back down. "Now, let's go home."

EPILOGUE

Aram shifted from foot to foot under the cooling shade of the tree. It had been almost a year since Malus had fallen and the Hidden thwarted, and his days traveling with his unlikely band of friends—now heroes—felt a lifetime away. His leg still ached sometimes when the weather was wet, and even though Drella's gift had healed the worst of his infected wound, he would walk with a slight limp for the rest of his days.

Drella.

Even though he could still feel her presence when he closed his eyes and conjured his nature magic, he missed her. Sometimes, when he stared out the window in his room in Lakeshire, dreaming wistfully of adventures yet to come, he could hear her whisper to him, reminding him to be grateful, reminding him to appreciate the family he had there in the cottage.

Things had changed for them, too. Ceya and Robb were going to have another child, and Robertson and Selya didn't just look up to him as a big brother now, but as a *warrior*. His younger siblings asked constantly about Murky and Hackle, asking when they would see their frog and puppy friends again.

"I don't know!" Aram had shouted at them the last time they pressed him on it. He couldn't help but lose his temper; he didn't even know when *he* would see his friends again.

After the battle in Outland, Aram was relieved to return to his quiet, safe life in Lakeshire. Greydon escorted him there, of course, but then he and Makasa left shortly after for Stormwind. The king needed to know about the Hidden plot, and the lengths Aram and his friends had gone to stop the Burning Legion's latest attempt to destroy Azeroth.

A month later, Aram received the fanciest document he had ever laid eyes on—a scroll stamped with the royal seal of King Varian Wrynn. The king, in his own hand, thanked Aram for his service, for his sacrifice, and for his dedication to all things just and honorable. The messenger delivering the scroll bowed after giving Aram the message, and handed the boy a finely wrought dagger of folded steel, chased with gold filigree and real inset sapphires. A lion's head roared from the crossbar.

"A gift from His Majesty," the messenger said, doffing his feathered cap. "A replacement, he says, for the blade you fought so hard to reforge."

The Diamond Blade. The naaru had been restored, its prophecy fulfilled, and now it could rest. Before parting, his sister

Makasa broke apart the blade and gave each of their party one of the shards to hold. Their crew agreed that no one person—no one side—should wield the weapon. Makasa was the one to take the largest shard, the hilt, to Stormwind, where she told the king that the blade had been shattered beyond repair in the battle against Malus.

"Hide your piece somewhere safe," Greydon told them all solemnly. He had chosen to stay in Stormwind, as an advisor to the king. Something he called "useful retirement." "Hide it. Somewhere only you would know. Guard the secret with your life."

After a tearful good-bye, Hackle and Murky had set off together to return to Kalimdor with the gnoll and yeti army. Galena and Telagos would accompany them as far as the edge of Feralas, then veer north to begin their long journey to the Moonglade. Galena had much to report to the Cenarion Circle, and she seemed more confident in her druidic abilities, having fought so bravely against the Hidden. Traveling with a dragon didn't hurt, either.

Aram glanced at the sun, painfully aware of how much time had passed since he reached the Northwatch Expedition Base. Gazlowe had agreed to take him from Lakeshire back to Kalimdor, and this time, the goblin actually got paid in diamonds, a gift from the Stormwind treasury for his part in thwarting the Darkstorm threat. The outpost teemed with

Alliance soldiers, but Aram's stomach had still twisted with fear as he approached on foot, remembering the ambush that had greeted him last time. The soldiers offered him water and food, and a place to stay, but Aram didn't linger, venturing back down the hill to sit beneath the vivid pink tree and wait. And wait.

He reached out and touched the soft, pale bark. An electric feeling shivered through him. A family of birds had taken up residence in the branches above, and they chirped down at him cheerfully as he looked down at his fingers.

"The soldiers say you bloom year-round," he said quietly. "They call you the Forever Tree, but I know your real name. I miss you."

"Urum!"

Aram glanced up, searching the shrubs along the road until he spotted Murky there, bright green as ever, his back laden with a loaded traveler's pack, his trusty net hanging there, his spear in hand. As soon as the murloc caught sight of him, he broke into a run. Hackle followed not far behind, grinning lopsidedly, his war club resting on one shoulder.

"You came!" Aram called, kneeling and accepting a warm, slimy hug from the murloc. "Have you seen any sign of the others?"

"Hackle no see and no smell." The gnoll embraced Aram with a side hug, then gazed up at the beautiful, flowering branches. "Hackle glad to see tree still here."

"Murky glal," the murloc said with a nod. "Murky hgla verr-rooga goloa gogler."

"He say he have much to tell you," Hackle translated with a grin. "Many adventure. Murky known by all murloc now, big hero."

"And the Woodpaw?" Aram asked. "They must respect you even more now."

The gnoll puffed out his chest, gazing into the horizon. "Hackle known to all gnolls, all yetis. Most respected brute in all forest."

"I'm glad to hear it. You both deserve it." He put a hand over the gift from King Wrynn, the dagger tucked into his belt. It wasn't the same, perhaps, as being known all throughout the Eastern Kingdoms as a savior of Azeroth, but it was enough.

"Why fur so short?" Hackle barked at him, noticing that Aram had cut off his long locks, choosing to flop his brown hair back over his forehead. "You shed summer coat?"

"No, Hackle, I just wanted a change," Aram said. "What do you think?"

"Short fur is better. Long fur too hot, too stinky."

"Murky lglgl!"

"Murky like, too."

Aram didn't know if the opinion of a gnoll and murloc would help him much with the village girls back in Lakeshire, but it couldn't hurt. They passed the time trading stories, Aram letting them know they were very missed by his family, and that soon they would have a new Glade to impress. Murky and Hackle were delighted at the news, and told Aram all about life back at their homes.

He was beginning to wonder if nobody else would show, when the air around them became suddenly tense. A strange breeze drifted down toward them, growing in intensity until Aram's new, shorter hair was blown back off his forehead and Murky had to grab his net to keep it from blowing away. A blue shape darted down toward them, then hovered, the dirt around them spinning as Telagos arrived, his wings beating the air before he landed, shaking the ground.

"What an entrance," Aram called, watching as Galena tumbled from the dragon's back.

"Oof!" she cried out. "Sorry. Still bad at landing that way."

Telagos shrank, wings distorting into arms and blue skin bleeding away as he resumed his human form, dusting his shoulders lightly. "I think it's an elegant way to travel."

"I'm glad you made it!" Before Aram could say anything else, Galena had been mobbed by Murky, and Hackle greeted them both warmly. Aram hadn't spent much time at all with Telagos, but he shook the young man's hand, feeling as if the dragon could see through him with those intense pale eyes.

Now they just needed Makasa. The afternoon flew by, everyone absolutely brimming with stories and news. Galena had redeemed herself with the Cenarion Circle for her part in the battle against the Hidden, and they were incredibly impressed that she had convinced a blue dragon to meet with them in the Moonglade. Telagos spent his days studying the druids just as intently as they studied him.

"I never thought I'd live that one down," Galena finished with a laugh. She noticed Aram staring off into the setting sun. "I wonder where Makasa could be?"

"Maybe she's not coming," Aram said. "Let's give her a little while longer."

Murky was in the middle of describing their voyage to the tree meeting place, and the trouble they had gotten into with some quilboar, when Galena interrupted him, bouncing up and down excitedly, pointing toward the east.

"Look!" she cried. "They're here!"

Makasa had indeed shown, and so had Valdread, his dark leather coat and trousers changed out for a fashionable sailor's coat and accoutrements of deep purple. He still wore a hood, likely to conceal himself from the Alliance soldiers standing watch above them on the cliff. Makasa wore a similar outfit, though hers included a purple vest, a weathered black captain's hat sitting jauntily on her head.

"You're late!" Aram teased.

"Only fashionably," Valdread drawled. The undead had doused himself in perfume for the occasion, and he was wearing his shiniest black boots.

"What took you so long?" Aram asked as he and Makasa

hugged tightly. She clapped him on the back, then pulled away and nodded back the way they had come.

"I've got a surprise for you," she said. "That's why. What did you do to your hair?"

"What did you do to your nose?" he countered. A little gold hoop glimmered around one nostril.

"Hackle like!" the gnoll bayed. "Very popular with lady gnoll."

"Well, the lady gnolls couldn't be wrong, could they?" Makasa winked, then let Murky wrap himself around her leg for a good five minutes while he sobbed uncontrollably, screaming, "Mrksa! Mrksa!" until the Alliance soldiers called down to them, asking if all was well.

"So what's your big surprise?" Aram asked.

"Later," she said. "Let's pay our respects, first."

And so they did, standing quietly in a semicircle in front of the tree. Even Valdread seemed moved, standing with his head bowed and his hands tucked in front of his belt.

As the sun dipped behind the mountains, bathing them in cool shadows, Aram cleared his throat, then lifted his head, singing as best he could, trying to do justice to Drella's lullaby.

There I was
In the wood
With sunshine so bright.

His voice shook. He wasn't a strong singer, but it was important to him that he do what he could to tell Drella that they were there and that they hadn't forgotten her. He inhaled deeply, singing the next verse, surprised that his friends joined in with him. Telagos sang beautifully, in a voice that made the hairs on Aram's arms stand up. Murky was . . . Murky, and he gave it his all. Makasa had spent most of her life singing shanties, and didn't miss a beat, confident and loud, hitting the notes with a sailor's spirit.

> *There I was,*
> *Not alone but alive.*
> *There I walked in my grove*
> *With hope and pride.*
> *There I shall stay*
> *When I fear the rising tide.*

Aram sank down, running his hands over the damp earth at the base of the tree, then took something from his pocket. A shard from the Diamond Blade. It was the shard he had been tasked with protecting, and he knew exactly where it belonged. He dug down into the earth with his hands, then nestled the shard in the space, covering it up with a few pats. Before he could stand again, the tree shifted, creaking, the roots reaching up through the ground, twining around where he had buried the shard and then descending again, no doubt bringing it deeply, safely into the very heart of the tree.

"We'll be back again next year," Aram whispered. "I promise."

"We should celebrate our reunion," Valdread suggested, already taking a flask from his pack. "Perhaps now is the time to reveal your secret, Makasa."

"Oh! Sure!" She smiled, devilish. "Come on, it's not far."

Aram groaned.

"What?" she cried. "We've certainly gone farther!"

They marched after Makasa and Valdread, listening to father and daughter recall what they had done in the year since the battle in Outland. Aram couldn't believe how easy they seemed with each other, but he was happy for Makasa. After the loss of her brothers, it must have felt good to gain more family in her life. Though it was a strange sight, seeing them laugh and banter together, but he would get used to it. Eventually.

By the time they reached the shore south of the Charred Vale, it was full night. Galena lit one of her glowing white orbs of moonlight for them, and Aram did the same. He had been practicing his druidic magic each night. (His orb didn't glow quite as brightly as hers, but it was a start.) Telagos helped to ferry them some of the way after Murky complained of sore feet.

"There!" Makasa said. The salt air hit them, the sound of the waves carrying on the breeze. "What do you think? Isn't she beautiful?"

"Oh my!" Galena gasped, covering her mouth with both furred hands. "Is that yours?"

Makasa snorted. "Of course it's mine." Then she sidled up to Aram, draping an arm across his shoulders. "So? You in? We've got space enough for everyone. But if you'd rather go back to Lakeshire . . ."

"No!" He could hardly believe his eyes. The ship was beautiful, new and polished, a fast, angular vessel with gold and green sails snapping in the wind. He couldn't wait to draw it. "I'm definitely in!"

The figurehead at the front was carved masterfully, into the perfect likeness of Drella, her arms embracing the sea, her face friendly but coy. He could almost hear her bell-like voice singing, "Hi, friends!"

Crew stirred on the deck, noticing the light of their orbs on the sand. A dinghy bobbed not far into the water, waiting for them to take it across to the ship. Makasa started down toward it, the others following, Murky expressing his desire to be first mate.

"Got one already," Makasa said with a chuckle, pointing her thumb at Valdread. "Watch out—he'll fill your boots with tar and pour salt in your gruel. It's a bit out of hand, really."

"One has to find amusement somewhere on the open seas," the Forsaken replied. "I'm only keeping the crew on their toes. Where they belong."

Aram drank in the ship for one last moment, wanting to see it in all its glory before he boarded the dinghy, where Hackle, Murky, and the others waited. Makasa stood next to him still, no doubt enjoying his awe. She had done well, and she knew it, and Aram felt nothing but pride for his sister, and excitement at all the adventures they had yet to come.

"What did you name it?" he asked.

"The *Dryad*," Makasa told him. "Like it?"

Aram nodded, grinning across at her. He was so glad to see her again. It felt like being home.

It was right where he wanted to be. Where they both belonged.

ACKNOWLEDGMENTS

I would first like to thank Kate McKean for the opportunity to work on this tremendous series and other dream projects. The teams at Scholastic and Blizzard have been wonderfully patient and nurturing, and it's been such an honor to work with these two talented groups of people. It's been inspirational to see their passion for Azeroth and publishing. Chloe Fraboni—thank you for your patience, sense of humor, understanding, and creativity; it's been a joy to work with you on this novel. A huge thanks to Cate Gary and the editorial and continuity teams at Blizzard; I've had a blast playing in your vast and exciting sandbox.

I would also like to acknowledge Greg Weisman, Samwise Didier, and Stephane Belin for laying the groundwork for this wonderful series.

And finally, a huge thanks to Diandra, Karen, my boys, and my friends and family. An author is only as good as the network that surrounds and supports them.

About the Author

Madeleine Roux is the *New York Times* bestselling author of the Asylum series, which has sold over a million copies worldwide, and whose first book was named a Teen Indie Next List Pick. She is also the author of the House of Furies series, *Allison Hewitt Is Trapped*, *Sadie Walker Is Stranded*, and *Salvaged*. Her short story contributions can be found in collections such as *Star Wars: From a Certain Point of View*, *Resist*, and *New Scary Stories to Tell in the Dark*. Madeleine is a thirteen-year *World of Warcraft* veteran and a noncombat pet enthusiast, and she was briefly known as the Slayer of Incompetent, Stupid, and Disappointing Minions. She spends all her DKP on treats for her beloved Core Hound in Seattle, Washington.